NEURAL WEB

Dima Zales

♠ Mozaika Publications ♠

Published by Mozaika Publications, an imprint of Mozaika LLC.
www.mozaikallc.com

Cover by Najla Qamber Designs
www.najlaqamberdesigns.com

e-ISBN: 978-1-63142-304-8
Print ISBN: 978-1-63142-305-5

CHAPTER ONE

I'm seventeen thousand feet up, on the 102nd floor of one of the newer tourist magnets in Manhattan, One World Observatory. The crowds around me are flattening their noses against the floor-to-ceiling glass to gulp down a view that can turn a normal person acrophobic. I join in and stare. Every borough is visible under our feet, like a detailed 3D map of New York City.

A vague sense of déjà vu sweeps over me, filling me with overwhelming dread. It's hard to say if I'm scared of the heights, the large crowd, or something more ephemeral.

A dark shape moves in the crowd, and I pivot on my heel to deal with it.

I'm faced with a man with two noses. He has pierced nostrils where his eyes should be, and a cyclopean eye in the center of his face.

My facial recognition app reports an error, and the biological equivalent of a system failure happens in the part of my brain responsible for recognizing faces.

The nose-eye man takes out a gun, and before I can theorize how he got it through the security downstairs, he raises it, aligns the sights with his one eye, and squeezes the trigger.

Without the earplugs I typically use at the gun range, the gunshot blasts my eardrums, likely hastening age-related deafness by at least a year. The humongous window next to me shatters into small pieces that twist and oscillate, doing their best to cut as many tourists as possible.

I ignore more shots fired, as well as the blood and screams all around me, because another man with the same eye-and-noses face appears right behind me. I spin and try to punch the abomination in the one eye, but he dodges.

I do a double take. If I used Photoshop to duplicate the eye, delete the extra nose, and move it all to the right places, the face in front of me would look a lot like the face I see in the mirror every day (minus the nose piercings).

My attacker uses my distraction and momentary lack of balance to push me toward the broken window.

I scream, but it's too late. After a cartoon-like moment during which I look down and take in the impossible height, I begin to fall.

This building is so tall there are clouds around me. The feeling of déjà vu gets stronger as I race past the surrounding skyscrapers. From here, they look tiny. The Statue of

Liberty is like a toy in the nearby water, and the people on the streets are too small to see, like bacteria.

My heart realizes I'll splatter on the pavement in around ten seconds and tries to evacuate my chest cavity while it still can. The terror in every cell of my body deepens the feeling of déjà vu.

I choke on my scream as a fiery figure swoops in from nowhere, like the legendary Firebird from the Russian legends. As it approaches, I realize it's a glowing human being. In a whoosh of fiery wings, it cradles me in its arms, and we hover around the eightieth floor of the skyscraper.

My savior's hair forms a telltale Einsteinian halo around his head. When I recognize the AI's face, I instantly know what he's about to say.

Sure enough, he announces with a German accent, "You're safe. As part of your nightmare reduction therapy, I'm letting you know that this is a dream. You also wanted me to suggest that you try lucid dreaming, which would require you to stay asleep."

"Of course." I barely resist smacking myself on the forehead. "That's what that déjà vu feeling was about. I've had this nightmare before."

"You've had other dreams of falling as well." Einstein's glow is completely gone, and he no longer possesses fiery wings. "We can discuss your dreams later. Your window of opportunity for lucid dreaming is closing fast."

He's right. If I want to take control of my dream world as all the books on the subject suggest, I need to act now.

First, I focus on turning my unpleasant dream of falling into a dream with a similar physical action but nearly opposite subjective value. I wish to fly, and a moment later, I find myself soaring through Manhattan and enjoying views that passengers on a tourist helicopter tour would envy.

The now-ordinary Einstein and I form a flock of two, his arms in front of him like Superman and mine out like wings.

"This is awesome," I tell the AI. "If falling feels overwhelmingly stressful, flying is pure joy."

"Just watch out," Einstein replies. "Exhilaration can wake you just as easily as—"

I wake up in my bed, a rat nose at my back and Ada's warm body spooned in front of me.

"You have been unconscious for two hours and thirty-seven minutes," Einstein's voice says.

"Another nightmare?" Ada whispers over her shoulder.

"Nothing bad," I say—a euphemism I use to mean I didn't dream about family members being slaughtered in front of my eyes nor any of the other horrors I've dealt with. "Just some weird faces and falling."

"I bet it's a manifestation of stage fright. After all, our trip is the day after tomorrow." She switches on the soft bedroom light with a mental command to Einstein and turns to face me, her amber eyes glinting with a surprising level of alertness for the time of night.

She might have a point. We're going to be doing presentations about our company in several new markets, and I've been increasingly dreading these trips—and not just because, like any normal human, I don't like speaking in front of huge crowds.

"I'm actually more concerned about telling our off-spring," I say to Ada in a private Zik message. Illogically, I feel like our son might somehow overhear us if I so much as vibrate the airwaves in the house. "It's right after his birthday, and I don't want to ruin the big event for him."

"Don't worry about that for now." She strokes my shoulder. "If you'd like, I'll be the bad one this time around—anything to help you sleep."

"You're the best wife ever, but this is something we'll have to tell him together. Now let's sleep."

"In a few minutes." She shifts closer, and as her lips approach mine, I realize what she wants. My anatomy reciprocates—strongly. "After you fulfill your marital duties, you'll sleep even better," she adds in a huskier voice, making sure her lips brush mine as she talks.

"VR or for real?"

"Why not both?"

She yanks down the blanket with a flourish, and sleep becomes but a distant memory.

CHAPTER TWO

"S *dnyom rozhdeniya*, Alan," Uncle Abe says to my son and raises his shot glass.

"Happy birthday! Four years old." Mom also raises her vodka excitedly. "You're such a big boy."

Flanked by Gogi and Joe, my progeny is standing next to his avatar, which he has made visible only to Ada and me so that we can privately see him roll his eyes.

"Be nice to your grandma." The newest version of the Telepathy app allows Ada to sound kind, firm, and slightly scolding at the same time—something you can't do with just voice. The emotions the app conveys have nuances that can only be understood and felt by people with Brainocyte-enhanced brains. "If you really were as mature as you think you are, you wouldn't mind phrases like 'baby' or 'big boy,'" she continues.

"Or 'kid,'" I add, winking at Alan. "Or—"

"Thanks, Grandma," he replies on a public thought channel, without a hint of negativity. His public Zik message shows proper gratitude and happiness; it's scary how good of a liar my son can be. "You're right, of course, Mom," he adds in our private chat. His avatar's head bows impossibly low and his foot paints an arc in front of his body, telling me he's overacting his contrition. "Some words and phrases just seem to trigger my inner primate—something I'm working on."

I look over my son, both his real-world visage and his digital representation. If you take Ada's amber eyes and double up on the mischievous twinkle, you get Alan's real-world eyes. If you take my smile—specifically, the smile I get when I've done something truly devious to someone who totally deserves it—you get Alan's smile. The rest of his face is a mixture of my wife and me with a slight simian twist, as though we'd spliced capuchin monkey genes into our offspring (which we didn't, though we now have the technology to do that or anything else Dr. Moreau would be jealous of). Alan must be able to see the monkey in his own face as well. How else to explain that "inner primate" comment?

In contrast to his tiny real-world self, Alan's digital avatar looks like a twenty-year-old man who, quite literally, is a mixture of Ada and me. He created this avatar using a neural net he designed a few weeks ago, a specialized AI whose sole purpose was to scan every picture of Alan's parental units and produce a 3D face that perfectly blended our features. He didn't use us as inspiration for his body, though, opting instead for something he must've seen on a cover of some magazine—hence the broad shoulders, chiseled abs, and precancerous tan.

Everyone in the real world clinks their glasses together, and I join in.

"You know," Mitya thinks at me privately, his real-world self chewing on a caviar sandwich, "it's crazy that we have a table filled with Russian cuisine in the middle all this."

I look around and acknowledge that Mitya is right. This party doesn't belong here, in the dinosaur exhibit of the Museum of Natural History. When I rented *Night at the Museum* a few weeks ago, I didn't realize how obscenely expensive that movie rental would turn out to be. Then again, what's the point of being one of the richest people in the world if you can't rent your son a museum on his birthday?

"Do you like my gift?" Muhomor asks after he stops grimacing, something he does after every shot of vodka.

Muhomor is wearing the latest model of his Brainocyte-controlled power suit, which means he can walk for days nonstop, run a hundred marathons, and beat a world record in sprinting. If he wanted to, he could leap up and dance a jig on the skull of that giant dinosaur skeleton that happens to be the centerpiece of this enormous hall. Golan Dahan, our Director of Nanotech, thinks we're mere months from fixing Muhomor's spine—and the spines of anyone else who needs it.

"Who doesn't love reading about blockchains?" Alan's private avatar rolls his eyes again. "I always wanted to know how bitcoin works in as much detail as possible."

Only Ada and I can detect the sarcasm in Alan's real-world voice. Muhomor takes his words at face value and grins as though he managed to hack yet another bank. Ada and I exchange glances and decide that since we ourselves roll our eyes at most of Muhomor's statements, we should let Alan's impertinence stand. After all, he learned this behavior from us.

"I just want to make sure this 'gift' doesn't include any ideas on how to hack bitcoin's cryptographic functions." Ada's pointed smile makes Muhomor nearly choke on his lamb kebab. "I hope we all agree that something like that would not be suitable as a gift for a four-year-old?"

Alan suddenly looks a lot more interested in his gift. Muhomor hastily gestures at it, and the virtual gift box changes, the new one noticeably smaller.

I consider having one of the myriad parallel instances of myself examine the gift in detail but decide against it. Instead, I think to Ada, "If Alan were to set his sights on bitcoin, it would be toast anyway."

Alan got Brainocytes as soon as he was born, long before US laws set eighteen as the minimum age for Brainocyte eligibility (our expensive lobbyists are working on overturning those laws, along with any other hint of legislation against our products). Alan also got Respirocytes with the rest of us. The only thing we didn't give him—because he's still developing—are Bone Servers. That's what Dahan, our Director of Nanotech, calls the beta product that allows us to have stronger bones that can serve as computing resources in a pinch.

In any case, when it comes to brain enhancements, Alan got as many as the rest of us in the Brainocytes Club inner circle—and that's an impressive number indeed. He was also the first human to have his complete brain connectome mapped in a digital substrate, though the rest of us followed shortly. Like with us, his digital brain parts in the cloud far outstrip his meager biological parts. His mind is distributed among the top-of-the-line servers that only enhanced brains could've developed in such a short span of time.

As a result, Alan has as much in common intellectually with a typical four-year-old as we do with a vanilla, unenhanced human being. Alan could speak Zik when he was a month old. He recently completed his PhD thesis in Computer Science and plans to study more fields. If he wanted to get into hacking, he'd be a frightening force, but I don't think that activity would be stimulating enough for him.

"He won't bother with something as mundane as hacking," Ada says, echoing my thought. "He has more interesting projects to keep him busy."

It's true. Alan's current intellectual challenge is advanced video game environments that use virtual reality—or as he likes to call it, world simulations. I think he first got interested in this when he learned I used VR to help me cope with PTSD-like symptoms. He has now created a whole virtual world for Mr. Spock and the rest of our enhanced rats to roam. This world is a rat nirvana, and Mr. Spock and his kin now spend most of their time there. In fact, Rat World is where they are right now, virtually, though their actual biological bodies are at home. Being stimulated like that helps enhance rat life expectancy, as do the nanocytes that we're experimenting with (and which we'll eventually use to triple human life expectancy). The most interesting part about Rat World, though, is that Alan populated it with virtual rats with brains mimicked at such detail that the resulting creatures are, for all intents and purposes, real rats (unless you want to get philosophical about it, which Alan likes to do). When I walked through Rat World and saw the multitudes of his rat creations, it wasn't hard to picture my son growing up to create whole universes, like a self-made deity.

"Nor does he have a financial incentive to crack bitcoin," I add when Ada looks at me expectantly.

"Exactly," she agrees.

Ada and I set up a multi-billion-dollar trust fund for Alan a year ago. His monthly allowance is in the millions. However, he won't need our funds for long because his many businesses will soon show profits. The kid has more patents than Thomas Edison.

"If it's gift time, I have something for the little bunny," Mom says, and I notice JC, her new husband, touch her elbow in warning. He understands Alan better than she does. "Here"—she grabs a box from under her chair and brings it out with aplomb—"it's from your grandparents."

Mom insists that Alan think of JC as his grandpa, but Alan insists on calling JC by his initials like everyone else does. In part, this is because Alan supersedes JC on the Human++ corporate hierarchy. JC still leads Techno, which is now just a small part of the giant corporation that Mitya, Ada, and I formed together, while Alan is a major shareholder of that corporation.

"It's a knitted sweater," real-world Alan says without a hint of the disappointment that even I feel on his behalf. "Thank you."

He walks over to Mom and kisses her cheek, and she promptly melts into a contented puddle. I sure hope he never turns evil, because that move would make Machiavelli proud.

"My turn." Uncle Abe pulls out a wrapped package that's obviously a skateboard. "Here you go. It's so you can play outside more."

Unlike the rest of the family, Uncle Abe didn't join the new Human++ megacorporation, and he's refused advanced versions of Brainocytes. It took a lot of convincing to even get him to accept the newest, FDA-approved Brainocytes delivered via a transdermal patch—the Tier III ones Human++ has been giving away for free to billions of people. His lack of understanding of Alan's mental capabilities is why he miscalculated his gift so dramatically; otherwise, he'd have known that Alan assessed the risks of skateboarding and found the scary statistics unacceptable—or at least I hope that's what happened.

Oddly, Alan looks genuinely grateful, which is worrying. I privately think at Ada, "Hon, we should create a virtual reality experience of riding that thing for Alan so he doesn't get tempted to split his head for real."

"I'm pretty sure he's only planning to ride the board using one of his robo-avatars," she replies calmly. "My other thread can see his favorite body walking this way."

I check the museum security cameras and confirm that one of Alan's "bodies" is indeed walking our way. More reminiscent of a Terminator skeleton than a human being, this advanced model has sight, hearing, taste, smell, and touch sensors that pass for their human equivalents. But unlike a human body, it also allows us to sense electrical and magnetic fields, perform echolocation, detect changes in air moisture, and a couple of other things I haven't tried yet.

On a whim, I spawn another instance of myself, take possession of one of the robot bodies I left on standby, and walk it toward Alan's metallic avatar.

Embodying this equipment still gives me an eerie feeling, much more so than when I operate avatars in virtual environments. In part, that's because I have hundreds of virtual personae running at any given moment, whereas I only rarely need a physical robot body for business or recreational tasks. Still, to my expanded consciousness, the robot body is quite serviceable, and its senses are surprisingly lifelike. Riding this body really nails the idea Ada has been trying to sell to everyone for ages: that the human body is a machine like this robot, just made from meat.

"Will you let me ride your skateboard?" my robot self asks Alan's robot instantiation. My synthetic voice is almost indistinguishable from that of a human.

"Of course, Dad." As an addendum to his words, Alan's avatar's metallic face tries to smile at me, something that still looks ghastly on this particular model. "But I go first."

"Hey, it's your birthday." I make my robot wink.

"I got this for the little warrior," Gogi says in the meantime and pulls out a box. If the newly arrived robots made

Gogi nervous, he doesn't show it, unlike white-faced Uncle Abe.

As his robot body skates away, the tiny human version of Alan rips into the wrapping of Gogi's gift with age-appropriate enthusiasm. As a rule, Alan and Gogi get along, having bonded over violent video games. Not surprisingly, Gogi's present turns out to be a pair of little boxing gloves—another not-so-subtle hint that Alan should begin training in self-defense in the real world. In the virtual world, the kid wipes the floor with Gogi already, and I bet if Gogi were able to control a robot, which he can't, Alan would beat him that way also.

Ada frowns at the gift. I grab her small hand in mine and gently squeeze, saying privately, "If Alan learned to box, it would only make him safer."

She doesn't seem pacified but doesn't say anything.

Joe clears his throat, indicating that he must also have something for the birthday boy.

Ada's frown deepens. Despite Joe's recent improvements in his business dealings and temperament, she's still not his biggest fan.

"Here," he says to Alan. "I hope it fits."

Alan unwraps Joe's box with even more enthusiasm than Gogi's, but when he looks inside, his whole posture seems to deflate. With excitement I can clearly discern as fake, he says, "A bulletproof vest. Wow. Thanks, Uncle Joe."

In our private virtual reality, Ada and I exchange a meaningful glance, and I secretly say, "You know, it could've been something worse—like a knife."

Unlike his father, Joe has the more advanced Tier II Brainocyte suite that gives its user a wider range of utilities, including a modest brain boost. Tier II is a perk for all Human++ employees, and as Head of Security, Joe was one of the early adopters.

Tier II brain boost has had an interesting effect on my cousin. The guy now seems to possess a conscience, albeit a rudimentary one. There are a couple of theories as to the cause of this, and all of them assume he didn't have a conscience before. Mitya believes Joe is simply mellowing with age, but we all think that's baloney, as the "mellowing" happened in the last four years. I think that the experience of getting smarter makes one realize that violence is sometimes not the best solution, but my friends think that's too simplistic an explanation, as plenty of intelligent people have committed violence over the years.

Ada thinks the older Brainocyte brain boost methodology is behind the changes in Joe, as we still employ the older method for Tier II. The old boosts use simulated computer brain regions to enhance brainpower, meaning Joe is getting more brain that isn't his original brain and thus somehow gaining empathy or whatever else he previously lacked. If she's right, we may want to be careful about how, when, and if we give Joe Tier I access, as that uses the newer method for the boosts.

Out of necessity, Tier I Brainocyte capabilities are still available only to the four original members of the Brainocytes Club, plus my son. It's not because we're trying to hoard power, though. We want everyone to become Tier

I eventually; we just have a bottleneck when it comes to computer resources.

The Tier I brain boosts are different because of advancements in brain scanning technology. We let existing Brainocytes scan our biological brain in minute detail. Then, when we build computer models for the extra brain regions, we base them on the scans of our brain circuitry. This new and better method of enhancement cuts down on the negative side effects that Tier II people experience, such as pre-cog moments. The new method also decreases the boost adjustment period to a matter of hours instead of days. But it's computationally much harder to accomplish, and we can't afford to give it to everyone yet.

Additionally, this brain scanning gives us backups of our brains in case something happens to the fragile tissue, like a stroke or a blow to the head. Mitya has become obsessed with this line of research and already has his whole biological brain backed up. It's this obsession of his that was behind the protocols that ensure our prodigious non-biological brainpower is backed up on a regular basis. I think he's wasting his time worrying so much about his meat brain, as Ada calls it. Our biological brainpower will soon become but a tiny part of what we are, so small that we might not miss it if we suddenly lost it.

"You're multitasking too much again." Ada's complaint pulls me out of my thoughts.

"No."

My reply is too defensive, and I take in a breath to examine myself. Ada's been trying to get me to be more in the moment. She worries that I don't get any quality time with her and Alan. I don't like to think that I'm the kind of father and husband who needs reminders like that—even if I sometimes do.

"I'm merely coding that new app we discussed"—the defensiveness is completely gone in my thought-speech—"testing our surprise gift, reading work emails, and having a psychotherapy session with Einstein. That last one was something you suggested."

Using Einstein as a shrink is a new service we're about to roll out to the worldwide Brainocyte user base. It's going to be part of our freemium model, and we expect it to bring about a lot of good in the world, as this therapy has been instrumental in curbing my nightmares and relieving my post-traumatic stress.

Ada looks placated enough, and we companionably watch Alan open a gift from JC, which turns out to be, of all things, a yo-yo. Alan seems to appreciate it and starts doing tricks with it immediately.

"Our turn soon," Ada says with a wink. "You might want to reduce your workload a little more. For whatever reason, you seem a bit distant."

Ada claims that heavy multitasking takes away from each activity. Since she designed the system, it must be true. On my end, though, I rarely feel the distractedness. I stopped feeling as if I'm doing multiple things at once a couple of years back.

The term multitasking is misleading for what we can now do, anyway. The me who's talking to Einstein in the virtual therapy room feels very different from the me who's watching the current proceedings. It's as though I exist in multiple places at once, but later I have the memory of all these bits of myself. Of course, rationally I know that each of these instances of myself uses dedicated computer resources, and that if these resources are overloaded, something will happen to all instances of me. That something could easily look like distractedness to an outside observer.

"Didn't you design the system to prevent a thread from being created during resource overload?" I ask her.

"I did, but once your resources are allocated, they are never taken away. If you start doing more with your resource allotment, you can get distracted."

I stop some of my tasks. I know better than to argue with Ada about Brainocyte tech. She's still the world expert, so if she says multitasking leads to being distant, it's probably true despite my feelings to the contrary.

"Let's let Mitya go next." I make myself look as alert as I can. "We want to end this gift giving with a splash."

"Show off, you mean?" Her private avatar, the one that looks like a punky panda bear, smiles.

"Maybe," I reply, realizing that my earlier list of activities didn't include skateboarding with Alan—a sign that I honestly am distracted right now. "You're proud of our work too. It's okay to admit it."

A smile touches Ada's real-world amber eyes, and I can tell she's anxious to see her son's reaction to our surprise.

"My gift is something everyone might enjoy," Mitya says, and we switch our attention to him. "I've secured a deal between Human++ and Disney. The folks at Disney are going to build a huge virtual park that Brainocytes users can visit in VR, without the need to fly to places like

Orlando. This"—a huge golden ticket flies toward Alan in the shared VR environment—"is part of that deal. Alan gets VIP access pass to the park—for life."

Now that most of the human population has Brainocytes in their heads, many companies have chosen to create apps and experiences tailored for Brainocytes, so Disney's jumping on the bandwagon isn't a shock to anyone. Still, Alan seems thrilled at the prospect of seeing what the folks at Disney will create. My guess is he has professional interest as a world creator—and probably also thinks a Disney park will be fun.

"Looks like it's our turn." Ada gets up and I follow.

"You'll be able to enjoy our gift right away," I say to Alan. I give Mitya a narrow-eyed stare—he knew what Ada and I had prepared for Alan, yet he chose a gift that's very similar to ours. "I'd like everyone to pay attention to the public VR."

Ada lets me launch the B-Day app, and the museum around us comes alive.

CHAPTER THREE

A flock of pterosaurs swoops toward our big table, and Mom squeals in excitement. The giant skeleton in the room grows meat and muscle, and is seconds away from manifesting skin. When the monster dinosaur begins to move, it gives Godzilla a run for her (or is it his?) money.

"Our room is but a small part of the world Ada and I put together," I tell the awestruck guests. "Other rooms in the museum are also animating right now. Here are some highlights." I share screens with everyone so they can see the walking mummies, the giant blue whale that sings its song as it splashes the virtual water on the first floor, and Ada's least favorite, Lucy and the other early hominids hunting animated mammals and dinosaurs from other exhibits.

For the first time today, Alan behaves as I imagine a four-year-old should: he jumps to his feet and runs to check out the rest of our creation.

Before Ada can notice and disapprove, Joe nods to a couple of his security people, and they follow Alan at a perfectly calculated distance.

The fact that our son is physically running is a testament to our gift's success. The kid is a master of distributing his mind into robots and cameras, to the point where Ada and I sometimes worry about his lack of physical activity.

Ada and I both take a bow, and the rest of the guests clap with genuine enthusiasm, even Muhomor. We sit back down, and Gogi pours another round of drinks across the table as giant virtual dragonflies swarm around his head.

"I don't mean to spoil the merriment," Joe says with a cold carelessness that contradicts his words, "but you should at least be aware of the protestors outside."

I suppress a groan as adrenaline surges through my veins. If there's a consequence of our success I could do without, it's the protests. If one is really happening outside the museum, it would be an especially unpleasant surprise. We tried so hard to keep this event a secret from the public.

It takes me just a moment to find the best camera from the myriad available outside. After a quick examination, my adrenaline levels stabilize. "These are the anti-GMO people," I say privately to Joe. "They're harmless."

My cousin doesn't bother showing his disdain for my opinion. He probably spent all his disdain on the protestors outside.

I inwardly sigh as I take another look at the crowd of haters. Despite the obscene money Human++ regularly spends on PR, these kinds of protests have been happening more frequently. It's shocking how many of our gifts to humanity have been met with hostility. In part, this is because certain technologies have been villainized by books, Hollywood, and special interest groups. Robots are a great example of the former, à la *The Terminator*, while GMOs are a good example of the latter.

What people don't seem to get is that we're smart enough to avoid Skynet scenarios and purposely keep Einstein's intellect far behind our own. Also, our genetically enhanced plants are different from the GMOs of old, in which foreign genes were introduced into traditional domestic plants. We use CRISPR and other gene-editing technologies to merely tweak certain genes in semi-domesticated or wild plants. The wild legumes and quinoa at this very table are the products of this work, and they're amazing—and the fact that they're being eaten by the richest and smartest people is a good indication of their lack of risk to human health. But it's hard to convert people who have turned their hatred of GMOs into a quasi-religion.

Ada nervously spikes her hair. "The Real Humans Only crowd is also outside. Joe was right to be concerned."

"Maybe those guys are not as violent as we think," I tell her, wishing I could believe my own words. "At least the RHO's cause is easier for me to understand." Seeing Ada frown, I add, "Though not agree with or condone."

Her frown deepens. "They're basically Luddites under a different name, except the machines they want to break are in our heads."

It's true. Like the original Luddites, the RHO worries that jobs will go away as a result of our technology, and there are good reasons for that. One Brainocyte-enhanced lawyer can do the workload of ten unenhanced lawyers; ditto with doctors and almost any other profession. Given that the world needs a limited number of doctors, some jobs could disappear. And it's not just experts in danger; regular workers will be impacted as well. Our tech now allows one person to control a group of robots that can do many of the difficult, dangerous, and dirty jobs that formerly required teams of people.

"Will this make it hard for the other guests to arrive?" I ask Joe. "Alan has an after-party planned."

"The after-party people are already here and have been vetted," Joe says.

Alan runs back into the room, catches his breath, and rattles out, "That was awesome. Thank you, Mom. Thank you, Dad."

"You came back just in time," I say to Alan as I spot the baker navigating his way into the hallway. No doubt he has also been vetted. "Prepare your wish."

Instead of saying something like Happy Birthday, Alan, the cake states P vs. NP in yummy chocolate sauce.

"What does that mean?" Uncle Abe asks. "And do I even want to know?"

"It's just a computer science problem I want to solve when I grow up," Alan replies with false modesty. "In a nutshell, this asks if every problem that can be quickly verified can also be quickly solved."

"By quickly, he means polynomial time," Muhomor says, though it's clear Uncle Abe couldn't care less if he actively tried. "I think we can all agree that P does not equal NP."

"You're just saying that because you hope it doesn't," Alan replies teasingly. "Tema would be beatable if P equals NP."

Alan and Muhomor begin to argue computer science theory, and everyone else focuses on their own conversations as they consume large quantities of dessert.

"You should let the after-party people in," I tell Joe when the last of the cake is gone. "The family portion of the festivities looks to be over."

As though on cue, everyone gets up and attempts to overcome their impending food comas by walking around the museum to check out Alan's gift. Alan, Ada, and I remain behind, since we already know what it looks like. Waiters attack the big table, and within minutes, the space is ready for the cocktail-style after-party.

"It's going to be great to see some of my friends for the first time," Alan tells us excitedly.

"Are these online-only friends?" I look my son up and down.

His mischievous expression turns defensive. "Do I have any other kind?"

"And did you tell them what you actually look like?" Ada asks sternly.

Alan starts to reply but stops when a man enters. The guy appears to be in his thirties, with the air of a college professor about him. I use face recognition to confirm my intuition; indeed, he's a tenured professor of philosophy at Columbia. His name is John Moore, and he isn't on any sexual predator lists—not that Joe would let him live, let alone enter this room, if he were.

John confidently walks over to me and holds out his hand. "Alan, it's a pleasure to finally meet you."

"Well, that answers that question," Ada tells me privately. "They don't realize they've come to a four-year-old's birthday."

"Hello, John." I give the man a warm handshake. "I'm not Alan."

"You're not?" He looks at Ada for help. "You look a lot like your avatar." He looks at her more closely. "I'm so sorry, are you Alan? You also look like that avatar, but I thought you were a man. Not that—"

"I'm Ada," she cuts in. "This is Mike." She gestures at me. "And this"—she points at our son—"is Alan."

"I really enjoyed our discussion about the Cambridge Declaration on Consciousness," Alan tells John, his eyes beaming with mischief. "I just sent you details for our party VR session. If you enter it, you'll be able to see me in the guise you're more comfortable with."

Once John's eyes stop threatening to jump out of his sockets, he uses his Brainocytes to see Alan's adult avatar.

"I hope you don't begrudge me this surprise," Alan says both in VR and the real world. "I decided my birthday would be the perfect time to come out as a four-year-old. I couldn't figure out a way to explain it online."

"But how?" John whispers. "Is this a prank?"

As Alan explains about his Brainocytes, Joe glides over silently and grasps John's shoulder so firmly John cringes in pain.

"If I may have a word," Joe says. "Now that you know who you came here to see, I just want to say—"

I don't hear the rest, because he leans in and whispers into John's ear.

John's previously awestruck expression changes, and his pale face turns an almost purple shade of terror. It doesn't take a lot of imagination to figure out that Joe must've told him something like, "If you touch my nephew in any way, especially the wrong way, your short and painful life will not be long enough to get onto the registered sex offenders list."

"Joe," Alan says, obviously realizing the same thing, "stop bullying my friends."

Joe reluctantly lets go of John's shoulder and stalks to the far corner of the room.

To diffuse the tension, I look up the Cambridge Declaration on Consciousness and learn that it states that many animals are conscious and aware.

"The number of scientists who signed the Cambridge Declaration on Consciousness is truly impressive," I say casually. "Their list of species is great too. Besides mammals, they included birds and even octopuses."

"Maybe this means people will finally understand this basic, self-evident truth," Ada grumbles. "Animals are just as self-aware as we are."

"But not necessarily as intelligent," John chimes in, his demeanor turning professorial. "Consciousness does not equate to intelligence."

"No, but admitting that animals have consciousness should at least be enough for people to enlarge their circle of empathy to include them." Ada plants her feet wider apart and regards John belligerently. "We don't eat unintelligent human beings, do we?"

John blinks and pushes his glasses higher up his nose. "I see where Alan gets some of his views. I understand what you're saying, of course, but you can't downplay the role of intelligence."

Alan glances at his mom worriedly. Like me, he's aware this is a touchy subject. "Can we try another thought experiment, John, like usual?"

John looks at the real-world Alan and rubs his temples. "I'm still adjusting to the fact that you're you. But sure, let's hear it."

"Let's say there existed a rat who was smart," Alan begins. In our private VR, he winks at me. He's obviously talking about Mr. Spock and his relatives, but John doesn't know that.

"Okay," John replies. "I can picture that."

"Now let's further assume this rat is intelligent by most definitions of the word. To simplify, let's say this rat is smarter than most of my peers."

"Right," John says. "What you describe is a scenario where we'd have to be very nice to such a rat. We'd treat the rat as a person. If such a magical creature existed."

"So you claim the fact that the rat is intelligent, not the fact that he's conscious, is the criterion for giving him nicer treatment?" Alan asks. "According to the Cambridge Declaration, all rats are conscious, since they're mammals."

"I'd say my position is more nuanced, but yes, I guess that's what I believe." John takes a step away from Ada, who's not even trying to hide her dislike of his philosophy.

"Forget the rat, then," Alan says. "Suppose there's an entity, an intelligent creature that's smarter than a human by the same factor that a human is smarter than a rat."

"Okay," John says hesitantly.

"Would such a creature have the right to treat human beings as 'nicely' as humans currently treat rats?" Alan steeples his tiny real-world fingers. "Run experiments on them, develop special poisons to try to wipe humanity out of existence, place sticky traps that will cause people to die horrific deaths, and so on?"

"Well," John says, rubbing his temples more vigorously this time, "I think that—"

Someone coughs, and John doesn't get a chance to finish his thought. A woman has come in and is peering around the crowd.

"Margret?" Alan yells. "We're over here."

Margret seems even more confused than John when she realizes how old her online friend is. According to face recognition, she's a theoretical computer scientist working at one of the larger NYC hedge funds. Her specialty is Big Data, which is probably what she and Alan talk about. He has an uncanny ability to see patterns in large quantities of data and is always trying to understand how his mind does what it does.

More people arrive, and the conversations move toward Alan's favorite subjects of identity, consciousness, and the technological singularity.

"If we define the singularity as the point when a regular person can no longer keep up with technology," Margret says, "my mother is already experiencing it."

"I define the singularity as the point when things radically change and the speed of advancements skyrockets beyond anyone's wildest dreams," Mitya says. "Right now, things are moving fast—but when the singularity hits, our progress will seem like a snail's pace in comparison. I agree, though, the term 'singularity' is definitely beginning to mean different things to different people."

John adjusts his glasses. "To me, it means AI running amok and causing something like the technological Armageddon. It's the start of a dystopia where humanity becomes extinct."

"I didn't realize you sympathized with the people outside," Alan says. Of course he knows about the RHO protestors. "I see the singularity as a point when humanity finally matures and becomes something it was always meant to be, something more than thinking meat… something rationally transcendent." He looks up at the adult faces, and when he sees everyone listening, he continues with fervor. "We can be a way for the universe to become aware of itself. Brain enhancements and integration with our AI and other technology is just the first step. In the long term, I see us becoming first a planet-sized conglomeration of minds, then a galaxy-sized intellect, and on and on, as far as the laws of physics allow."

"There may be as many definitions of the singularity as there are people," Ada says as she gazes proudly at our son. "My own vision is closer to that of Alan's, because I know we can bring it about and avoid any apocalyptic scenarios."

I nod at her words. "We take the concept of 'the world is what you make it' to its full, logical extreme," I say. "With us watching over it, I think the singularity will usher in a new step in evolution, a time when we'll take everything we cherish about being human and push it to an eleven out of ten."

"Even if these rosy predictions come into being," John says with the tone of someone who doubts it very much, "will the beings that inhabit the future actually be human?"

"Why not?" Ada asks. "Though even if they weren't, they would in the worst case be, in the words of Hans Moravec, our mind children."

She glances adoringly at Alan, and when she notices I've followed her gaze, she locks eyes with me and winks.

"I still have to respectfully disagree," John says. "Being human is so closely tied to being biological that I think becoming pure technology will turn people into machines."

"Perhaps I can take a stab at it," Mitya says. "You're a fan of thought experiments, so why don't I try one?"

"Sure," John says with an eagerness only a philosophy professor could possess. "Please."

"Imagine that someone has invented an artificial neuron," Mitya says. "Now also imagine that someone has taken one of your biological neurons and replaced it with the artificial one. You'd still be you, correct?"

"I'm familiar with this idea." John sips from his champagne glass. "It's called the neuron replacement thought experiment. Once I agree that I'm still the same after getting a single artificial neuron, you'll ask, what about a hundred? Then what about a billion? And soon after that, what if we replaced all of them?"

"Well, just because you know it doesn't mean it's not persuasive," Mitya says. "You'd still be you, even if the substrate of your brain were artificial."

"I can only counter this with a thought experiment that is just as persuasive," John says with a smirk. "It's called the Chinese room argument, postulated by John Searle…"

I tune out the rest of the discussion, because this topic reminds me that Ada and I still must break the news of tomorrow's trip to the birthday boy. Our regular work-related travel is a source of upset for Alan, mainly because he thinks he's now old enough and mature enough to join us.

"When do we tell him?" I ask Ada after I pull her into a private VR room that is the exact replica of our living room.

"Let's not ruin the party," she says without clarifying the what or the who, a sign this topic is on her mind as much as it is on mine. "He's having such a good time."

Since Alan is currently poking holes in John's best arguments, I'm forced to agree. The kid loves winning arguments, though it's harder when he debates someone as augmented as himself.

"He'll be mad if we tell him at the last minute." I plop into a replica of my favorite rocking lounge chair and stare at the replica of our awesome Manhattan view.

"I'd rather he be mad on a less special day—like tomorrow," Ada counters. She breaks the VR room's consistency by magicking herself a replica of her office chair to sit on. "I still vote for tomorrow."

"We can always blame Joe again and say he's the one who thinks it's not safe. It's mostly the truth." I rock back and forth in my lounger. For some reason, Alan's puppy eyes work much better on me than on Ada, and I'm not looking forward to this unpleasant task.

"We should tell him in VR," she says ruthlessly. "Tomorrow afternoon, when we're on the way to our destinations."

"You mean so that he won't be able to strong-arm us to take him?" I fight the urge to get up from the chair and start pacing.

"No." She pushes her chair closer and reaches over to clasp my hand. "We tell him that way so that it comes off as the law of the land rather than a topic for debate."

"That might be too authoritarian. I thought we were trying to be authoritative instead."

"I knew it was a mistake to have you read those books on parenting styles." She squeezes my hand. "How about we tell him in the morning at breakfast? Then it can be a back-and-forth, as long as the two of us agree that he's not going this time, no matter what he says."

"Agreed." I feel bad for Alan. He has no chance of winning against this conspiracy of parents.

"I didn't realize that having a preschooler would be this tough." She drops her hand. "It's much worse than those books on child development said."

"If you think this is bad, let's see what happens when he's a teenager."

We both jokingly shudder, but we're all too aware of the Russian proverb: "There is part truth in every joke."

CHAPTER FOUR

The island country of Curaçao is among the shrinking number of places without widespread Brainocyte adoption—hence my reason for being on this stage.

I survey the huge crowd gathered in front of me and activate a special version of the BraveChill app that's custom made to counteract stage fright. As soon as I'm calmer, I let myself gaze into the distance, where smoke chugs from factory pipes incongruent with the idyllic Caribbean Sea beyond.

"Dear friends." I begin in English and instantly say it again in Dutch and Papiamento, mainly as an easy way to demonstrate some of the things I'm about to present. "My name is Mike Cohen, and I'm here to tell you about Human++ and its gift to you and the world. Specifically, I want to discuss our paradigm-changing product, Brainocytes, and our free-energy project that will greatly improve your skies."

I point at the smoke pipes, and the crowd cheers. I wait for them to calm down before I proceed with the rest of my speech, a spiel that's been carefully crafted by our PR department. I tell the crowd that they're going to get free electricity, the same free electricity that most of the world already enjoys. This is the easy part of the talk, because most people find the idea of free energy easy to understand. Here in the Caribbean, people picture themselves using as much AC as they want; elsewhere, they imagine leaving all their lights on and never paying the electric bill.

I explain some of the bigger but less intuitive consequences of free energy, like no more paying for gas after switching to an electric car. When I talk about the possibility of nearly free fresh water, I get cheers and clapping. The clapping turns into a standing ovation when I proceed to explain how few will go hungry as the price of food production plummets.

Joe's security people pass a mic into the crowd, and a wise-looking woman asks, "If all this is free, how do you make your money?"

"That's a great question," I reply. "We use a freemium model. Most private individuals and small businesses will get electricity for free, but bigger businesses with heavier consumption will incur some cost. But that cost is still going to be a fraction of what they're used to, so everyone is happy in the end."

"This part of the lecture isn't playing as well here in Bahrain," Mitya says in our private VR meeting.

The VR space perfectly mimics our favorite conference room in the Human++ tower, right down to the touchscreen boards, ultramodern furniture, and dazzling view of the Manhattan skyline. Though every one of us is physically conducting a similar presentation somewhere around the globe, it's become our policy to keep one instance of our virtual avatars sitting in this room. Muhomor, Alan, Ada, and I are almost always in this room in some fashion anyway, but Joe only joins on days like today, when his security guys are on high alert.

"This part of the spiel never does well in places where oil helps the economy," Ada agrees. "Here on Iturup Island, we're close enough to Russia for people to also be a little wary."

"They might be wary because some of them grew up hearing about free stuff," I say.

"Yeah, that's how most understood what communism would be like," Mitya says.

"Why did Ada get to go to the Kuril Islands again?" Muhomor grumbles. "I still say it should've been one of us native Russian speakers. As you just made obvious, we don't just speak the language natively, we understand the culture—"

"If it's complaining time now," Alan says, "I resent staying back in the States."

"Resent" is a polite word for his actual feelings on the subject. He nearly threw an age-appropriate temper tantrum when we told him that no, he would not be presenting. He doesn't understand our possibly irrational parental worry about sending a four-year-old overseas by himself. Besides, how seriously would people without Brainocytes take such a tiny presenter?

The large virtual screens behind my friends show the crowd and their surroundings at each location. Mitya's crowd in Bahrain is probably the largest, and even through the virtual window, I can almost feel the heat of his dusty yellow surroundings. Ada's gathering on Iturup Island is the smallest, though that could be an illusion thanks to the never-ending sea in the distance. Muhomor's location is a lot like mine, minus any industry; he's on the tropical island of Les Cayemites in Haiti. Each of us have Joe's security people around us, and a couple of robot surrogate bodies as well, in part for security but also for my favorite part of the demo, which will happen toward the end.

On a whim, I embody the robot to Ada's left and use its sensors to savor the crisp, salty air. I then possess a robot next to Mitya and confirm the low humidity and heat.

"Now let me tell you about Brainocytes," I say into the microphone. I can feel the crowd grow more alert; this is probably what they came to hear about.

I explain that Brainocytes are nanomachines that interface with the brain. Once my listeners have an idea what the signature tech does, I move on to dispel some common worries that always come up about our products.

"No brain surgery is required to get Brainocytes." I reach into my pocket and pull out a little square piece of fabric I have prepared for the presentation. "The current delivery method is transdermal patches like this one." I wave the patch and put an image of it on the big screen behind me.

Meanwhile, in the VR room, our conversation contin-ues full on. Ada looks at Mitya. "How are things going on the delivery front? I'm tired of explaining these patches."

"We'll be able to put Brainocytes into the drinking wa-ter shortly." Mitya has been driving this initiative, and it's clear he takes great pleasure in showing off how quickly he's accomplished this task. "We've honed it to the point where Brainocytes will only activate in adult humans, but I still don't think we ought to put it in water where people don't want or know about Brainocytes."

This is an old argument between Mitya and Ada, one that the rest of us haven't taken sides on. Ada wants to put Brainocytes into the water supply in places where the government oppresses the populace, as these are usually also places where the government doesn't let us deliver or market Brainocytes to willing customers. But Mitya thinks that despite the tyrannical regimes in those places, we have no right to put machines into people's bodies without their consent, even if they would provide greater freedom for said people.

"It's going to be a moot point soon," Alan chimes in. "Every dictator and tyrant now has Brainocytes in his head anyway, so eventually they'll want it for their people too."

"Ah, the naïveté of the young." Muhomor's VR shades hover in the air without temples or a nose bridge, mak-ing him look like a poker player from space. "Just as with any other form of power, the dictators will want to hoard Brainocytes for themselves."

"You're wasting time on these arguments," I interject. "We know thousands of patches got smuggled into even the most closed-down countries. Once the dissidents, or whoever the users are, tell regular citizens about the benefits of our tech, people might start a revolution to get their hands on Brainocytes."

"Which segues well into our next real-world point," Ada says.

She's right, because I say out loud in Curaçao, "At the very basic level, this technology can replace a personal computer of any kind, as well as your TV, your music player, your smartphone, GPS, AI assistants such as Siri, Alexa, and Cortana, devices like the Kindle, gaming consoles, and pretty much all other gadgets. We're revolutionizing education and how people work. Widespread Brainocyte adoption is taking the internet revolution to the next level..."

"Our PR people have dumbed down the message," Alan complains back in the VR room. "When I finally get a chance to speak at these conferences, I'll write my own speech."

"So what does the wise toddler think we should be saying?" Even through his shades, it's clear Muhomor just rolled his eyes.

"People might worry about self-replicating nanotechnology," Alan says. I feel proud as a father on a couple of levels but particularly when I realize how stoically Alan just ignored Muhomor's insult—proving that in many ways, Alan is the more mature of these two. "You should tell them about our nonreplicating nanofactories and how—"

"Too technical," Muhomor counters. "And if we tell them why we're being careful with nanotech replication, they'll just get scared."

"Then we should at least tell them about the opportunity to get premium services." Alan's avatar now resembles Ada, and I wonder if he's created an algorithm that morphs his face based on the topic of conversation.

My son is talking about Ada's initiative: paying people to create content that's beneficial to humankind. Ada wants to encourage people to write wiki pages and blogs, to create original art, and to even put up nice pictures of themselves so that other people might enjoy them. The idea, as she puts it, is to "encourage an era of cultural expression." To that end, we created a version of Einstein to trawl the internet for such activities. When he finds any, he rewards the content producer with special points that can be turned into cash or premium services.

"That program makes us seem too Machiavellian," Muhomor says. "And we don't want people to know the truth about that." His glasses float upward, and when they clear the middle of his forehead, his right eye winks conspiratorially.

"You also don't mention some of the benefits of Einstein." Alan's face now morphs to more closely resemble mine—I guess because he knows I like Einstein's features more than Ada does. "Einstein's getting to know each user better than they know themselves. He's on the cusp of helping people with critical decisions. He'll be a sort of digital consciousness for many. He might tell them whom to date or remind them not to make deals when their blood pressure is too high or their dopamine levels too low."

"It makes Einstein sound like Big Brother," Ada says.

She so rarely agrees with Muhomor on anything that everyone in the room exchanges glances.

I chuckle. "Alan actually sees Einstein as a big brother—but in a literal sense, not in a *1984* way."

"If our users wanted to fear anyone, it should be us, not Einstein," Alan says.

"And therefore, you shouldn't write your own speeches," Muhomor says with finality. "If Marcus in PR heard what you just said, his Brainocytes would explode out of his brain."

We move on to less contentious subjects in the VR room, while in the real world, I explain how Brainocytes will work with Global Terahertz wireless internet, a Human++ freemium product Curaçao already utilizes. Global Terahertz will keep Brainocytes users connected to Human++ servers at all times (unless some evil scientist puts them in a Faraday cage with thick lead walls). Many eyes light up as I explain the potential, including voting with one's mind, crystal clear air in large cities, VR dating and relationships, and a slew of other sweeping societal changes.

The conference is going smoother than usual, yet something begins to bother me.

The events of four and a half years ago taught me to trust my paranoia. I put an end to all my parallel activities, leaving my attention on the VR conference room and the real world. In a fraction of a second, I beat ChessMaster, the world's best AI algorithm, and refuse it a rematch; I complete four Rubik's Cubes I've been solving in parallel; and I stop writing my fifty-sixth novel and submit all the unfinished code I was just working on to source control.

As often happens, the extra attention I now direct to the real world gives me the illusion that I'm watching reality in slow motion. On the surface, everything looks routine, like the many conferences we've done before. Yet despite the BraveChill app, I'm overcome with a strong sense of dread.

Parts of my mind are identifying dangers before my conscious awareness can catch up.

Frantically, I scan my surroundings through the eyes of the robots next to Ada, Mitya, and Muhomor. At first, I can't even verbalize what I see. Then my vision zooms in on a guy in the crowd around Mitya, and I understand what's been bothering me.

This guy's clothes are way too bulky for the unforgiving Middle Eastern heat.

Now that I know what to look for, I see men wearing something similar at every location, including my own.

"Suicide bombers!" I shout in the VR room.

In an instant, I text images of the suspects to Joe and his security teams in every region, and put them up on screen in the VR room. If I'm wrong and these aren't suicide vests, I'd rather apologize for being paranoid.

While everyone's reacting to my revelation, the guy in Mitya's crowd inches toward the stage with wild eyes. I jump my awareness into a robot, using his camera eyes to zoom in on the man's hands, and my metallic robot jaws clench with an audible clunk.

He's closing his hand around a device clutched in front of his chest.

I analyze the device in a picosecond. It can only be a detonator.

The man's features contort in fear.

Someone else, probably Mitya, takes control of the bulkier robot to my right. I make my robot follow his and prepare to jump toward the bomber.

I don't need a brain boost to realize that the robots will not make it in time.

"Run!" I scream through metal lips as my robot flies through the crowd.

"Run!" I yell at Mitya in the VR room.

The robots might as well be miles away, because the bomber's fingers finish squeezing the detonator.

All cameras at Mitya's location show a flash of fire.

I leave my robot before it's ripped apart, but not before I get a horrific glimmer of flesh exploding around me. The microphones roar with soul-piercing static. Then all video and audio goes silent at Mitya's location.

"Mitya!" I scream. "Are you okay?"

Mitya doesn't reply.

We all stare at Mitya's VR room avatar, who stands wide-eyed and uncomprehending. Then the avatar lets out an inhuman scream and turns pixelated—like a ghost inside a machine.

CHAPTER FIVE

I've never felt this disjointed.

It's as though there are four distinct versions of me operating completely independently of each other. One, a purely emotional one, is beginning to grieve for Mitya, whose avatar is still disappearing from VR like a mirage.

In complete contrast, the other versions of me exemplify bloodthirst and pragmatism. Enraged, I slam my consciousness into a robot at Ada's right and leap for the bomber in her crowd. I'm glad we overdesigned the strength and speed of these metallic bodies, as I'm flying at an incredible speed. But even this breakneck rescue might not be fast enough.

No.

What just happened to Mitya isn't going to happen to Ada.

I won't let it.

I operate on pure instinct. Grabbing my left robotic arm with the right one, I rip it off. The swell of pain is sharp, but I ignore it.

Teeth clenched, I hurl the separated limb at the approaching bomber.

The metal arm whooshes through the air and smacks into my target's right shoulder. The man stumbles back, the trigger device clattering to the ground.

Before I can rejoice, he recovers and crouches to pick it up with his uninjured left arm.

I'm grateful the crowd flees from the bomber, because no one impedes my progress. The one-armed robot body lands in front of the crouching man, and I use its remaining left hand to punch into the mushy human body of my enemy. My metal fingers rip through the rib cage and close around a piece of pulsing flesh.

"He was about to kill Ada," I say grimly in VR, as though someone were about to criticize my actions.

No one replies as I pull the asshole's beating heart out of his chest like a priest in some macabre Aztec ritual. The people around us scream. A video of this kill will undoubtedly end up on YouTube, confirming all the fears the paranoiacs have about our robots, but I'm beyond caring.

Back in my real body, I reach into my pocket for the gun one of Joe's people handed me earlier today. The security team around me already has their weapons out, but my training at the range pays off yet again. In less time than it takes the bomber to blink, I put a bullet in his brain.

In the past, I might've worried about taking a life, but paradoxically, it's my respect for life that makes me take the headshot. If the bomber got the chance to squeeze the trigger, hundreds of people would've died. And hey, the asshole was in the process of killing himself anyway. If Ada gives me crap about this later, I can truthfully tell her that a headshot was the best and safest solution.

At the same time as I'm rescuing Ada and myself, I also take charge of a robot near Muhomor. But as soon as I begin to move, I see that I'm too late.

The bomber squeezes the trigger.

All the blood drains from my face.

"I'm sorry." My voice cracks in VR. "I tried."

"Don't worry about me." Muhomor manages to sound smug. "I found a way to jam that signal."

Stunned, I realize the bomb didn't go off. And though my robot is no longer running toward the bomber, another one is.

Wild-eyed, I scan the VR room. "Who—"

"It's me," Alan says. "I think—"

In the real world, the bomber realizes his bomb isn't going to work, so he pulls out a gun and aims it at Muhomor. In the time he takes aim, I've blocked my friend with my robotic metal body. Joe's security people also move to shield him, but Muhomor is already on the move, his exoskeleton legs outpacing even the robots.

The bomber must've realized he won't be able to hit him, because he turns the gun in his own direction.

It takes me less than a millisecond to recognize his plan. The bomber wants to plant a bullet in his own chest, probably to activate the bomb. I have no time to research if this maneuver will succeed or not, so I assume the worst.

Though Muhomor is running quickly, he can't outpace the spread of an explosion. Frantically, I grope for solutions as the bomber's hand continues its deadly arc, but nothing comes to mind.

This is when Alan's robot lands next to the bomber. Before the bomber can finish turning the gun at his chest, Alan rips off the guy's suicide vest with the smooth motion of a hungry ape insta-peeling a banana.

The bomber stumbles back, his gun turning upward.

"Alan, stop him!" Joe yells in the VR room. "I need him alive."

But it's too late. Before Alan can command his robot to do anything, the bomber aims the gun under his chin and presses the trigger.

The shot is deafening, bits of blood and brain matter flying everywhere. In every crowd, people are screaming in different languages, but their behavior is uniform: everyone is trying to get away from the bombers and the stages.

Overwhelmed, I allow Joe's security people to take over. In Curaçao, I'm ushered backstage and swiftly led to a bulletproof car. Through the eyes of the robots, I see everyone else getting into other bulletproof cars.

As we speed away from the presentation sites, I finally recover my wits enough to say dazedly inside the VR room, "Someone coordinated an attack on us."

Alan nods gravely. "There's also an anomaly going on with our Ohio data centers. It might—"

"You're both focusing on the wrong thing," Ada says hoarsely. Her punky avatar is sitting in the corner of the virtual room, her knees clasped tightly against her chest. "Don't you remember? Mitya is dead."

I freeze, feeling like I've just been hit by a tsunami of ice. The heat of battle pushed Mitya's fate out of my mind, but it's all I can think about now. My chest is painfully tight, my heart like a block of lead inside my ribcage. Mitya's avatar is still evaporating, one pixel at a time, and in desperation, I wonder whether Ada could be wrong.

Maybe my best friend isn't truly gone.

Filled with sudden hope, I tap into satellite imagery and zoom in on Mitya's position. As soon as I get a clear view of the blast site, though, I have no choice but to accept that Ada is right. Our smart bones are stronger than regular bones, and the Respirocytes in our bloodstreams allow us to go for a while without breathing, but none of these advantages could've helped Mitya. The pieces of charred human flesh around the stage leave no room for doubt.

Not a single person on that stage could've survived.

The pain is so intense it steals my breath away. I feel like I'm about to shatter. It's too much, too overwhelming—the horrified faces that mirror mine in the VR room, the knowledge that I was too late to save my friend.

That I'll never see him again.

Dragging in a shallow breath, I wrap my arms around my real-world body, and in VR, I create a separate room to be alone.

The worst part about my pain is that Brainocytes allow us to manipulate what and how we feel. Ada has been experimenting with apps that expand her circle of empathy, as she calls it, so that she's able to fully empathize with the suffering of non-humans. In this moment, I'm tempted to manipulate my experience in the opposite direction with an app that would make me numb. The only thing that stops me is knowing that if I feel numb after learning my friend is dead, I might as well be effectively dead myself.

It quickly becomes clear that seclusion is not helping, so I do what I always do when I feel down: I invite Mr. Spock into the room. The rat is now savvy enough with the VR interface that he has an avatar, a largish white rat that looks much fiercer than the real Mr. Spock. As soon as my furry companion runs up to me, I make my own avatar small enough that I can hug him to my chest like a teddy bear.

"What's wrong?" he asks in Zik. He and his kin now have the vocabularies of unenhanced four-year-olds. "Are you cold? Are you hungry?"

I hug him tighter. I guess he can tell I'm not in a talkative mood, because he begins to brux, a behavior I've grown to find soothing.

"Maybe we should have an unscheduled session?" asks the accented voice of Einstein's shrink instantiation. True to his current role, the AI looks and sounds more like Freud than the famous physicist.

"Maybe later," I tell him grimly. "Let me be."

In the real world, Joe's people move me from the bulletproof car into a helicopter. I go along without complaint.

Being with Mr. Spock helps me get a grip on my chaotic emotions, and I return to the joint VR room. Ada's avatar is quietly crying, so I approach her and pull her into my embrace, feeling awful for leaving, even if it was only for a brief time.

Mitya might not have been her best friend, but she needs consolation as much as I do.

As I hold her, gently stroking her back while I battle my own grief, I notice something strange. Mitya's remaining pixels have stopped dissipating. In fact, they may be slowly regenerating. His avatar is re-solidifying, like the Cheshire cat from *Alice in Wonderland*.

I wait for a few moments to be sure, then clear my throat. "Guys, if Mitya is dead, what's going on with his avatar?"

"I don't think of myself as dead," says the reappearing avatar, and goosebumps spread all over my body as he continues. "I prefer to think of myself as facing some physical challenges—or whatever the current politically correct term is for an invalid. Think of me as an amputee who just happens to have lost every part of his body."

CHAPTER SIX

I gape at the avatar as questions pepper Mitya from the rest of the room.

"Dude, I see your charred remains," I manage to say when I regain my voice.

Mitya's avatar is now completely solid, and there's a hyperrealism to it, like when you switch from regular TV to ultrahigh definition. Also different are his clothes. He's wearing something reminiscent of a toga and a helmet with a swan on top, and he's carrying a double-headed axe and a shield with a bull's face etched on the front.

"Okay," he says, interrupting the nonstop questions. "Here's the deal. As you guys know, I've been worried about my biological brain."

"Right," I say for everyone. I already know what he's about to say, but we all need to hear him say it before we can officially start to process the information.

"I last backed up the biological connectome when I went to bed yesterday," the strangely dressed avatar continues. "When my unfortunate disembodiment occurred a few minutes ago, a special set of instructions was activated as soon as my Brainocytes declared official brain death—a set of instructions you people would have thought paranoid."

"You figured out a way to run your mind without the biological brain?" Ada gasps. "I thought you were still far away from making that work."

"I settled on a prototype solution about six months ago. Just didn't have a good way to test it." He lets go of his axe and shield, and they hover in the air. "Is this so hard to believe? Only a small fraction of your mind is biological now, anyway."

Muhomor looks him up and down a couple of times. "It's not just the brain that makes us what we are. There's also the rest of the body."

"Speaking of that," Alan asks, clearly intrigued, "how does it feel to be without a body?"

Mitya grimaces. "I can't tell you for sure, because I was only without a body for a few subjective milliseconds. Now, though, I'm running an ultrarealistic simulation of the real body"—he spreads his VR arms—"plus I'm inside a couple of our top-of-the-line surrogate bodies as we speak—though I have to say, we'll need to further this line of research immensely, else I can forget about going on a real-world date."

He doesn't seem too put out, but that's not surprising. Even when he had a body, Mitya mostly used VR for intimate encounters because of an obsessive fear of sexually transmitted diseases.

Muhomor stares pointedly at the axe. "Okay, I'll be the asshole to ask: what's with the getup? This is not how you used to dress when you were a real boy."

"Since I'm pretty much pure mind now, I figured I'd make myself look like the Slavic god of wisdom." Mitya pointedly grabs the axe and shield from the air and waits expectantly. When no one says anything, he says with clear disappointment, "Radagast."

I can't help but look up the god in question.

"According to what I just read, Radagast was a god of hospitality," Muhomor says, beating me to it. "Hence the 'Rad' part, which is Russian for 'happy,' and 'gast' for 'guest.'"

"It's also very likely that such a god didn't exist," Alan adds, "at least according to what I see on the Russian Wikipedia page. Radagast might've been the name of a town that an ancient chronicler accidentally turned into the name of a deity."

"And most importantly," Ada says, finally smiling, "Radagast was the name of that wizard in *The Hobbit* movies, the one who lived with a bunch of animals in the woods. Then again, I guess I do see some resemblance." She puts up a screen with the likeness of the crazy old man in question.

Mitya's avatar momentarily shimmers, and a moment later, he's standing there in a very typical jeans-and-hoodie outfit. "I didn't expect this much teasing on the day I die."

"Jokes aside," I say, staring at my lifelike, sort-of-dead friend, "you're going to be legally dead. What does that mean for your fortune? For your status in human society?"

"Funny you should bring that up." He stands up straighter. "I'm discussing this very thing with Mr. Kadvosky right now. Hold on, let me pull him into this room."

A man with noble, eagle-like features appears—an avatar we all recognize as the favorite of Nathaniel Kadvosky, recently appointed Head Attorney at Human++. The avatar exudes gravitas to such a degree that no one dares mention that in the physical world, he looks more like a plucked sparrow.

"This is a historic case," Kadvosky says without so much as a hello. "Supreme Court judges would have a hard-on if they heard of this—at least those of them able to get hard-ons."

"It won't be that difficult to build a case." Mitya sounds as if he's continuing whatever conversation they began earlier. "I don't have a will—"

"Nor do you have children or close relatives," the lawyer says. "No one benefits if you're declared dead—aside from, perhaps, your business partners." He looks pointedly at the rest of the people in the room.

Mitya visibly saddens at the mention of his lack of family. His parents were murdered a while back, and he didn't take the loss well. It might even have been the trigger for the obsession that led him to research how to remain alive after death.

To pull him from his momentary funk, I say as confidently as I can, "Mitya's not dead, as far as I'm concerned. I would not challenge his share of the company."

"I feel the same," Ada says.

Muhomor nods. "He's as lame now as he's always been. I wouldn't declare him dead, that's for sure."

"So no heirs," Kadvosky sums up. "That's good, but that fact alone doesn't hand us the case. What will help is your idea of presenting this as a disability. There's a man in Florida who lost half his brain in an automotive accident, but he's fully functioning, thanks to Brainocytes, and no one disputes his personhood or that he is alive. We have quadriplegic people who move around on Human++ legs and eat with Human++ arms; no one challenges their status as living, either."

"Yeah, we can coin a new term: quinqueplegic, or septemplegic," Mitya says.

"I notice you skipped the term for six." Muhomor chuckles. He expectantly surveys our humorless faces, then defensively adds, "Because in that case, the term would sexplegic."

"If anyone here were sexplegic, it would be you," Ada tells Muhomor. I bet it's taking all her willpower not to smack him on the back of the head, something she feels she can let herself do in VR because it's not real violence.

"The actual term is irrelevant," Kadvosky says, and I'm impressed at the admirable job he's doing at pretending Muhomor isn't even there. "We can use whatever term the PR department decides would have the best resonance with the public."

"But what about the question of identity?" Alan asks. "I don't think we want to abandon the question of inheritance so quickly."

Ada and I exchange proud glances. Kadvosky seems to be lagging behind Alan's train of thought.

"What do you mean?" the lawyer asks.

"Knowing Mitya, he's probably already figuring out a way to copy himself," Alan says. When Mitya smiles mischievously, my son adds, "That's what's happening with the servers in Ohio, isn't it?"

"No," Mitya says. "The Ohio servers took the brunt of running what used to be my biological brain. All our servers are running at peak capacity now, which is why I wouldn't worry about my copying myself for a while."

Alan looks back at Kadvosky. "You need to plan for when he does clone himself. Who will own his money at that point?"

"Your other selves will certainly only get one vote during our Brainocyte Club meetings." Muhomor crosses his arms across his chest.

"I can remain a singleton for a while," Mitya says with a hint of disappointment. "Or I can design a new mind modality where me and my clones will become a sort of hive mind. But long term, yeah, this is something we'll need to work out—just not now. I'm sure a new copy of me should get some resources from me, a little bit like a child does from a par—"

"Why don't we focus on the immediate issue of your corporealness?" Kadvosky moves to adjust his glasses, then remembers he doesn't wear any in VR. "I don't think the

Supreme Court would find the fate of your copies as interesting as the status of your current self, though I personally find the implications fascinating and would gladly discuss them further."

"What is the worst-case scenario?" Mitya asks Kadvosky with a seriousness unusual for him. "Can the law decide I'm software that can simply be deleted?"

"No need to get so dramatic," Kadvosky says. "In the worst case, your legal status would be akin to that of Einstein. Before we let the AI drive cars and drones, we made sure it has the same legal rights as corporations. In other words, you will still be able to own things, be sued, and sue other people. You'll also be able to give money to political campaigns and so on."

"But corporations can't marry," Mitya says.

I can't resist. "If you find the right girl, you can have a merger."

Kadvosky gives me a scathing glance. "I have a lot of work ahead of me. I'm going to have to leave you to continue this conversation on your own. Just keep telling yourself that brain amputation is not death."

Without waiting for a reply—or perhaps dreading one—Kadvosky poofs out of the VR room in a manner most VR users would find rude. Leaving the room through the virtual door is quickly becoming the custom.

Alan responds to Mitya's subdued expression with a worried look. "Am I the only one who's looking on the bright side of this? You won't need food or to use the bathroom. You can run drug trial simulations on your simulated brain with no harmful side effects. You can boost your mind to a degree we can't even dream of. You can—"

"Young man," Ada says to Alan in her stern maternal voice, her hands on her hips, "don't even think about ditching your biological body, not over my d—"

Joe's avatar slams the conference table with such force that the virtual glass shatters and the table breaks into pieces.

"Enough of this bullshit," he says through gritted teeth. "It's time you apply your sorry excuse for enhanced brains to the actual attempt on your lives."

CHAPTER SEVEN

Ada and I exchange guilty looks. Joe is right. Someone put together a coordinated attack on us, one that spanned the whole globe.

"I already did some investigating," Mitya says defensively. "My thought process is at least double what it was when I was slowed down by a biological br—"

"Dude, stay on topic," I say, noting how Alan's eyes shine with avarice at this tidbit about Mitya's new state of being.

"Right." Mitya manifests screens with the faces of the four bombers and reads the bio as he points out the bomber from Bahrain. "This is Hamad Marhoon. He's a programmer for the Al Baraka Banking Group. He was the first of the bombers I thoroughly—"

"Racial stereotyping," Ada grumbles. "Great."

"If I were stereotyping, it wouldn't be that big of a leap." Mitya looks at me for support, since I was in Manhattan that day on 9/11. When I don't support him in time, he adds, "This doesn't seem to be Jihad-related—or whatever the politically correct term is for that type of terrorism."

"I agree," Muhomor chimes in. "Bahrain is a progressive coun—"

"Right." I nod. "Plus the other people involved in this make it seem unlikely." I already knew some of this from the facial recognition app that's always running in my head, but I haven't had the chance to analyze it yet.

Mitya points at the next man. "This is Vurnon Corsen. He's a Curaçao native who does security and IT for Campo Alegre, a legal brothel. He's a Catholic and a father of four. Nothing in his profile hints at why he'd want to hurt us at all, and I have a hard time picturing someone recruiting him to be a suicide bomber for any cause, let alone some radical Islam group. Even less suspicious is Garcelle Derulo, a Haiti national who worked for Royal Caribbean Cruises as a nurse. The man was a saint—he worked almost a week straight, pro bono, helping the recent earthquake victims. They wrote about him in the papers."

"I just checked the NSA files," Muhomor says. "None of these people were on any terrorist watch lists. Checking the Russian sources next."

"Speaking of Russia, this is Ermolai Ruzatov, and I think he's our best lead." Mitya motions at the pale face of the third bomber.

I realize I've been avoiding this bio because the man's face invokes conflicting emotions. On the one hand, he almost killed Ada, so he got what he deserved. I'd kill him again to keep her safe. On the other hand, I ripped this man's heart out of his chest—not something I would've imagined myself capable of, even if the situation demanded it.

"Ruzatov is a quality assurance engineer for Gazprom," Mitya reads. "He's never been religious and has no living family and only a few friends outside work."

"He doesn't belong to any terrorist groups, either." Muhomor puts up a bio in Russian, something he must've gotten from the "Russian sources" we'd rather not know about.

Ruzatov seems boring, as far as Russian government interests go. He's never criticized the current regime or done anything worthy of notice.

"Why did this Ruzatov come to our conference?" I ask. "He's from Vladivostok. He would have no trouble getting Brainocytes there."

Muhomor looks smug. "They all had Brainocytes, every one of the bombers. But that and their fascination with technology in general is the only thing I can see that links them all—and they share that fascination with billions of other people."

Ada rubs her temples. "I won't ask how you know they had Brainocytes."

We pride ourselves on the privacy we provide to our users, so the fact that Muhomor can get that information so quickly isn't something we'd ever want the public to know.

"Don't be so paranoid," he says. "I simply extrapolated their Brainocytes status based on how they used easier-to-hack technology."

"So," I say before Ada can have a fit of righteousness, "did they ever email each other? Or call each other? Or meet in person?"

"No. At least, not prior to getting Brainocytes. Afterward, it's harder to say. Everything sent out is Tema-encrypted."

"What about the bombs?" I look at Joe. "There are ways to track those."

"Working on it," my cousin says. "But the local police departments aren't being very helpful. Did any of those four people show any interest in the Luddite movement?"

Muhomor looks thoughtful for a moment—probably querying his prodigious resources. "Ruzatov had a coworker named Eugene Blinov who's part of the Green Party. That's the closest connection I could find. But the Russian Greens aren't that interested in Human++."

"Why, Joe?" I ask, recalling the protestors outside the museum on Alan's birthday. "Do you think the RHO or someone like that is behind this?"

"I don't know." Joe kicks a large piece of the virtual table glass, and it shatters against the wall. "I'll find out soon, though."

"It's feasible," Mitya says. "The Unabomber was anti-technology, and his manifesto sounds like the same crap you might hear from the RHO."

"I'll deal with the RHO," Joe says with barely disguised menace.

"Don't hurt anyone," Ada warns.

"Not without evidence," I clarify.

Ada gives me a narrow-eyed glare.

"I could use some help investigating in Russia," Joe says without dignifying our comments with a reply.

"I'm not going to Russia," Muhomor and I say at the same time.

Muhomor is a wanted man there, and I still have nightmares from what happened the last time I was in the country.

"Uncle Joe doesn't want you to go," Alan chimes in. "He'd have a hard time protecting you there. He probably wants you to use one of our robots—so can I help?"

Joe gives Muhomor and me a look that seems to say, "How is it that a four-year-old is so much smarter than the two of you?"

"That's a great idea," Mitya says. "I can help also. The only trick is getting some avatar bodies. Because of the laws against them, we have very few operating in Russia and none in Vladivostok right now. I should be there in a couple of hours, though."

"You start on that," I say. "The rest of us will think through other possibilities and explore other angles."

Everyone gets busy, and as things quiet down in the VR room, I get a private telepathic message from Ada: "Please join me in the Bedroom."

The Bedroom is a euphemism for the virtual reality sex room Ada and I use for intimate encounters when we're not in proximity to each other (our Manhattan penthouse also has a non-virtual room designated for sex only, separate from our bedroom).

As soon as I think about it, I find myself there. Out of habit, I enhance my muscles in the way I hope Ada likes and put on an outfit she designed for me to wear here (one I wouldn't be caught dead wearing in the real world).

As soon as I see the expression on my wife's face, I realize this isn't going to be the usual sort of session we have in this room. Her eyes look puffy, and there are deep worry lines on her forehead—incongruous details among the sex toys, swings, mirrored walls, racks of lingerie, gallons of scented oils, and ultrarealistic VR characters with slack expressions and varying degrees of seductive nudity.

Seeing Ada like this instantly makes me wish we could be in front of each other in person. But I still have a few hours of flight time before I reach New York City, and her flight is longer still.

"I thought I would lose you." Her hands are visibly shaking as I take her small, cold palms in mine.

"It's okay, babe." I try to sound as reassuring as I can. "You're stuck with me forever."

A hint of a smile lifts her lips. I build on my success and grab her in a large hug. The benefit of the hug is that she can't see my face, because I suspect I don't look that reassuring. Now that we're past the battle and the shock of Mitya dying, I allow myself to contemplate the horrible possibility of Ada's death, and the stupid thought fills me with an ocean of dread.

Fighting it, I pull away and gaze down at her. "Whoever is behind this, I'll make sure they—"

She presses a finger to my lips, then slides it down my neck and across my chest. She then rises on tiptoes, and our mouths intertwine, the kiss more urgent than usual, almost primal.

"I want to finally test the Join app," she tells me telepathically. Her Zik messages' emotional undertones are still on the sad side. "Please?"

The app is something she first thought of years ago, but it turned out harder to implement than she originally conceived. The idea is to use Brainocytes to merge two or more minds. The melding, or whatever the proper term would be, is an extremely complex process. The simplest aspects include the heavy simulation of mirror neurons for both parties. Both participants experience one another's memories and emotions by sharing a lot of nonbiological brain regions, in part to swap sensory data and in part to process neurological data together. The basic idea is that I'd experience the world as Ada does, and she would get the reverse experience.

A month ago, Ada finally decided she was happy enough with the app to test it on our rats. The rats, especially Mr. Spock and Uhura, liked the experience a lot and now run the app continuously. As a result, Mr. Spock got a bit more mellow, for lack of a better term. Sadly, though, the rats aren't yet smart enough to properly explain how the Join app makes them feel—at least beyond terse descriptions like Kirk's "I just feel better," McCoy's "It makes me feel never alone," Scotty's "It's more fun than Alan's Rat World—and I like Rat World," Uhura's "It makes me happier," or Mr. Spock's slightly less cryptic "It makes me love Uhura more." To me, the idea of having Ada inside my head seems scary. Despite my therapy with Einstein, I'm afraid that what she finds there could scare her away.

"It's unfair to ask me today," I whisper once our lips unlock. "Why don't we do that zero-gravity position?" I begin the gesture to disable gravity in the room, but she puts her hand on mine to stop me.

"I really need this." She's still speaking virtually. "It will take our relationship to the next step, I know it will, and I want to do that because life is unpredictable, and—"

"It's okay." I lose myself in her amber eyes again, grateful she didn't alter their color today. "If it means so much to you, I'll do it."

I stop myself from adding something like, "It was going to happen eventually, anyway." I learned long ago that I can only tell Ada no for a very short time, and the whole process is full of guilt and other subtle unpleasantness. There's an old Russian saying that goes, "The husband is the head, and the wife is the neck." That's our relationship in a nutshell: I turn where Ada wants me to turn and see what she wants me to see. Not that this means I imagine myself as the head of our family. Ada is both the head and the neck in our household, while I might be something like the gallbladder.

A giant new icon shows up in the room, and I psych myself up to activate the Join app. If I look at it through Ada's eyes, this is a way to get closer to each other. Seen that way, the whole business doesn't sound nearly as scary. Besides, Ada already knows what I did five years ago in Russia and a few months later in the US. She also saw what I did earlier today. Hopefully, she won't hold any of my memories against me. And she's going to see how I feel about her, which is worth something. We don't say the L word to each other as much as other couples, so that reas-surance might be a nice bonus.

Perhaps as blackmail, or as extra motivation to get me to start the app, Ada VR-magicks her clothes away from her body.

I instantly get rid of mine as well.

"This is how I've always pictured this," she says, step-ping toward me.

Without voicing my doubts, I give in to the call of biol-ogy, and as the pleasure begins, I launch the Join app and close my eyes.

CHAPTER EIGHT

Brainocytes allow us to experiment with safe psychedelic experiences, and Mitya has made it his personal mission to blow our minds with a set of LSD-like apps of ever-increasing potency. But none of Mitya's apps, real drugs, or even the horrific truth serum cocktail used on me four and a half years ago could've prepared me for this assault on my sense of reality.

My senses feel completely crisscrossed—though that's not quite accurate. What's really happening is that I'm trying to sense through Ada's eyes, skin, ears, nose, and mouth, while in a strange, recursive loop, I'm also feeling what it feels like for her to experience my own senses. It's like placing a mirror in front of another mirror. We each get lost in our experiences of each other's experience of the other person's experiences, down infinite levels, until we simply forget there's a difference between Ada and Mike—which I think is one of the goals.

It quickly becomes clear that sex is not the best way to first experience this app because of the sensory overload that comes with intimacy. A part of me that's more Ada than Mike disagrees and thinks we'd be equally overwhelmed during a session of knitting or playing solitaire.

The boundaries between the being who is Mike and the glorious entity that is Ada blur more with every second, yet I still feel that I'm myself at the same time. Although I'm used to being in many places at once, what's happening now feels completely different. In a strange way, I feel more in the moment in multiple places at once, more alive in multiple places at once, and again paradoxically more myself, even though I'm merged with someone else. I can't shake the feeling that this is how I'm supposed to be, that this is the real me. Finally free. Finally home.

As my mind adjusts to this roller coaster of newness, I begin to see myself through Ada's eyes. I feel what she feels for me, and I feel what she's feeling as we make love, here in the VR room. I knew she loves me, but because she doesn't like to overuse the words to express her feelings, sometimes I'm open to doubt. I will never doubt again. Ada loves me with an intensity I might not be capable of myself, though I must be wrong, because she swells with contentment when she experiences how I feel about her.

They say that as couples live together, they become like rocks polished by a river. Any differences and problems between them smooth away. I'm not sure if there's any truth to that metaphor, but in this VR room, in one instant, we understand and move past whatever tiny flaws we've noticed in each other. We forgive all grievances by seeing the world through the other's eyes. We become more as one than a couple who have lived together all their lives.

This is when the oddest part begins. A surge of Ada's memories flood my awareness. I recall a nice day in Central Park when she was walking over a scenic bridge and musing about her deadbeat father, who left her mother and was never heard from again. Her conflicting emotions are familiar to me, and I soon realize that I have had almost identical musings about my own father, a man whose death I still relive with intense guilt. I recall Ada's memory of sitting in the hospital, her love for her mother swelling her chest, and I remember myself in similar circumstances after Mom's accident.

Not all the memories pull us closer. Some memories are almost opposites: Ada worried after losing her virginity as a teen, while I worried that I'd never get the chance to lose mine. Some are completely foreign to me, like the ordeal Ada experienced when she lost her mom to cancer.

Tears stream down my face, both in VR and in the real world, as I relive her struggles. The pain she felt is unlike anything I've ever experienced, carrying me to the verge of panic.

Soon, though, the sad memories are over, and happier ones move to the forefront. I witness Ada discovering coding, her first love. I recall her first kiss in a forest camp and her first crush on a young professor in Intro to Java class. I remember how she felt the first time we had sex, and when she said her vows during our Hawaiian wedding—and the first time she held a screaming Alan in her arms. I understand that Ada is most defined by her happier experiences, and I hope she finds the same to be true about me, though it's probably not the case.

If it were possible to feel yourself evolving into a better person, this is what it would feel like. There's no jealousy when I recall the men and the one woman from Ada's past. I would hug them and thank them if I met them now—a reaction I can't believe I'm having. I also now understand Ada's abhorrence of violence, having felt her conviction of how precious life is and how even the worst person in the world is still deserving of love and kindness.

Ada has been trying to get me to meditate, and in the process, I've learned a little bit about Buddhism. Now, using the Join app, I feel as if I've reached enlightenment, or how I imagined it would feel, although I probably had a very reductionist view of that spiritual term.

Experimentally, I open my eyes in the real world. The plane is still in the air, and when I try to introspect, I feel normal. I feel like an individual—that is, until I try to feel one with Ada. Then the feeling of enlightenment rushes back full force.

I open my eyes in the VR room and see Ada's naked body reflected in all the mirrors. We're still joined in this way, too, our virtual sweat glistening on our ephemeral bodies.

Something new becomes possible, and it demands my attention. As the intensity of the Joining lessens, I discover that we can think as one, at least for a moment. Unimaginatively, we jointly contemplate, "We think, therefore we are."

"Wow," I reply. "Our hive mind is a philosopher."

"Amazing," she agrees. "I know that neither of us came up with that thought, yet we thought it."

"I need a way to reference self," the hive mind thinks to themselves (or herself or himself or itself).

"How about The Cohens?" I suggest.

"The Cohens would make more sense if we Joined with your uncle, cousin, and mom," it counters. "But fine, it will do."

Somehow, a reminder about the rest of the family during sex doesn't seem gross or even weird. It feels completely neutral, like thinking about clouds. Perhaps this is part of an evolved state of being, though it might also be because sex is the last thing on our minds now, even though we're still making love.

"Can more than two people Join like this?" I ask. "I mean, the Join app, not—"

"The more people, the more complete we'd become," answers the being code-named The Cohens.

"Besides people, we could even pull in other beings, like Mr. Spock," Ada adds. "But perhaps after we finish."

I don't get to make any bestiality jokes because we're getting to the climax of the physical—well, the virtually physical—part of our Bedroom extravaganza, and it's becoming impossible to talk, even telepathically. I pray nobody is watching me on the plane right now, or if they are, I hope they don't record my facial expressions or consider my reactions some form of sexual harassment.

Though I've become acclimated to Ada's senses, now that she's this close to release, I begin to feel overwhelmed. What I feel intermingles with what she's feeling, and I'm eager to learn what this part will feel like from her perspective.

Then she performs a maneuver possible only in VR (though she claims she's going to start doing Kegel exercises to replicate this in the real world). My response arrives like clockwork, and for a moment, I forget the hive mind named The Cohens or even my own name.

At some point during Brainocyte development (maybe around the seventh brain boost, though it might've been the eighth), we cloud-replicated the parts of the brain responsible for orgasms, giving us a much greater capacity for appreciating this already miraculous experience. Without the Join app, I'd say what I usually feel is at least a hundred times more intense than an unenhanced orgasm. With the Join app, however, I feel Ada's reactions as well as my own enhanced ones. Our minds meld into pure bliss with no boundaries or limits and an intensity thousands of times more powerful than anything we've ever experienced.

What feels like a hundred heavenly years later, I catch my breath and reflect on how hard it is to become winded when you have Respirocytes doing the job of your red blood cells. Then again, I just got winded in VR, so oxygen efficiency obviously isn't the main factor.

"Not my best idea," Ada whispers as soon as she's able to make coherent sentences again. She VR-magicks herself a virtual cigarette, more as a jokey prop than because she has any physical need for it. "The Join app on its own would've been enough."

"It might've been one of your best ideas," I say, my voice thick from the experience. "Should I shut down the app?"

"I think so," she murmurs. "Though it would make The Cohens go away."

"We'll use this again," I say. "The Cohens will return."

"I'm glad that part of the app actually worked," she says with noticeable enthusiasm.

I gaze at my brilliant wife with pride that borders on worship. "You utilized our idle brain regions, didn't you?"

Her eyes shine with mischief. "That's a very primitive way of looking at it, but something like that. I leveraged Einstein to provide this app with a platform to self-organize our unused resources. Clearly, it worked."

"Fascinating," state The Cohens. "We're intrigued about bringing more minds into ourselves."

"Good idea, but not now." Ada releases the smoke from her cigarette. Instead of the usual toxic fumes, the cloud has a soft, vaporous quality and smells like bergamot tea with a slice of lime. It probably tastes that way as well, since that's Ada's favorite morning pick-me-up. "How about we shelve the Join app experiments until we figure out who's trying to kill us?"

"I agree," I reply. "The Cohens will also have to wait."

"We do not fear nonexistence," The Cohens reply.

"You won't not exist," Ada says. "You're us. As long as we exist, you also exist."

"However long it takes for you to Join again will seem but a moment to us," The Cohens say enigmatically.

"On that note, I'm turning off the app." I match mental actions to my words.

I instantly feel a sense of loss. The being that was The Cohens is gone without a trace. Until it disappeared, I didn't realize I felt it was a part of me. Given Ada's pained expression, I can see something similar is happening to her.

"Is the app addictive?" I ask.

"We just need to readjust to being alone," she replies softly. "But I can now see why our rats run a version of this app all the time."

"Me too. I wonder what their version of The Cohens is like."

"Their Join app doesn't have that part. I actually wonder if it's safe to have in our version. What would happen if we Joined with more than a few thousand people at once?"

"Because The Cohens would be too smart to control or comprehend?" I yawn demonstratively. Post-coital bliss always hits me hard, whether the coitus is real or virtual.

"Exactly," she says. "We should run this by the others at the next Brainocytes meeting."

"Sounds like a plan. What do we tell them about this app for now?"

"Nothing, if you don't mind. Let me prepare to tell them about it properly."

"Fair enough." I can't help another yawn. "Can we sleep?"

"Our friends probably think we fell asleep anyway," she says through another puff of yummy smoke. "So yeah, why not? It might actually be a good idea."

"I have enough left of my flight for a decent nap." I yawn so temptingly that she yawns as well.

"I actually have time for a substantial rest," she says after another contagious yawn. "Let's just check on everyone before we fall asleep."

We rejoin the VR conference room and learn that nothing interesting occurred while we were away discovering a new state of consciousness.

"Time for a nap," I say in the VR room, fighting to stay awake.

"We'll wake you up if you're needed," Joe says flatly.

"I had no doubt you would," I mutter under my breath. Joe has no problem having his people slap me awake if that's what it takes.

Stopping all multitasking, I leave my mind firmly in my real-world environment, and my thoughts turn to the change in my marriage. Now that I've seen the world through Ada's eyes, I don't think I can ever have an argument with her again—not that we normally have many. I must also admit that, although I loved Ada before the Join app, my feelings are now almost frighteningly intense. Fully understanding her has made me see how sacred her mind is, how sublime. It's as though Ada is a literal part of me, her well-being irrevocably entwined with my own.

I might be a better husband than before. Perhaps even a better human being.

Another yawn makes my jaws crack and interrupts my self-aggrandizements, so I decide to just sleep. Usually, I use an app designed to help me fall asleep, but I don't need it today. Instead, I simply run a utility app called Do Not Disturb, which basically disables hearing and vision for the duration I want—in this case, five hours.

As soon as it turns on, Do Not Disturb creates the effect of being in a deep underground silo. Not a single photon hits my eyelids, and not a fraction of a decibel titillates my eardrums. I open my eyes because I still find it fun to see how Do Not Disturb makes the space around me pitch dark even with my eyes wide open. Then I close my eyes again and drop like a stone into unconsciousness.

CHAPTER NINE

The hall of mirrors stretches as far as my eyes can see. A camera inside a drone above my head shows me that this space has taken over the whole world, horizon to horizon.

I run, barely breathing, my heart rate squarely in the anaerobic zone. When the place tries to be a maze and puts a mirror in my way, I shatter the offending surface with a well-placed kick. My goal seems to be to not see myself in any of the reflections, so I do it again and again as more mirrors pop up.

When I kick the tenth mirror, pain explodes in my leg, but the cursed glass doesn't even crack. The pain breaks my concentration, and I catch the reflection staring back at me—and regret it instantly. The baleful glare on Joe's face makes his everyday coldness seem warm and fluffy.

My whole body freezes in panic as Joe's face stares back at me with varying shades of wrath from the infinitude of mirrors. A scream escapes my mouth, vibrating the air so violently the mirrors around me ripple and explode in a chain reaction.

I'm on the verge of some great epiphany when the image in the mirror that refused to break morphs.

First, Joe's military cut grows into tufts of white hair that spread like a halo around his head. Next, his features soften into a wrinkly smile. Soon, Einstein's famous face is staring at me, eyes twinkling with wisdom and mirth.

"This is a dream," I tell Einstein, my fight-or-flight response already calming down.

"We discussed this one in therapy," says the AI's German-accented voice. As usual, in the context of psychology, it comes off sounding suspiciously like Freud. "You're not becoming a monster."

"Make a note to discuss this again when I'm awake. For now, I want to try lucid dreaming again."

Einstein nods and disappears. After a moment of concentration, I soar upward toward the drone still flying in the empty, mirrored sky.

CHAPTER TEN

I wake with a start to the sight of Gogi's face too close to mine. Given that I can hear a car's engine and see my friend, the Do Not Disturb cycle must be complete.

My cheek burns. He must've tried to smack me awake, one of the few ways to bypass the Do Not Disturb app—but not needed in this case, since mine was no longer on.

"You have been unconscious for five hours," Einstein says. "You had one minute of REM sleep, and I estimate that your sleep debt is still a full night's sleep of eight hours, which I suggest you get as soon as you can." Mitya has been incorporating emotional cues and contextual information in this latest version of Einstein, and the AI's voice sounds annoyingly caring and consolatory. "Current time is 7:36 p.m."

I'm jealous of Ada, who's still napping thanks to her longer flight. Rubbing my eyes, I wonder if I can order Gogi to let me sleep but decide against it, since my chances of getting quality sleep during the short ride are slim to none. Besides, given the time of day, it might be best if I suffer for a few hours and then sleep when it's dark out. For now, I might as well catch up with my friend.

"If I had a ruble for every time I dragged you from the plane to the car, I'd be able to retire," Gogi says, a smile visible through his Stalinesque mustache.

"You can retire now," I answer groggily, unhappy that the Do Not Disturb app made me miss my landing. "You own a piece of Human++."

His face turns serious. "What's with trying to get yourselves killed when it's my turn to babysit?"

"Next time I'll try to get bombed when you're around." All remnants of sleep flee from my mind. Realizing I might be channeling negativity at the wrong person, I add in a conciliatory tone, "You can help find and deal with the people responsible. How are you at controlling the robots?"

"The kid has been training me," Gogi says. One of the robots inside Zapo X (at least I assume that's what we're driving) gives me a salute.

I give Gogi a rundown of the recent events as I proceed to multitask, a part of me rejoining the VR room to check on the investigation.

"I secured four robots," Mitya says. "Your cousin is already walking one to speak with the bomber's Green Party coworker." He points at a screen where people are staring in awe at the shell of Joe's robotic body stalking through the Russian streets.

"Excellent job," I tell him. "Gogi just volunteered to take one, and so have I."

"It might be best if you take one to speak with the bomber's mother." He warily eyes Joe's VR avatar. "This task might require some finesse."

What goes unsaid is that Joe and Gogi are not above torturing the poor woman, who doesn't yet know she lost her son, for information. Even before mingling my mind with Ada's, I firmly believed the sins of the parents don't transfer to their children and vice versa. With my post-Join outlook, I want to help this woman instead of interrogating her. The only issue I see is that I'm the one who killed her son. Facing her might be hard, though I probably deserve whatever discomfort I feel.

"I'm going to try to locate his father," Mitya says and puts up another screen showing a robot that also begins moving. "The dad is a drunk, and the mom divorced him a long time ago. But who knows? Maybe this Ruzatov guy stayed on speaking terms with his old man."

I take possession of my designated robot, an older model that reminds me of a microwave oven mixed with a Cylon from the original 1978 *Battlestar Galactica*. I plug the mother's address into the GPS app and start clanking down the street. The GPS interface is the same as the Brainocyte one we put into wide use a couple of years ago.

As I walk the Russian streets, I'm overcome with déjà vu. Though my native Krasnodar is nearly six thousand miles from Vladivostok—a distance possible only in Russia—I might as well be walking the streets I remember as a kid. This is what happens when you recycle architectural designs the way the Soviets did: cookie cutters seem original by comparison. In America, some of the government-built housing, such as the projects in New York City, evoke this kind of feeling, only this part of Vladivostok is much grayer and danker.

To avoid becoming depressed, I look with my real-world eyes through the limo window at the streets of midtown Manhattan. Compared to Vladivostok, this is another world. In a strange way, when I swap points of view, I get the sense of traveling into the future, then back into the past—and I mean years, not just the switch between day and night brought about by the fourteen-hour time difference. Of course, this isn't a fair comparison. Moscow is a lot like New York when it comes to the adoption of new technology and would make a fairer match; comparing a backward Vladivostok street to Manhattan's Midtown is like comparing New York City to Nowhereville.

New Yorkers have adopted every single one of Human++ innovations and still crave more. Though it's long after most offices have closed, robotic commuters still litter the streets, a vast improvement for folks who live in the boonies yet whose jobs require their physical presence. No one so much as blinks at their metallic figures, and it's clear that the future is going to look a lot like the movie *Surrogates* (but hopefully without the societal issues). For every robotic wearer, thousands of people are using VR to work remotely. All the big firms not only allow but encourage this form of telepresence, which allows them to hire the best people regardless of where they are in the world. Also, it helps that VR space is much cheaper than real-world office space, especially for companies based in Manhattan.

VR's presence is affecting more than the way people work, of course. Tourists on the street are using both augmented and virtual reality, their expressions blank as they tune in to the tours engineered to trigger near popular sights. The natives are just as affected by the new tech. Instead of keeping their noses in their smartphones and other devices, everyone is "in their heads." People who can afford premium Brainocyte services are able to multitask while walking, and they watch the new, fully interactive movies that have more in common with video games than with the movies of old. Those using free entertainment end up sitting in cars and public transportation while doing the same.

The cars, including ours, are all electric, silent, and self-driving, and most of them are commandeered by Einstein. For the first time in over a century, there are no traffic jams to speak of in Manhattan. The air is as clean as in rural areas, and even the noise pollution is down, thanks in part to Brainocyte-enabled telepathic communication that's quickly redefining the way people interact.

The relative quiet of the street is short-lived, however, because when we get to 42nd Street, we see a crowd of protestors. Their shouting is hard to discern, but signs like Brainocytes Steal Your Soul and Humanity Is Lost leave little room for doubt that this is yet another demonstration by the RHO or a similar group.

"Is this a coincidence?" I ask in the VR room. "Or should we reroute the car?"

"You should reroute in any case," Mitya replies instantly. "I just calculated the travel time to your apartment, and your current route is the slowest."

"Are you going to become our Einstein replacement?" I ask.

"I can integrate with Einstein much better now," Mitya says. "It's now clear to me that the biological brain is a bottleneck of a sort. I can think much, much faster already, and I've only just begun to tweak my capabilities."

"We're walking through this crowd," Joe says without even a hint of interest in this fascinating update on Mitya's condition. "No one here is wearing bombs."

He must be using a sniffer device, a gizmo designed by one of the enhanced engineers at Human++ R&D. Sniffers are orders of magnitude more reliable than a dog and, to quote Ada, "don't require canine slave labor."

I authorize Einstein to take the path Mitya recommends and ask, "If Joe is in that crowd and Gogi is in the car, who's watching Alan?"

"I'm with Dominic, Father," Alan replies grumpily. "Also Jacob and a slew of others."

"Alan, you're smart enough to realize security is necessary," I say, figuring it beats "watch your tone, young man," which was my initial instinct. "Plus, you like Dominic."

"Yeah, yeah." His petulant expression looks odd on his adult avatar's face. "Just get home already."

Though I don't say it out loud lest I upset Gogi and Joe, Dominic may be the most qualified person to stay with Alan, and not just because of their friendship. A schoolteacher back in his early twenties, Dominic enlisted in the army after 9/11 and eventually became part of the Special Forces. That's how his path crossed with Joe's, but their personalities couldn't be any more different. Dominic is as straight an arrow as I've ever come across. An IED explosion left him in a coma, which he came out of two years ago, but the traumatic brain injury he received left his body in a completely locked-in state, unable to move any muscles. Unlike some people in that condition, he didn't even have the ability to blink yes or no in response to questions.

Brainocytes gave Dominic back a form of sight, a way to communicate, and an exoskeleton that allows him to move around—that is, until Dahan, our Director of Nanotech, works out an even better solution, enabling nanomachines to repair the damage he received. A state-of-the-art bionic arm replaced the one Dominic lost in that explosion, and he claims he's unable to tell the difference between his left and right arms anymore.

In large part because of what he regained thanks to our help, Dominic is probably the most grateful and loyal person who works for us. I've grown to trust him almost as much as I trust my closest friends and family.

Almost ready to stop worrying about my kid, I remind myself that Alan mentioned that Jacob is guarding him as well. Jacob is extremely competent. His quick reactions saved Muhomor's life in that hospital four and a half years ago, and he's moved up rapidly through our security ranks ever since.

"I've built Dominic a VR world," Alan brags to me privately. "It's doing wonders for his PTSD, and I think he'll be able to walk up to cars soon without feeling any panic."

"Let me know when your VR therapy worlds are ready to be turned into a product," I tell him. "They're helpful for me. I'm actually now walking in Russia and don't feel any dread."

The truth is that I do feel some negative emotions as I walk the morning streets of Vladivostok, but this isn't due to irrational leftovers from my misadventures in Russia. I worry because a crowd is walking menacingly toward me. American protestors can look plenty angry, but these Russians seem even scarier in their emotionless movement.

I make the robot cross the street, and the lynch mob crosses the street at the same time, leaving no doubt they're up to something sinister.

I turn my robotic head and see another, smaller group of people flanking me from behind.

"Joe." I cram my telepathic message with apprehension. "Look at what my robot is seeing."

"It's not just you." Joe's telepathic reply is calm but foreboding.

He's right. In the VR room, everyone's screens show their robots under pursuit by people who look a lot like the mob approaching me.

"We're in different parts of a large country," I say, confused.

"Yes, I know." Mitya sounds just as puzzled.

"None of these people seem to even know each other." Alan points at a large screen where he's posted hundreds of face recognition profiles.

"If they destroy the robots, it will take days to procure more," Mitya says. His crowd of people looks even more sinister than mine; they remind me of the pitchfork-wielding villagers approaching Frankenstein.

"This attack has to be government sponsored." Muhomor scares away a couple of scrawny cats as he cuts through a side alley to get away from his pursuers. "The Russians still hate us for developing Tema. Maybe this is payback?"

Part of me agrees with Muhomor's assessment. It's not just Russia; every government wishes the Tema cryptography didn't exist. Still unbreakable, Tema makes the ability to surveil your own or another country's citizens a thing of the past—one the governments of the world dearly miss. Some countries tried to outlaw Tema, but once we made the algorithms, theory, and even the software open source, outlawing this system became like trying to outlaw the Pythagorean theorem.

"I find it hard to picture these people working for the government," Alan chimes in as I cast another wary look at my robot's pursuers. "The majority are alcoholics and can barely keep a shitty job."

"Hey, watch your language," I tell him privately, doing my best to embed fatherly disapproval into the Zik message. "But you're right, they don't look impressive."

"At least we found something they have in common," Mitya says. "Because the kid nailed it. A lot of these people recently recovered in hospitals from alcohol poisoning. I guess Russia got rid of *vytrezvitel*.'"

"*Vytrezvitel* is a detoxification center where cops take drunks to sober up," I tell Alan. "The fact that the Soviet

Union had a need for such facilities tells you a little bit about the culture at the time."

"Was Ruzatov an alcoholic?" he asks. "Though even if he was, I fail to see how it sheds light on any of this."

"He drank every now and then, but normal amounts." Mitya's robot dodges a red brick flying at his head and increases his pace. "For a Russian, anyway."

"He did get committed to a hospital." Muhomor finds people waiting for his robot at the end of the alley, so he turns back. "A week ago."

"His blood alcohol level was .10," Alan adds.

"Like I said." Mitya's robot dodges a broken bottle this time. "That number is normal for a Russian."

"He had some head trauma," Muhomor says. "Maybe he was in a drunken brawl?"

"Speaking of a drunken brawl," Alan says. "You should all focus on the trouble in the real world. We can pause the meeting for now."

He's right. Though all of us can carry on a conversation in VR and deal with these attackers, it's best to focus, especially considering what Mitya said about the difficulty of getting new robots.

I stare at the cracked asphalt street. The first set of pursuers is but a foot away. Using the robot's sense of smell, I verify the stench of stale vodka on the breath of the nearest man.

"I don't want to hurt anyone, but I need this robot, so I won't let you break it," I rattle through the robot's mouth in Russian.

"Monster," yelps the nearest drunk in a strange falsetto. "You'll regret your sins."

As though emboldened by this cry to action, the two groups surround me and close the distance. My real-world heart forgets the difference between physical and robotic bodies, because it slams against my chest like a hydraulic motor after a power surge.

CHAPTER ELEVEN

When the first man strikes my metallic face, I realize that things might not be as dire as we fear. The guy's fist is bloody, yet my robot's diagnostics show no ill effects. To my shock, the guy hits me again, his bone crunching against the chest chassis. I see no pain in his face, just determination to hit me repeatedly.

"He must be drunk right now," I yell in VR when the same man headbutts the metal, his nose spraying blood onto the camera that serves as my eyes.

"Watch out for that one with the crowbar," Alan shouts. I instinctively duck, and the metal of the blunt weapon skitters along the top of my metallic skull.

"Einstein, turn on Battle Mode," I mentally command. "Adjust it to this robotic body."

"Done," Einstein replies. "Do you want to turn on the Emotion Dampener as well?"

"Let's save Emotion Dampener for a much worse situation."

Battle Mode—or BM, as we sometimes abbreviate it to—is something I've been working on ever since I mastered the martial arts that now make up my personal, still-to-be-named fighting style. It's a merger of my acquired skills and technology—a way to leverage Brainocyte-enabled, superluminal decision-making in a combat situation. Emotion Dampener—which we *never* abbreviate to ED—is an add-on to BM. It's an optional subroutine that approximates what happens (or doesn't happen) in Joe's mind when he fights. It makes the regions of the brain responsible for empathy take a back seat, so users are free to maim and kill without compunction. It's a scary enough app that I never told Ada about its existence—though in a way, the fact that I need an app like this proves I'm a good person, doesn't it?

Battle Mode starts by highlighting the trajectories of all the nearby fists, bricks, crowbars, and booted feet in my Augmented Reality. It then overlays a ghostly outline for the various dodges and strikes I can make. Each offensive and defensive choice is based on my own brain regions and thus polished by countless hours of fighting Gogi, Joe, and the best sensei that money can buy.

The tricky part, and the reason I choose not to use the Emotion Dampener add-on to Battle Mode, is that I don't want to hurt these people too much. After all, they don't pose any threat to my life. Ultimately, the only thing they're guilty of is trying to damage some (albeit important) corporate property. I don't even have evidence that they're in league with the bombers, though it does seem likely.

Before anyone gets a chance to blink, I choose Action Option 50 and allow the robot body to begin moving. As expected, a fist misses my head and crashes into the shoulder of a drunk behind me. A kick does land, but at such an angle that I feel only the barest vibration in the robot's left side. The owner of the foot probably has a broken toe.

"They're ignoring all damage to their bodies." Mitya's frantic private thought echoes something that's been gnawing at my awareness for a few seconds now. "Like the bombers, these idiots are utterly dedicated to their cause—or crazy."

"Not that there's a difference," Alan mutters.

I don't reply, because my robotic ears ring with the bang of a gunshot that comes as a complete surprise. I hadn't registered anyone with a weapon when I scanned the crowd earlier.

The bullet hits the right side of my metal head, and I'm grateful that I only feel a fraction of the pain I would've experienced if this happened to my real-world flesh. Still, it's as bad as the sparring session last week when Jacob landed a hit on my jaw.

Battle Mode gets help from Einstein when it comes to ballistic trajectories, and soon I have the location of the shooter highlighted in my view, as well as the movements I'll need to take to reach him. I begin to execute the suggested maneuver, even at the cost of getting smacked by a nearby crowbar. The crowbar dents my robotic shoulder blade, but I manage to grab and crush the gun, along with the guy's hand.

Unfortunately, Battle Mode is only good at anticipating rational behavior. It cannot foresee the drunk with missing teeth who purposely drops under my feet while some assailant behind me tackles me with the intensity of a football player on cocaine. Both men will likely end up in the hospital after this, but they accomplish what they set out to do, because I begin to fall. Waving my metal arms reflexively, I manage to bring down two people along with me.

The attackers savagely kick me, and though most of the kicks reach my metal body, some of them end up striking their fallen allies, presumably by mistake. Here again, these people are causing more damage to themselves than the robot (especially if you count all the toes they're breaking right now).

Someone lands a lucky kick that hits me in the joint of my metal neck with a loud clang. Emboldened by the sound, someone smashes a red brick against the same spot, and the diagnostics complain about structural damage.

I struggle to get up, but a couple of heavyset men are hanging onto my robotic legs, so all I accomplish is a half roll on the ground. I use my arms to throw off some of the nearest attackers. I'm clearly beginning to forget about the desire not to hurt people over a robot, because my flailing breaks a dozen bones and dislocates a handful of shoulders.

Undaunted by the damage I dish out, the drunks keep pounding away at me. They remind me of a starving man with a can of tuna but no can opener. Slowly and methodically, they begin to damage my metal body, unde-terred by the cost to themselves. One insane man bites my camera, losing some teeth but loosening the sensor enough that the next man's kick leaves me blind.

It doesn't take long to locate a security camera in a nearby liquor store, but all that viewpoint does is allow me to see the robot massacre continuing to unfold.

"My robot is dead," Mitya says. "Joe's will soon be a goner also."

"Not much better on my end," Muhomor complains.

I remove my mind from what's left of the robot body. "Same here."

I look through everyone's views. Joe is the only one whose robot is still semi-functional, and that's only be-cause he wasn't hesitating to kill the drunkards over it. Completely covered in blood and brain matter, his robot slips on gore and finally goes down. The drunks still alive proceed to beat the poor machine with the dismembered limbs of their comrades, proving without a doubt that they are at least as crazy as the people who were willing to blow themselves up earlier today.

Two more waves of onslaught extinguish the last spark from Joe's robot.

When I get back to the VR room, Joe has broken the virtual glass table again, and no one has run the app to repair it because he looks like he'd break it again, possibly with his glare.

I look at the grim faces one by one. "Seems like some-one really doesn't want us investigating in Russia."

"I wouldn't rule out a group that hates technology." Alan's grown-up avatar seems smaller, almost frail. "The savagery they showed toward the robots smells like fanatics to me."

"We'll soon have someone to talk to about that," Joe says, his eyes such that I could swear his VR avatar is about to morph into a lizard.

"This whole thing doesn't make any sense," Mitya says. "Those drunks out there wouldn't have the resources to locate each of our robots on their own, no matter how much they hate machinery."

"Can we hire people who live in Russia to investigate?" I ask, looking warily at Joe. "Gogi has those Georgians."

"All dead." Joe squeezes a fist so hard I expect blood to pour out of his palm. "All our Russian contacts are gone. And this"—he puts up an image of an explosion—"is what's left of the Human++ Moscow office."

We stare at the ruins in silence. I have trouble processing the horror of it. There were at least a thousand employees in that Moscow building, including a dozen people I worked with on a weekly basis and a management team that I personally interviewed.

I feel a bout of nausea in the real world, and frantically scan my physical body's surroundings. Zapo X is pulling into my home building's parking lot, and Gogi is staring at my green face with solemn determination. He's clearly in the loop about the events, including the death of his Georgian comrades.

I get Einstein to stop the car so I can open the door and make a mess of the otherwise spotless pavement. As I do so, I make a mental note to give a huge tip to the janitor.

Feeling a modicum of relief, I close the door, resume the car's parking progress, and speak both in VR and out loud. "We need to go on the defensive. I want Alan and Ada in that bunker we bought in New Jersey. I think all of us should stay there. We must also evacuate everyone in the Human++ buildings and send a mass email for everyone to work from home tomorrow."

Mitya and Muhomor nod, but Joe just stares.

"Route the arriving planes to the airport nearest the bunker," I say. "Joe, can you have your man in Ada's plane wake her up so we can tell her what's happening?"

In the real world, Gogi frowns. "We're not just going to run with our tails tucked between our legs."

"I'm not suggesting we stop the investigation," I say. "Just that we take safety precautions, regroup—"

"And then strike with everything we got," Gogi and Joe say in unison, one in VR and the other in the car.

We exit the car, and Gogi is herding me toward the stairs when a screech of tires echoes through the parking lot.

My gun is in my hands before I make any conscious decision to take it out, and Gogi and I leap behind the nearest parked cars, prepared for battle.

CHAPTER TWELVE

Before either of us gets a chance to shoot anything, I recognize the old-school (and now illegal) manual-drive Ford Mustang that must cost Joe a fortune in tickets and gas. Once electricity became nearly free, oil production plummeted and prices skyrocketed, as expected for a luxury item.

I lower my gun.

Joe gets out, stalks toward his back seat, and grabs something there. I expect it to be many things, but not a small, curvy, and seemingly unconscious woman.

"Who is that?" I ask in a stern tone I've never used on my cousin before. Reasonable scenarios, such as "drunk friend," don't even cross my mind.

Joe ignores my question, strides to Zapo X, and deposits the woman inside. I find both the way he carries and puts her down creepily gentle, as if he's afraid she might break prematurely.

"According to facial recognition," Ada says to me privately, "that's Tatum Crawford. She's a de facto leader of the Real Humans Only group."

"You're awake." I confirm what Ada said with my own facial recognition. Indeed, the round and highly symmetrical face belongs to the RHO leader.

"Woke up to a nightmare," Ada says. "They told me about Russia—and now this."

"I guess we now know why Joe went to the protest," I reply telepathically. Out loud, I say, "Joe, I thought it was understood that Human++ is not in the kidnapping business."

He doesn't deign to reply. Taking out a syringe, he rolls up the woman's sleeve. After a barely perceptible hesitation, he pushes the needle into the exposed pale flesh, presses on the plunger, pulls the needle out, and closes the door. He then turns around and must issue a command to Einstein, because Zapo X's back window rolls down.

"Nice touch," Ada says. "He doesn't want his captive to suffocate."

"A real humanitarian." I match her sarcasm in my telepathic undertones.

"In his defense," Gogi whispers when Joe is no longer within earshot, "these people are at the top of our suspect list, so talking to their leader might be just the thing we need."

"Joe," I call out and head after him. "You can't just pull something like this and say nothing."

"She's just our guest," he says when I catch him by the elevator. "If this has nothing to do with RHO, you can let her go."

I eye his security people guarding the elevator, but they show no sign of listening.

Frustrated, I stab the elevator button. "It's not that simple. She'll press charges and crucify us in the news. Also, as soon as you let her wake up, she'll use her Brainocytes to summon the authorities."

"Her Wikipedia page states that she doesn't have Brainocytes," Mitya says to everyone in VR. "Those RHOers are crazy." When Ada focuses her displeasure on him, he adds, "Not that I approve of taking her captive, of course."

Joe's icy stare makes the hairs stand up on the back of my neck. Maybe I overestimated how much conscience his brain boost granted him.

"Hope you didn't just convince him to kill the poor girl," Ada privately states. Not for the first time, her telepathic message echoes my thoughts.

"Let's deal with one problem at a time," I say more calmly as the doors to the penthouse open wide. "Getting our family to safety comes first."

"Mishen'ka!" Mom exclaims from the living room. "Dominic is saying something about a road trip to New Jersey."

"Hi, Dad." Alan is right behind his grandmother, an unreadable expression on his tiny face. "I'm ready to go."

"Sir," Dominic says telepathically after I hug my mom and son. He can speak through a special voice box in his exoskeleton, but he prefers mental communication. "Get whatever you need so we can head out."

Joe looks at his man approvingly. As per Dominic's preference, I'm using Augmented Reality to overlay his real-world face with a virtual avatar that looks exactly as he would have if not for explosion. The avatar's noble features look worried—and if Dominic is worried, we mere mortals should be peeing our pants.

"What about Uncle Abe?" I ask Joe as I look around for anything I should take with me.

"We'll pick him up on the way." Joe moves to the large safe where he and his people stash weapons and begins openly unloading a large arsenal of guns and rifles.

Mom eyes me questioningly, so I give her a simplified rundown of the situation, downplaying the danger as much as I can. Mom's blood pressure has been a real issue lately.

"It's mostly a precaution," I finish. "I prefer to think of this as a fire drill. This way, we'll know what to do in case of a real emergency."

"What about Mom?" Alan asks telepathically, mindful not to worry his grandma.

"Still flying back, but when she lands, I'll be there to pick her up," I reply.

"Can we bring the rats with us?" he asks, still telepathically.

"Of course." I give him a real-world wink. "Just make sure your grandmother doesn't see them."

Alan asks Dominic to help him "with something," and they head to the eighth bedroom in the penthouse, also known as the Rat Room—a room my mom likes to pretend doesn't exist, since Mr. Spock and his kin have made it their home.

It takes me only a minute to get ready. It's amazing how few physical possessions a person needs once they have Brainocytes in their heads. For another ten minutes, I gather all the stuff Ada requests, even though I'm ninety-percent sure our personal assistants have already gotten these items for the bunker—even Ada's high-powered blender that I nicknamed "The Chainsaw."

The most urgent tasks complete, I walk the hallways Ada and I jointly decorated. The ultramodern design, with all the blues and grays and the smart home devices at every turn, feels like home. Thanks to the million sensors spread around the place, "feels like home" takes on a new meaning for me because I can literally feel the apartment when it comes to temperature, lighting, water and chemical levels in the indoor pool, the contents of the fridge, and even how much dust is on the floor. I hope we don't have to stay in the bunker too long, because I'll miss this place.

"Hi, friend," Mr. Spock says in Zik as he scurries up my body into my pocket. "Can I ride on you?"

"Most would ask before diving for my pocket," I tease. "But of course you can."

Mr. Spock rewards me by bruxing, then gives me an update on where his family is hiding from Mom.

The trip downstairs is quick. After I get Alan into the car, I hold the door open for my mom.

"Who is this girl?" she asks as I take what would be a driver's seat, if this car needed one. "Is she okay?"

I give Joe a narrow-eyed look. When he ignores the question, I say, "She's Joe's friend, Mom. She's just napping after a red-eye flight."

"Hmm." Mom looks over Tatum Crawford's plump, petite frame. "Josya's friend." She looks like she's tasting the idea. "She's pretty."

I debate correcting her but decide there's no harm if she thinks Tatum is Joe's girlfriend. That implies two nice fantasies: that Tatum isn't kidnapped, and that Joe is capable of feelings that lead to having girlfriends.

"In the Caucasus Mountains, where our friend Gogi is from," Mitya says in the VR room, "they have a famous but barbaric custom of kidnapping brides—"

I don't find out the punchline, because my attention ricochets back to the real world as the sensors in the penthouse scream in the smart-device equivalent of horrific pain. The roar of destroyed door sensors quickly follows the screeching of malfunctioning appliances, and sparks blind every camera.

It's an explosion—one that shakes the building with such intensity the car alarms in the parking lot start blaring.

CHAPTER THIRTEEN

Not being in the building, we're alive, so I capitalize on this small bit of luck and bring up the most up-to-date version of the Batmobile app to steal control of Zapo X from Einstein. The tires squeal as the heavily customized limo catapults onto the Manhattan street.

Taking over one of the myriad delivery drones flying around, I assess the damage and immediately wish I didn't. As I feared, the explosion came from the penthouse. The place is totaled. Our extra-thick, hurricane-proof windows are raining down on the street in tiny shards.

People on the street are gawking at the flames, their faces pale. Many New Yorkers, including myself, get unpleasant flashbacks when an explosion happens in a high-rise building.

Mom's voice quivers. "At least we all got out in time." She puts a shaking hand on my shoulder, as though I'm the one who needs consoling.

"Yeah, Dad," Alan says, nodding at her words. "We can replace material stuff."

His words reassure me that he's okay—child or not, my son is more mature than many adults—so I push aside my shock and telepathically reach out to Ada. "How are you?"

She opts to show up as an AU avatar next to Alan, her eyes suspiciously puffy. "Intellectually, I understand that it's just stuff. But I still feel like I just lost a piece of myself."

I swerve onto Lexington Street as we ride in silence.

After I recruit a couple more delivery drones as air support, I notice that everyone in the car is privately asking me to check out the news, so I do. The media is already obsessing about the Midtown explosion, as they're calling it.

"My inbox and voicemail are filling up with questions from the government and the media," Mitya complains.

I check and realize the same is happening to me.

"We don't know if we can trust the authorities," Joe says. "Don't tell anyone where we are and especially where we're going."

"In that case, I wouldn't even take calls or open emails," Muhomor chimes in. "We don't know how sophisticated our adversary is."

I turn onto the West Side Highway and speed up. By the time I reach the tunnel, I've earned a couple of thousand dollars in speeding fines, not to mention several tickets for manually overriding the navigation system. Despite being hosted in our data centers, Einstein squealed on me just as he would on any other driver.

We fly through the tunnel. One advantage of self-driving cars is that you can race around them easily. When they know a human driver is near, they treat that car like it has rabies.

As I drive, I also go through the building's security footage. It takes mere seconds to locate the suspect, since he's wearing a suicide vest nearly identical to the ones from the earlier attempts on our lives. I get a good shot of his face and scan the report from the face recognition software.

"Are you watching the news?" Gogi asks out loud. He glances at Joe's captive and telepathically asks me, "Do you still think we don't need her?"

I tune in to the news and confirm what I just learned from facial recognition: Lennox Dixon is a prominent member of the RHO. In fact, there are pictures of him and Tatum all over the news, so I learn another tidbit: the authorities are looking for Tatum, which may further complicate Joe's kidnapping of the woman.

"First a protest, then blowing shit up," Muhomor says. "The RHO does not look good right now."

"I just hope they know we have their leader." I get onto the Brooklyn-Queens Expressway. "So they stop trying to kill us."

"Even if the RHO is behind this, Joe had no right to do what he did," Ada says.

"We'll deal with that when we're safe," I reply, careful not to tell her my theory that the worst for Tatum is still to come. Joe is undoubtedly planning to question her using dubious methods.

I spot an emergency vehicle in the distance and race ahead to perform a maneuver that was popular in New York before self-driving cars. Catching up to the EMT van,

I get behind it so that when it gets the right of way, I can take advantage of the window in the traffic.

Something bugs me, though—something to do with the recon I'm getting from the drones above us. I'm not sure what I'm seeing yet, but I've learned to trust my intuition after being the only one who noticed government surveillance four and a half years ago.

"Guys," I say in the VR room, as that's where the quickest-thinking group is. "Something is off."

I put up feedback from the drones I appropriated, and everyone adds their own—turns out each of them was also providing air support.

"There and there," Alan says. I recognize his facial expression—this is how he looks when he's absorbed in a video game. "We're in trouble."

I consult the screen and realize what the oddities are: we're not the only manually driven car on the road. There's a green SUV swerving around the self-driving traffic in a way that leaves little doubt there's a human involved. What's worse is the giant Peterbilt truck steamrolling onto the ramp at triple the speed limit.

"The truck will block you from speeding up." Mitya shows us a screen where he models what he thinks is going on—an impressive feat that must be possible thanks to his newly nonbiological mind. "The SUV probably contains a suicide bomber ready to blow up when he catches up with you."

I send a frantic message: "Joe, Gogi, join VR."

They obey, joining almost instantly.

Mitya repeats his theory, and Joe's grim expression leaves no doubt that he concurs with what's about to happen.

Joe's security team from the car shows up in the VR room. Muhomor nods at Jacob; after the big man saved his life, they became friends. Dominic looks like a regular person here in VR, and it's eerie to see his shoulders droop. His exoskeleton doesn't have the capability to express emotion in the real world.

"You"—Joe gestures at Dominic—"secure Alan, while you"—he points at Jacob—"look out for my aunt."

He proceeds to give more orders, and I'm pleased to see he's treating me as one of the security people. I'm to stay alert and react to the situation. Then again, he might not have ordered anyone to secure me because I'm in the front by myself.

"Gogi and I are going to take care of the SUV," Joe says. He looks around as though challenging anyone to contradict him, but no one dares.

"I should drive," Mitya says once the plan of action is solidified. "My reaction times are now at least double any of yours."

I shudder as I recall the last time Mitya drove in a life-or-death situation. Still, reaction time is the key metric here, so I hesitantly agree.

"We go back to real time on three." Gogi wipes sweat from his virtual mustache. "One. Two. Three."

Unlike the guards, I don't need the countdown to pay attention to the real world. I'm already there, double-checking my seatbelt.

Jacob buckles up my mom, and Joe even finds a moment to put a seatbelt on the unconscious RHO leader, though he's probably less concerned for her safety than preserving the pleasure of torturing her later. Meanwhile, Dominic takes Alan into his arms as though he's trying to give the kid a hug. Given that Dominic's body is mostly titanium, Alan should be more secure than in any kind of kiddie car seat.

Joe and Gogi are the only people unbuckling their seat belts. I know what they're about to do, so I open the side windows in the back of the car.

They move in sync, like dancing partners. Both jump up and slide to the window on their side. Both take out their guns seemingly at the same moment. Their simultaneous shots merge into a single eardrum-damaging bang, and the SUV's tires blow out—Joe and Gogi's marksmanship is app-enhanced.

Unfortunately, the SUV appears to have new tires designed, ironically, by Human++. Sparks fly as metal grinds against pavement, but the car doesn't slow down quickly enough—not if we want to keep a far enough distance from a potential blast radius.

"I'm speeding up," Mitya says. "I think that's the only option. If the truck gets off the ramp ahead of Zapo, you're toast—and at the moment, we don't have the resources to run anyone else's minds in the cloud besides mine."

"Wait, hold on," I yell at my friend in VR. "We're going to be by the ramp at the same time. The truck will be able to ram straight into us."

Mitya either doesn't hear or doesn't care.

Zapo X zooms forward.

CHAPTER FOURTEEN

Before I recover from whiplash, Mitya swerves into the middle lane. Does he think the truck will have trouble with a few extra feet of distance? Then I realize that puts a car between us and the truck—an empty self-driving red Toyota that works for Uber.

"I had to speed up," Mitya says in VR as we watch the slow-from-this-perspective progression of the truck on the ramp. "If the SUV driver is another suicide bomber, going faster is your only option."

"The problem is the truck driver might be a suicide bomber as well," I counter.

"I don't think so." Mitya's left eye twitches. Even in digital form, he retains his signature poker tell. His face is calm, but I'm not buying it. "Let's put it another way. If the truck driver has a bomb, you're all dead anyway."

I realize that he and I are both right.

"Joe, Gogi!" I scream in the real world. "Get back into your seats."

The trucker has no bomb, but he's still suicidal. He's realized he can't get ahead of us, so he's now speeding up and clearly intends to crash into the red Toyota that currently separates us. The trucker must think that hitting the Toyota won't slow him enough to keep him from reaching us. My heart rate speeds up as I realize he might just be right.

In real-world slow motion, the cars inch toward each other. I brace myself, cringing at the sight of Gogi and Joe still not in their seats.

Using the quantum servers, I model the upcoming set of collisions a couple of times. When the results come through the same on the third simulation, I shout in VR, "Mitya, Muhomor, get that ambulance in front of us to stop. We're going to need it."

Important task done, I squeeze my eyes shut and brace for the impact in the real world.

The truck almost pulverizes the empty Toyota. As the modeling showed, there's indeed enough momentum left to then ram into Zapo's hulk with notable force.

For some reason, my enhanced brain registers the sound first, a crunch that sounds as if a giant with diamond teeth decided to chew the bulletproof metal of Zapo with his mouth wide open. The jerk comes next, and every part of my body jolts forward, my neck muscles straining to keep my head attached. Shards of glass rain through the vehicle without cutting anyone, thanks to the patented shatter-without-edges technology that cost the equivalent of a modest car to install.

Through the drone cameras, I can see that Zapo has withstood the impact slightly better than the modeling predicted, though the suicidal driver got his death wish when he catapulted through his broken window. When I rewind the video, I see him somersault over Zapo's roof and land in a bloody splat of broken bones.

Unfortunately, the unsecured Gogi and Joe also behave as foretold in the modeling. As though continuing their earlier synchronicity, each man flies head first at the opposite wall and smacks his skull before collapsing into a limp bundle. The only differences between them are the blood pouring from Joe's head wound and the unnatural angle of Gogi's ankle.

I'm not sure how Mitya or Muhomor managed it, but the ambulance we've been following is backing up.

Then it hits me that I'm relaxing too soon. Surviving the truck still leaves us with the SUV behind us, a car with a suicide bomber behind the wheel.

"Dominic," I scream, "behind us!"

I don't think I needed to prompt the former soldier. He gently sets Alan on Jacob's lap and sweeps into action with a set of maneuvers that explain to me why the army is so keenly interested in the exoskeleton technology he now controls. With a powerful push of his legs, he leaps through the broken back window, reaches for his gun in midair, and lands with the softness of a feline predator. He then sprints toward the SUV, his biological hand holding the gun and his bionic hand extended palm outwards.

"I can't even imagine what he's feeling right now," Alan messages me privately. "Dominic has a deep-seated anxiety when it comes to walking up to cars, even parked ones."

Dominic's bullet hits the driver squarely in the head, but the car still has enough momentum to roll toward us, despite the naked metal of the wheels now gouging deep gashes in the pavement.

Dominic's palm connects with the SUV's grill. If his arm had been mine, enhanced bones or not, it would have snapped. But his state-of-the-art bionic arm holds the car without any problems and makes him look like a super-hero as he skids backward in his effort to slow the SUV. The bottoms of his feet are covered by the same titanium as the rest of his body, and the sparks from his feet rival those produced by the car's wheels.

In a fraction of a second, I use the quantum servers again to see if the rest of his exoskeleton will prevent his midsection from getting splattered if the SUV slams him into our vehicle. The answer comes out negative—he'll likely die if he doesn't stop the car. I frantically run another simulation to tell me if he'll manage to stop in time.

Dominic's back slowly draws nearer. Before I get the calculation results back, he stops, his right foot a millime-ter from Zapo's back tire.

Everyone in the car cringes. Though the driver can't activate the bombs now that he's dead, if his allies have an override, we're about to go up in smoke.

"They shouldn't have an override," Mitya says in VR, but it's clear he's unsure. "They didn't in earlier attempts."

"They might have adapted them," Alan says.

"I bet they had the bombs made ahead of time," Ada says, her Zik message hopeful. "That makes it harder to adapt, unless the driver was very handy with explosive-related gizmos."

"Get into the ambulance now," Muhomor says. "Don't wait to find out."

Dominic seems to have the same idea, because he jumps back into Zapo and picks up Gogi like a doll.

"The exoskeleton is now one of my favorite creations," I say in the VR, awestruck. "That, or Dominic is a biological marvel."

"I know." Ada doesn't seem to realize that she just bit a virtual nail. "The man isn't even out of breath."

An EMT emerges from the passenger side of the ambulance. "What's going on? We were responding to a heart attack when the car navigation started acting up and made us back up." Coming closer, he takes in the scene and asks, "Is anyone hurt?"

"Yes," I reply. "Please help."

"That rerouting sounds like Muhomor's work," Mitya says in VR. "Too bad someone's going to die because of it."

"The call was from a hypochondriac." Muhomor gives Mitya a defensive look. "I'm checking her out through her webcam, and Einstein agrees she's just having a panic attack."

"I'm making sure another ambulance double-checks Doctor Muhomor's diagnosis," Ada chimes in. "Meanwhile, take our people to the hospital."

Ignoring the emergency personnel, Dominic puts Gogi inside the ambulance and comes back for Joe. The

EMT guys gape at all this in fascination; they're undoubtedly used to doing all the work on their own.

The rest of us unbuckle our seatbelts, and I check that Mom is okay. She's been silent throughout the ordeal, and her pale face looks more frightened than the day we rescued her from that Russian facility. On a hunch, I reassure her that Joe is going to be okay, and that seems to return a hint of color to her cheeks. I wait another beat, and when her shallow breathing evens out, I help her stand up. Before she gets a chance to completely come back to her senses, I lead her out of the ruins of Zapo as Jacob carries Alan behind me.

"That was scary," Mr. Spock telepathically announces from my pocket. "Let's not do it again."

"I'd love not to do that again, bud," I reply. "The bad people didn't give me a choice."

"I don't like bad people," he says confidently. "Can I bite them?"

Mr. Spock has been learning human social mores, and the mere fact that he asks if he can bite before doing so is a huge sign of progress.

"I hope you don't have to bite them. They taste really bad," I tell him.

"You're going to need another vehicle," Muhomor says.

A white limousine promptly screeches to a halt in the opposite lane.

Dominic grabs the still-unconscious Tatum, steps over the road divider, and proceeds toward the limo. He opens the door and climbs inside. Moments later, a bunch of dressed-up teenagers file out, their expressions a blend of anger, fear, and confusion.

"I'm very sorry, but we need to borrow your ride," I tell the biggest kid. I take a few crisp hundreds from my wallet.

"Tell him another rental is on the way," Muhomor says. "A better, more expensive, and cleaner one, at that."

I relay what Muhomor says and hand over the money. "If you need a place to stay after the prom, I just rented you a couple of suites at The Beekman."

I bypass the stunned teenagers and get Mom comfortable in the front of the limo. The rest of our group sits in the back.

"Have the EMT drive to the nearest hospital that's not overcrowded," I tell my friends in VR. "Also, make sure a car rental is waiting for me there. I'm going to stay with Gogi and Joe while Dominic takes Mom and Alan to the bunker."

"My plane arrives soon," Muhomor says. "Can they pick me up?"

Dominic thinks picking up Muhomor might be safer en route, so I agree to that.

"I'm staying with Josya at the hospital," Mom says when I tell her the plan.

I shake my head. "No, Mom. I need you to be there when Dominic picks up your brother." I'm not just being manipulative. Uncle Abe might balk at going with the robot man, as he calls Dominic behind his back in Russian. "I also need you to get in touch with JC and have him double-check on office evacuations and then join us in the bunker," I continue. "This mess is looking worse and worse, and I wouldn't want them—whoever they are—to hurt any more people, especially your new husband."

I seem to win this fight. Mom looks distant, a habit when using her Brainocytes.

I patch into the camera in the EMT van. To my relief, Joe and Gogi's vitals are good.

Mitya keeps the limo on the tail of the ambulance all the way to Coney Island Hospital. We're not allowed to enter the emergency room driveway, so Mitya takes me to the main entrance instead.

"Alan, Mom," I say as I get up to leave, "I'll see you in the bunker. Love you."

"Let me know when you find out how Uncle Joe is doing," Alan says. "And Gogi too."

"What am I going to tell Joe's father?" Mom looks at me sternly.

"Maybe we'll know something by the time you have to explain," I lie. Uncle Abe lives on Brighton Beach just a few blocks away, and there's no chance Joe will be seen by a doctor in the time it takes the limo to pick up his father.

"Okay," she says. "Go make sure they take good care of him."

"I'm conscious." A telepathic message from Joe arrives without any emotional overtones.

"Great," I reply. "I'm going to come see you in a moment."

Entering the hospital brings back unpleasant flashbacks of my prior hospital visit, and I fight the hollowness in my chest.

"If any of us visit a hospital a few more times," Muhomor says, "they'll probably offer us a procedure for free."

My friend's joke fails to dispel my disquiet, so I get into a virtual room with Einstein in therapist mode. This version of Einstein is good at reading facial cues and body language, and right away, he gives me a soothing smile. His German accent is almost nonexistent as he asks, "How does it feel to be in a hospital?"

"I'm going to need a gallon of vodka." Gogi's grumpy telepathic message comes in at the same time. "Why the hell did you take me to the hospital? You know I hate these places."

"Stay put." I'm hugely relieved that Gogi has also regained consciousness. I also feel slightly guilty that I wasn't as relieved when I learned that Joe had come to. "I'm on my way to the ER."

"They're taking me and Joe someplace," Gogi says.

"To image your heads," Muhomor explains when I pass on Gogi's comment. "They didn't encrypt their ancient system using Tema, so I'm in there. I expedited things as much as I could. You'll see a doctor as soon as the imaging is complete."

"They're checking your brain for any damage," I tell Gogi. "Nothing to worry about."

In my post-adrenaline slump, the need for sleep presses like a weight against my eyelids. Fighting to keep from yawning, I walk up to the check-in window.

"Hi," says the tall receptionist as she looks at me through fake eyelashes. "How can I help you?"

"I'm here to visit my cousin. An ambulance just brought him in."

The receptionist looks at me with a gaze completely devoid of empathy. "If your cousin was just brought in, he won't be in the system yet."

"He should be in the system," I say, annoyed she didn't even ask for his name. "He's getting his head scanned."

"We can't let you walk in while the patients are getting scanned," she says in the same monotone. "Please take a seat."

"Muhomor." I rub my temples both in VR and the real world. "Can you get me through the red tape?"

Muhomor waves his hands like a conductor in VR, then says, "Walk up to the security guard and launch this app"—an icon that looks like a one-eyed pirate shows up in my AROS view—"and your Brainprint will confirm your identity as a doctor."

Brainprint was one of Muhomor's early inventions. It replaced most ID cards, log-in passwords, bank account PINs, and other identity-verifying security. Brainprint uses Brainocytes for biometric identification, as each person's brain is more unique than their retinas and fingerprints combined. In fact, Muhomor claims that Brainprint doesn't allow identity theft at all, and if he thinks so, it's safe to assume it's pretty much the case. But if you make up a fake person from scratch (something Muhomor can do), you can also create a fictional Brainprint for such a person—and add the Brainprint to the hospital database.

The screen next to the guard blinks green, and my name shows up as "Dr. Hui."

"Very mature," I mutter as I plod through the opening door. In Russian, *hui* is the vulgar word for male genitalia.

The guard consults the screen and chuckles. Given this hospital's proximity to Brighton Beach, he probably understands what my name means.

"Dr. Hui's first name is Richard." Muhomor's VR grin is annoyingly cheerful. "But friends call him Dick, of course."

"I hope you weren't stupid enough to give Joe an alias like that." I cross my VR arms over my chest. "You're about to be taken to the same bunker as he, and he's bound to be in a bad mood after getting his head bashed in."

Muhomor's smile disappears. "I didn't get a chance to give them fake identities. The EMT guys read their Brainprint before I could interfere."

"Did you at least delete them from the hospital database?" My voice jumps an octave. "The bad guys seem to be operating out of Russia, and this hospital is crawling with Russian-speaking staff."

"The security for patients is better than for employees," Muhomor says defensively. "They don't want to remove the wrong person's kidney due to an identity mix-up."

I shoot him an incredulous look. "So you can't hide their tracks?"

"If the brain imaging is clean, I'll make it look as though they were never here," he says. "If not, we'll figure something out. I guess I can create fake people with the same medical problem as Joe and Gogi and fake an admission trail—"

"I'm done with the scans." Joe appears in VR, his lizard-like eyes watching without emotion as everyone jumps.

"Gogi is done also," Muhomor says. "No skull fractures or brain damage for either, but Gogi's ankle is hurt."

"We need to get to the bunker then," I say. "Get a couple of our Human++ doctors to join us there in case we need them. Speak with Dr. Jarvis in particular, and tell him to bring his whole surgical team along with any equipment they might need."

"ER," Joe says. He disappears from VR.

When I reach the emergency room, Joe is already standing, ready to go.

"*Blyad*," Gogi mutters when his foot touches the floor. He tries to take a tentative step, then explodes into more Russian and Georgian curses that garner the attention of the Russian-speaking people around us.

"Here, sit on this," Joe says.

I'm shocked to see he's already pilfered a wheelchair. Gogi grudgingly sits, and Joe begins pushing, forcing me to follow.

"This place smells bad," Mr. Spock mentally complains from my pocket.

"We're leaving, bud." I gently tap him through my clothes, angry at myself for forgetting to give him to Alan earlier.

"Watch every camera in the hospital," I tell my friends in VR. "Every time I've been to a hospital lately, it didn't end well."

"Sir," someone shouts from behind us. "Stop!"

CHAPTER FIFTEEN

Whatever the nurse wants, we'll never learn, because we proceed forward as fast as the wheelchair allows. To my surprise and relief, no one bothers us once we get outside the ER, and our luck continues to hold all the way to the parking lot.

"My plane landed, and I got picked up," Muhomor says in VR. "In case anyone cares."

Dominic also reports that he, Mom, Uncle Abe, and Alan made it to the airport without any problems, and that Muhomor is now in the car and en route to the bunker.

"Lean on me," I tell Gogi when we locate the luxury Lexus rental car waiting for us. He lets me and Joe help him get into the front seat.

"For an ankle that wasn't seriously damaged, it sure hurts like a sonofabitch," he says as the car begins to move.

"We'll get you some ice when we get to the hideout," I reassure him. "Run the Relief app for now."

"We should expedite the research on nanocytes that reduce swelling," Ada says in the VR room. "Maybe once things calm down a bit."

"All our efforts should focus on computing resources," Mitya counters. "And we might want to start thinking about that now, not later."

"More hardware so that you can spawn more of yourself?" Muhomor makes an okay sign with his left hand, then spears it with his right index finger in a gesture vaguely related to reproduction.

"No." Mitya's avatar seems to become more solid, and his inability to keep a poker face shows me that Muhomor might've been right. "I want you guys to have the option of getting resurrected as I was. In the longer term, this option should exist for more people."

"He's got a point," Alan says. "We nearly died today."

"We have enough disk space to back ourselves up as you did," I say. "It's processing power that we lack."

"Yes," Mitya says.

"So if we die but have a backup"—I can't help but shiver at the thought—"you can still resurrect us once the processing power is available in the future."

"Of course," he says. "Obviously I can. But building new hardware will take a while—time that will seem like forever to someone like me, a mind whose subjective experience of the world is so much faster."

"Are you saying you'd miss us for an eternity?" Alan asks. It's unclear if he's teasing Mitya or is dead serious.

"You understand it better than most, kid," Mitya says. "I bet in your four years, you've experienced the equivalent of fifty subjective years."

"If not more," Alan says sagely.

Muhomor takes off his sunglasses and rubs his eyes. "Knowing that I depend on you for my resurrection, my fear of death is getting worse."

"That's right." Mitya rubs his palms like a supervillain. "You better be on your best behavior, or else you might wake up a hundred years from now. Or not at all."

"We should do the backups more regularly." I make a mental note to speak with therapy Einstein about my utter horror at being in a disembodied state like Mitya. "And I agree that we should work on the hardware problem, especially since that aligns with so many of our other endeavors."

"Anyone against?" Muhomor looks at Ada.

"We can make hardware a priority," my wife says, "but we should still work on nanocytes that reduce inflammation."

"Agreed," I say for everyone.

"Since no one is trying to kill you at the moment, how about we brainstorm?" Mitya says.

"Speaking of that," Alan says, "our car just reached the bunker."

I exhale in the real world and realize it's been many minutes since I held my breath in worry for my mom and son. "Great. In that case, let's talk hardware while I'm stuck in my own car. I've been thinking a lot about quantum dot cellular automata lately, so maybe let's start with that."

When Gogi first floated the idea of building the bunker four years ago, I told him he was bonkers. Now I'm glad Joe took his colleague's side, and we ended up with this impenetrable monstrosity. Originally a Cold War-era nuclear fallout shelter, the renovated space is a survivalist's wet dream. The entry door alone cost more than a modest house, and it's impervious to most explosions, which is what motivated me to come here.

Inside, the bunker looks like a malignant man cave that kept growing in someone's basement until it became the size of a small mansion. The comfortable plush furniture tries to trick you into thinking you're in a luxury hotel, but the lack of windows betrays the truth.

"If the zombie apocalypse were to happen tomorrow, this is where you'd want to be," Muhomor says to us in lieu of a greeting. "It looks darker and smells even stuffier than I imagined."

He's right. The place smells like a wine cellar where all the wine has turned to vinegar.

"Joshen'ka," my mom exclaims as she takes in Joe's bandaged head. "How are you feeling?"

"Fine." He takes off the bandage, sees his father's worried expression, and shows the side of his head. "Barely a bump."

We sit Gogi on the nearby couch.

"Does your foot hurt?" Alan asks him.

"Ankle," Gogi replies. "I'm sure it's going to be fine."

"Dr. Keeplan," JC calls from the grotto-like kitchen section of the bunker. "Please have a look at Gogi's ankle."

The portly doctor swings into action, and soon Gogi has an ice pack on his ankle and a Percocet in his bloodstream.

"Boss," Jacob says to Joe as he enters the space designated as the living room of the bunker. "Your woman—I mean, your guest. She's awake now."

Joe puts down the sandwich he's been munching on and is instantly on his feet. "Where?"

"The storage room," Jacob says. Looking down like a guilty schoolchild, he adds, "She's breaking a lot of pickles."

"Do we have a view into that room?" I ask my friends in VR.

"Yes." Muhomor sets up a large screen in the bunker's Augmented Reality, making it look like a giant flat-screen TV we used as recently as three years ago.

On the screen, Tatum's delicate features are twisted in a mask of fury. Like a wronged housewife, she grabs a glass jar of pickled tomatoes and hurls it against the pantry wall—and by the looks of the room, it's not the first one.

"I made those," Mom exclaims in a horrified whisper. "I used those purple Ukrainian tomatoes Ada brought for me."

Joe's expression is completely unreadable as he springs into motion. Before anyone can blink, he's in the camera view, opening the door to the storage room.

CHAPTER SIXTEEN

Tatum looks Joe up and down, her eyes narrowing. She must not recognize him as the guy who knocked her out, because the latest jar isn't yet flying at his head.

Instead of worrying about a potential projectile, Joe climbs the shelves. We all, Tatum included, watch his actions with morbid fascination. Only when my cousin's palm grows large does it occur to me what he's doing. When the camera is ripped out of its socket, I congratulate myself for being right. Maybe he's trying to win Tatum's confidence by showing her that she was under surveillance. Oh hell, who am I kidding—he just doesn't want us to watch.

Everyone stares at the blank screen for a couple of beats before Ada asks, "Is there another camera in that room?"

Muhomor shakes his head, and when I ask Joe's security guys the same question, they all claim there's no other camera.

I walk up to the door, hoping I can at least overhear something. Unfortunately, the thick, heavy wood blocks any noise from escaping.

"Maybe this means she's not screaming in pain," I say, only slightly joking.

"You can't let him do this." Ada's amber eyes glint dangerously in the VR room.

"Do what?" Mitya asks. "We don't know what he's doing. For all we know, they might be having a civil conversation."

"Someone is clearly in need of a brain," Muhomor says. "This is Joe. If she's not screaming, it's because he has her gagged. Or worse."

I wonder if Joe's people would obey a direct order to go check on Tatum, assuming I wanted to be the guy giving such an order, which I don't. Dominic might listen to me, but I can't help but notice he's not rushing to check on Tatum voluntarily.

We argue for a few minutes in real time, and Ada has almost convinced me to ask Dominic to break the door when said door swings open and Joe swaggers out. Hard to read in the best of times, his current facial expression is an enigma wrapped in the skin of the Loch Ness monster.

"She's not involved," he says over his shoulder as he strides past us into the gloomily lit kitchen.

I follow him in and watch as he swiftly finishes his uneaten sandwich, then proceeds to get more bread from the pantry and some cheese from the fridge. "What do you mean?"

"She didn't order the attacks," he says without looking up from spreading mayo on the bread.

"Are you sure?"

"Go talk to her." He angrily slaps some cheese onto the bread. "And give her this."

He hands me the sandwich, which I regard as if it might sprout tentacles. Oblivious to my confusion, he grabs a sealed bottle of Poland Spring water and hands that to me as well.

"I should at least check if she's okay," I say in the VR room after making sure he's not in there. "Plus it doesn't hurt to double-check if she really is innocent or not. I mean, she was our best lead."

"The RHO was," Ada corrects. "But maybe she's not its leader as everyone thinks. Or maybe they have independent cells that don't operate under her direct command."

I head over to the room where Joe's captive awaits. For some reason, the food and drink feel like lead in my hands. Why couldn't all this have waited until tomorrow morning? I'd pay a couple of million for a quick nap.

Alan is blocking my way. I look down at him questioningly.

"You might find this helpful." He hands me a tablet computer, one of those ancient relics that only the likes of my uncle still use. "No Brainocytes, remember? You won't be able to show her anything online without it."

"Thanks, son," I say on autopilot. I hold the sandwich in my teeth while I slide the tablet under my armpit.

Jacob opens the heavy door for me, and I momentarily hesitate, afraid of blood and whatever else I might find. The little spike of anxiety jolts me awake. Realizing it's not safe to keep the door ajar so long, I step in and enable my Share app so my friends can see what I see.

The woman is sitting on a stack of canned beans, her piercing blue eyes regarding me with a mixture of curiosity and disdain.

"Michael Cohen," she says in a pleasant singsong voice. "I should've guessed you're in charge here."

"The way she said your name, you'd think she was talking about Lucifer." Mitya manifests in the room's public Augmented Reality, choosing the little devil avatar he sometimes likes to use.

Tatum doesn't acknowledge him at all, confirming her lack of Brainocytes. Her attention is on my hands, so I extend the water and sandwich.

"Joe wanted me to give you this."

To my huge surprise, she doesn't shudder at his name. Instead, her eyes gleam with some undefinable emotion. Realizing I'm watching her, she quickly recovers her mask of disdain, but that doesn't stop her from grabbing both the sandwich and the water.

Taking a giant bite of the sandwich, she eyes me challengingly as she slowly chews her food. If she thinks she can bore me so easily, she's going to be disappointed. Thanks to Brainocytes, if the real world is boring (which it almost always is), I can do a hundred other things virtually.

I lean against the wall of canned beans and make sure Tatum can tell that I'm comfortable enough to stay here for hours, if she insists. I then reply to all the emails that have accumulated since these crazy events began, launch several processor designs since that's a new priority, initiate an important conversation with Ada about Alan's plan to earn another PhD from Yale, begin writing a couple of apps, get started beating several world champions at chess, and outline a few chapters for my latest publication.

Once Tatum figures out she can't bore me into leaving, she says, "At the rallies, I always said what you did was criminal." She unscrews the bottle cap and gulps the water with the zest of a desert dweller. "I didn't realize how literal that was."

"You have the gall to bring up criminal acts with me?" My voice hardens. I'm having flashbacks of the multiple ways I nearly died today, along with memories of all the favorite things lost in my deceased penthouse—like the Swiss armchair I'd sit in while in VR and the obscenely expensive Pollock and Dalí originals. What a ghastly loss. I take a deep breath of pickled vegetables and add more calmly, "Your people tried to kill me. Multiple times. You blew up everything I own."

Her look is so full of sympathy that I stop talking and blink in confusion.

"I'm sorry about what happened to you." To heighten the sincerity of her words, she momentarily stops chewing, though I get the sense that she's dying to resume. "The RHO is a peaceful organization, and I would never authorize violence of any kind, even against you."

"Then how do you explain this?" On the tablet, I pull up a picture of her and Lennox Dixon, the guy who blew up our apartment, and transpose it with the news articles about the bombing.

I hold the screen toward her, and she puts down the water and grabs the device out of my hands. If Joe mentioned any of this to her during his mysterious interrogation, there's no sign of it. She looks shocked, her eyes filling with tears.

"If this is a trick," she says, blinking rapidly, "it's very cruel. Even for someone like you."

"Can you stop saying that? I'm not the devil."

She glances around the storage room as if to say, "I'm here, a prisoner, and you're in charge—do the math."

"Your being in this room is just a misunderstanding," I say. "We'll obviously let you go as soon as we understand who's trying to kill us and why. Besides, didn't you catch the part where the authorities want to question you?"

"Why shouldn't I talk about you as though you're the devil?" she asks, her gaze hardening now that she's no longer staring at the tablet. "You're about to usher in the apocalypse for the human species. That makes you pretty much the textbook antichrist."

"So you admit you tried to kill me." I speak quickly, trying a persuasion technique I've used a few times on investors. "You wanted to prevent the apocalypse."

The miserable expression returns to her face, and she shakes her head, her gaze on the tablet once more.

"I would never do that," she says. "Nor would Lennox ever do something like that, for that matter." She looks thoughtful for a moment, then shakes her head again. "No, he really wouldn't."

I latch on to her hesitation as a clue. "Yet he did. There's something you're not saying."

"Lennox didn't have long to live," she says after a pregnant pause. "A brain tumor. But he acted normally. Besides, where would he get a suicide vest? Why would he bomb your apartment, where your family might be? It just makes no sense."

"And yet it happened."

In VR, I ask, "Why didn't we know about his tumor?"

"Unlike Coney Island Hospital, most doctors' offices encrypt their records using Tema," Muhomor says defensively.

"We should see if anyone else had a terminal illness," I say in VR.

In the real world, Tatum frowns at me uncertainly. "Maybe someone offered him money? He was worried about his dad, but I told him we'd take care of his family." She begins to cry.

I feel like a monster, even though I haven't really done anything. I fight the temptation to walk over and touch her shoulder reassuringly. Comfort from "the antichrist" would probably make matters worse. "Can you think of anyone who would've paid him to do something like that? Maybe a more zealous part of your organization?"

"We don't have bloodthirsty zealots like that." She wipes the remnants of tears from her eyes to make sure I register the scathing look she gives me. "Most of us are unemployed, thanks to you and your company. We're as useless as the rest of humanity is going to be soon, if you're not stopped."

"Tell her about our plans to allow people to make money as artisans in their fields," Alan says, raising one of his favorite topics. "Also mention our plans for universal basic income."

"No zealots," Ada says, her voice dripping with sarcasm as she ignores Alan's tirade. She appears as an angel avatar next to Mitya's devil and gives Tatum an unsympathetic once-over. "Ask her how they planned to save humanity, then. By being a nuisance?"

"If you truly believe that we're bringing about the end of the world," I say instead, "isn't it just a matter of time before someone gets violent?"

"If Gandhi could drive the British out of India with patience and without violence, we should be able to reverse the harm you're doing using the same methods," Tatum says. Her dimpled chin juts upward.

"Did she just compare herself to Gandhi?" The tiny Mitya devil lands on Tatum's right shoulder. "Why not the Dalai Lama? Or Santa, while she's at it?"

"I bet fifty bucks she's going to compare us to Hitler at some point in the next few minutes," Ada replies, matching Mitya's tone.

I do my best to ignore the commentary from Augmented Reality. "Do you still think I fabricated what this tablet is showing you?"

"No." Tatum visibly deflates.

"Then you agree that despite what you tried to do, violence happened."

She nods.

"Then help us figure out who's responsible," I say. "If RHO is innocent, then it would seem someone is framing you guys. You should be as interested in getting to the truth as I—perhaps more so, since the authorities are looking for you."

She's silent for a moment. Her nicely trimmed eyebrows move animatedly on her forehead as though they're a window into her brain. "I don't think you're fabricating this." She gestures at the tablet, looking genuinely miserable. "I just don't know how I can help."

"Joe is right," Muhomor says in the VR room. "She's useless."

"I agree," Ada says. "Let's let her go after I land."

"I'm not convinced." Mitya's avatar flies from Tatum's shoulder, grows to the size of a small dog, and lands a foot away from her legs. "The fact that she doesn't have Brainocytes does open an interesting possibility. We could force her to get Brainocytes with a modified AROS interface that has the Polygraph app running in the background. We could then find out for sure if she's telling the truth."

"No." Ada's angel grows bigger than the devil avatar and flies through the room to place herself between Tatum and Mitya. "We're not doing that."

The Polygraph app was a failure created by the intelligence community, designed to test its own people. It's a Brainocyte app that can accurately spot if the person running it is telling the truth. It's a million times more reliable than the polygraph exam from which it takes its name. Even before Brainocytes, tools like fMRI and other brain-scanning technologies were used in lie detection, but Brainocytes took such technology to new levels.

The reason the project failed was that we designed Brainocytes in such a way that no one can force someone else to run a specific app; you must rely on the person to do it on her own. That led to an easy way to thwart the Polygraph app: a spoofed version of the app that doesn't keep an eye on the user's brain but instead shows results that look like the output of the Polygraph app.

What Mitya suggests would work around the spoof problem because Tatum would get Brainocytes for the first time. As a new user, she'd not be able to figure out how and where to get the Polygraph-faking app. Also—and this is probably why Ada is so upset—Mitya is suggesting that her Brainocytes would run an app in the background without her explicit consent, something our lobbyists are trying to make illegal in as many countries as we can.

"That's an interesting idea," I say to my friends telepathically. "If we made sure she's not connected to the internet, we could be certain the Polygraph app is working as intended. Or that the custom AROS build wouldn't even have internet. Hell, we could even give her a normal AROS interface and just insist she run the Polygraph app without internet. This way—"

"I said no." Ada's head turns toward me, her amber eyes burning with ire. "It's extremely unethical."

"Oh, she'd like us to do that," Muhomor says. "Confirmation bias. She'd love it if we confirmed every fear the RHO has about us."

"No," I say to Muhomor. "I just read some of Tatum's blog posts, and I think Brainocytes would be her worst nightmare. I guess we're back at square one."

"I think you're telling the truth," I say to our victim in the real world. "My cousin said as much." I say the last bit out of curiosity. I'd still like to know what Joe did to her to reach his conclusion.

"You mean Joe?" To my shock, her expression is less dire than I would've expected at the mention of her tormentor. It's almost excited, even. "You're related?"

"His father is my mother's brother." I raise my eyebrows in VR as if to say, "What *did* he do to her?"

"I see," Tatum says, her expression unreadable again.

Ada, Muhomor, and Mitya all shrug.

"I'd like you to stay with us a little bit longer," I say after a long and uncomfortable silence, during which Tatum finishes both her food and water.

"Stay your prisoner, you mean?" she says. It's hard to say if she's really upset or she's just using the chance to poke at the antichrist.

"I'd prefer to look at it as giving you shelter while we figure out how to clear your name." I wave at the tablet.

"Since I don't have a choice, I don't see why not," she says. "Any chance I can take a shower, use the bathroom, and take a nap?"

Mitya sends me the bunker schematics with one room circled. "Nine suites, two of them unused. That one has a door that someone can guard."

"Let me see what I can do for you," I tell Tatum.

After some quick setup, Gogi takes her to the room Mitya picked out.

"Dominic," I say. "Do you mind taking the first watch?"

Instead of answering, he assumes his position. I believe his exoskeleton would allow him to stand like this for days, but I've never double-checked by asking if it's true. Dominic doesn't like to talk about his body.

"Hey, Dad." Alan is using his real-world, hard-to-resist kid voice, which means he's about to say something I won't like. "Can I speak with her?"

"Tatum?" I glance at Dominic for support, but the guard's Augmented Reality face shows no emotion. "You want to talk to the woman who might've ordered that bombing?"

"We decided she didn't do it." He speaks telepathically now; he knows that when it comes to arguing, you sound less persuasive when your voice is that of a four-year-old.

If I start arguing, he's probably going to get his way, as well as delay my getting to sleep by precious minutes. So I do the easy thing and give in.

"Put another guard at the entry and take Dominic with you when you go inside." I make sure Dominic gives me a little nod.

"Okay," Alan says reluctantly.

"And run the Share app, recording every word she says."

"Well, of course."

"You okay with this?" I privately ask Ada. "I'll be the bad guy and say no, if you want."

"Let him talk to her," she replies, her message almost free of anxiety. "Dominic will be with him."

I send Dominic a private message. "If she so much as looks at him wrong or says a mean word, pull him out. If she touches him in the wrong way—in any way—break her arm."

The big man gives me another nod.

"And can I pick up Mom when she lands?" Alan asks, his eyes glinting mischievously. He knows what I'll say, but he's testing me anyway.

"Absolutely not." I try to look as authoritative as I can.

"We'll discuss this after you get some sleep," he says. "You're not in the best of moods now."

"My answer will be the same."

"We'll see."

I send a private telepathic message to my cousin. "Joe, make sure to wake me up before you go get Ada."

"Obviously," he replies.

"And when we go, please have someone check the car to make sure Alan is not stowed away in it someplace. He's gotten it into his head to go with us, which I don't think is safe."

"I agree," Joe replies grimly. I get the feeling that if he does catch Alan in the car, my son might get his first-ever spanking. Or worse.

"Can someone interview the family of the Curaçao bomber?" I ask in the VR room with a demonstrative yawn. "And can someone else do the same in the other locations?"

"I now can control a dozen more robots than when I was corporeal," Mitya says. "I volunteer."

"All right. Then can the rest of you guys please watch over Alan while he goes to talk to that witch?" I yawn again. "I can almost get a solid's night sleep before Ada's plane arrives."

"Not fair," Ada says. "I'm exhausted and want to go back to sleep also."

"So?" Muhomor says. "You don't trust me to watch over the offspring in a bunker full of guards?"

"Fine." Her yawn is even more contagious than mine. "I'm sleeping for the rest of the flight."

"Anything else we can do while the two of you slack off?" Muhomor asks sarcastically.

"It would be nice to look into the people who drove those cars earlier," I say. "My face recognition app didn't catch their faces, but maybe you can hack into police department or the morgue to find out who they were."

"Fine." He looks embarrassed. I guess this is the first time he hasn't already thought of hacking the answers.

I gulp down a smoothie I made while speaking in VR, then make my way to the master suite and plop down on the bed. I make a mental note to upgrade it to the Mitya-designed WhisperAir mattress at some point in the future. This mattress is the ancient memory foam variety.

Then I realize I'm accepting the need for bunkers too readily. The terrorists (or whoever they are) are winning.

"Watch Alan," I tell Mr. Spock. "Make sure the woman he's about to talk to doesn't upset him."

"If someone hurts Alan, I will bite them," Mr. Spock says, his basic Zik message full of wrath.

"It might be enough to run up to her and squeak," I tell him. "If violence is required, let Dominic deal with it."

"If she makes me squeak, I might not be able to stop myself from biting," Mr. Spock says.

I'm very proud of Mr. Spock's self-knowledge. "Do your best, bud."

"Sleep well." He scurries out of the room.

As my eyelids close, I send Ada our usual telepathic good-night message and blank out.

CHAPTER SEVENTEEN

The hospice tries to be as cheerful as such a place can possibly be, but with every step, I'm drowning in sorrow. A long gray tunnel in front of me ends with a large door marking my destination. Each step echoes through the hallway, and my legs seem to move without my conscious consent.

I know what waits behind that door.

Mom is there, her body a battlefront of cancer.

I feel as if I'm falling instead of walking, and the feeling of falling makes something click in my psyche. I'm pulling the door handle when I become certain that this is a nightmare—a dream inspired by the Join app experience during which I saw what happened to Ada's mother through Ada's eyes.

Bright light hits my retinas as the door opens. Will I see Ada's mother or my own mom in this dream? Or is this a dream at all?

Instead of anyone's mother, Einstein's grinning face greets me. The AI is wearing a gown and has tubes attached, just like in Ada's memories.

"You're getting much better at recognizing and controlling your dreams," he says. "Will you be practicing lucid dreaming now?"

Instead of answering, I focus my attention and transform the room into a rose garden. Once a sweet-scented breeze replaces the stuffy fumes and there's no hint of the hospice, I manifest Ada into the scene.

"Haven't you had enough of me when awake?" dream Ada asks seductively. She loosens the right strap of her yellow summer dress.

"Never," I whisper and float toward her.

CHAPTER EIGHTEEN

"You have been unconscious for eight hours and for-ty-seven minutes," Einstein reports somewhere in my groggy brain. "Current time is 8:55 a.m."

I jackknife in bed and send Ada a frantic telepathic message: "Are you back? Did Joe go pick you up without me?"

She doesn't reply, so I put together another Zik message. "Joe, where are you?"

Joe doesn't reply either. As my real-world hand reaches for my pants, I pop into the VR room, hoping either Ada or Joe are there, but they aren't. The only person in the VR room is Mitya, but his avatar looks strange. His face is like that of a statue in Madame Tussaud's museum, his open eyes glassy.

"Dude," I say when I realize he hasn't blinked for an unnatural length of time. "What the hell is going on with you?"

Mitya's eyes slowly blink and recover some of their live-liness. In almost no time, they sparkle with their normal intelligence, and his face animates into a smile. "Oh, hey."

"Hey," I reply cautiously. "You didn't answer my question."

"What was the question?" He raises his arms over his head in a catlike stretch. "I'm afraid I was a little out of it."

"No kidding," I say. "What was up with your eyes being glazed over?"

"Is that what it looked like?" He stretches his neck, tilting his head side to side. "Since everyone was asleep, I figured it was as good a time as any to experiment with sleep and dividing my attention."

"So that was you sleeping?" I say. "Your eyes were open."

"Do you think anything about me has to do with this avatar anymore?" His body morphs into a row of miniature computer servers. "This is what I really look like now," he says in a slightly metallic voice. "Not this." His avatar is back in the room and continues to stretch his limbs as though nothing happened. "I don't need to breathe," he says on an exhale. "I don't need to worry about my weight." A banana sundae appears on the meeting room table. "I don't—"

"—need to sleep?" I'm eager to get back to the subject of Ada. "Did you rid yourself of sleep? Was that what you experimented with?"

"I'm still mostly an emulation of a bunch of brain regions," he says. "Since the biological brain needs sleep, I'm afraid to just give it up without due diligence. No one's figured out what sleep is for: consolidation of memory, practicing scenarios for the future, or other, sometimes contradictory theories. For now, I'm experimenting with allowing parts of me to sleep while other parts of me remain conscious—a little bit like dolphins, although unlike the dolphins' tactic of sleeping half a brain at a time, I'm trying to figure out a more distributed configuration."

"Okay," I say. "Sounds interesting, but I'm here for a reason. Have you heard from Ada?"

"I was fully asleep for the last real-world hour or two. I wanted to record everything that was happening with every part of my being. But before that, Ada was sleeping, along with everyone else. I checked because I wanted to share my Curaçao findings, along with research on the other bombers—but alas, you guys didn't wake up even for that. I must say, this first night as a spirit inside the machine was pretty boring overall, and I foresee myself making lots of new friends around the world if you guys keep on sleeping regularly like this."

"This is odd," I say. "By all rights, Ada's plane should've landed already. I was expecting it at 7:30 a.m. or thereabouts."

"Perhaps no one woke you up because severe weather delayed the flight?" Mitya says and then frowns. "I can't reach the pilot or any of the crew. That really is odd."

My breathing speeds up in the real world, where I'm still only in the process of putting a foot through my right pant leg. I telepathically ping Ada again, and then do the same with Joe.

Nothing.

Desperate, I try getting in touch with Muhomor and get an auto-reply that he's sleeping. This isn't surprising, as Muhomor's earlier nickname was Upir—Russian for vampire, because he strongly prefers night to day. I debate getting in touch with Mom, but she might have a heart attack if I tell her my current situation, so I abandon that idea.

After a slight hesitation, I write a Zik message to Alan, certain that he of all people would be wide awake, bright-eyed and bushy-tailed. The kid is like that Energizer Bunny from the commercials. He gets up at 7 a.m. even if he goes to bed after midnight.

As milliseconds pass without an answer, my real-world heartbeat picks up. "I'm going to focus on what's happening in real time, so I won't be fun to talk to. Can I ask you to check into their location on this level?"

"Of course," Mitya says. "Here are the views into everyone's rooms through the security cameras our bodyguard set up. I'll proceed by locating the plane, and then—"

I stop paying attention because I'm taking in everyone in their rooms, and I don't like what I'm seeing. Muhomor and Mom are sleeping, as I thought, as are prisoner-guest Tatum, Gogi, Dominic, and most of the guards. Alan, however, isn't in his room or anyone else's. There's no camera in anyone's bathroom (a camera in the bedroom is bad enough, even for an underground post-apocalyptic bunker), so I can't check to see if he's merely brushing his teeth—though if he's awake, why would he ignore my messages?

I fully ignore VR and pour all my prodigious attention into the act of putting on pants while hopping toward the door. I'm pulling my zipper up as I dash toward Alan's room, passing a snoring Jacob on the way. He's napping on guard duty, but I'll leave it to Joe to reprimand his man—assuming I can find Joe.

In person, Alan's suite is only slightly smaller than the one designated for me and Ada. The bed is still empty, and I run up to it to feel for warmth. He must've left the bed a while ago, because the silk sheets (his favorite material) are cold to the touch. I check the bathroom and don't find him there, either.

I grab Alan's tooth-rinsing glass and fill it up with chilly water, then retrace my steps back to the lounge chair where Jacob is still sleeping on the job.

"Jacob."

Unsurprisingly, he keeps on snoring. In case he is stupid enough to run the Do Not Disturb app on duty, I toss the contents of my glass into his face and follow it up with a bitch slap.

I must hand it to Jacob's training. He's on his feet instantly with a gun to my head. Irritated, I prepare to disarm him, but before I get the chance, his eyes widen in recognition and he lowers his weapon.

"What the hell?" he asks as he rubs his cheek and looks down at his wet shirt. "What's gotten into you?"

My worry transforms into sudden fury. "Where is he?" A speck of my spittle lands on Jacob's nose. "Where is my son?"

"Alan?" He blinks. "He's with Joe. You should know that."

"Where is Joe?" My hands clench into fists.

"He went to pick up your wife." All remnants of sleep are gone from his face, replaced by an expression of deep concern.

"Joe took Alan with him?"

"Yes."

"It didn't seem odd to you that Joe took Alan but not me?"

"Well." Jacob looks panicked now. I guess Joe being his boss means he didn't question what happened, but now that I've forced him to think about it, he sees that he's failed in his guard duty. "I didn't think—"

"I can't reach any of them." I'm shouting, so I lower my voice. "I can't reach Joe, Ada, or Alan."

The blood leaves Jacob's face, and his eyes widen to the size of quarters.

"Behind you." Mitya's private telepathic Zik message comes imbued with the urgency flags set to maximum. "Jacob isn't reacting to your words."

Mitya's right; Jacob is staring at something behind me. I turn my whole body instead of just my head so that whatever the threat is, I'm facing it head on. At the same time, I use Muhomor's app to locate the melon-scented security camera.

Gogi is standing there with a gun. His face lacks his usual good humor.

"Wait," I order telepathically, but it's too late.

Gogi presses the trigger.

A red stain spreads on Jacob's chest right below the water spot I caused earlier. Jacob's expression is a mixture of horror and confusion as he drops to the ground. Like me, he can't believe he just got shot by a fellow guard—and not just any guard, but Gogi, Joe's second-in-command.

I see new movement from the corner of my eye, but all my attention is on Gogi's gun, because he turns and aims at my frantically beating heart.

CHAPTER NINETEEN

It's almost cruel how many thoughts I can have before Gogi presses the trigger. Hell, I might have enough time to write a farewell letter to everyone I ever cared about in the time before the bullet reaches my head.

When Gogi shot Jacob, I didn't know what to think. Granted, I had momentarily felt like killing the guy myself when I learned he didn't stop Joe from taking Alan and leaving without me. But I would never act on such an impulse. Joe might've shot Jacob for this, but not Gogi—or at least, that's what I thought.

Now that Gogi is aiming at me, only one answer seems logical, but that answer makes zero sense.

Gogi is a traitor.

As difficult as it is to believe, the enemy has somehow recruited Gogi and either blackmailed or bribed him to kill me.

Another idea develops, but before I can consciously register it, I see something wonderful. Using his exoskeleton legs to move unlike any mortal man, Muhomor is already behind Gogi. He may have refused to learn martial arts all these years, but his metal-reinforced leg is able to kick away the gun, sending it flying under the nearby lounge chair.

Gogi's hand should be in excruciating pain, but the big man's face shows nothing.

"Jacob saved my life," Muhomor says through gritted teeth as he throws a punch at Gogi's face. "You—"

Though Muhomor hits his target, his unrehearsed punch doesn't stop Gogi's fist from slamming into his pale jaw in return like a baseball bat into a softball. Muhomor's outraged expression instantly slackens, and he slumps to the floor, clearly out.

Gogi lifts his foot to kick Muhomor, but I'm already leaping at him. He doesn't shift his attention swiftly enough, and I see an opening for a devastating blow to his larynx. Yet something makes me hesitate.

"He's your friend," Mitya comments privately, as though he's read my mind. "Of course this will be hard."

"I'm more worried about damaging his neck," I think back at Mitya. "I need him to be able to talk later."

Gogi takes advantage of my delay by throwing a punch at my shoulder. I twist away and counter with a kick, but I don't use the opportunity to break his leg. Something in his movements doesn't fully make sense. I file the oddity away to analyze when I'm not fighting for my life.

Despite all my training, I'm not prepared for what I encounter in this fight. I've always relied on disabling my opponent, typically by causing severe harm very quickly. But I can't bring myself to do that to Gogi. I'm not sure if it's because of the love for life I've caught from Ada during that Joining or the fact that Gogi has been like family for years. Whatever the reason, I'm pulling my punches, blocking his hits and countering with a force no stronger than I'd use during sparring.

In contrast, Gogi's attacks are all real, all aiming to leave me disabled. This is somehow more painful than his intent to shoot me earlier, because there's something more premeditated about fighting someone hand to hand. I can see that if I don't overcome my reluctance, he'll win this fight. Belatedly, I recall that I now have access to Battle Mode and enable it, but I'm wary of turning on the Emotion Dampener because I might then kill Gogi in the most brutal way imaginable.

"Gogi," I say out loud and via a telepathic message. "Whatever they're paying you, I'll double it."

He doesn't stop. His emotionless eyes don't even register comprehension.

Battle Mode highlights my possibilities. I choose an opening that will result in a painful but hopefully not-too-damaging kick in the family jewels. I've already begun to execute the maneuver when I realize my mistake: I've fallen for a feint. Gogi grabs my foot, and we tumble to the ground.

Battle Mode shows me how to position my body midflight to make sure I don't break my spine. My heart pounds against my chest a couple of times before I smack onto the bunker floor. Despite all my training and Battle Mode, I'm still no match for Gogi when it comes to wrestling. I'd be in trouble even without the handicap of my hesitation to hurt a friend.

Out of utter desperation, half based on my own intuition and half on Battle Mode, I slither out of his grasp like a Vaseline-covered eel. To my surprise, I manage to grab his ankle in a lock.

This is when it hits me: the guy hurt his ankle yesterday and could barely stand, yet he's showing no sign of pain during our fight. How much is it costing him to do this? And how much pain am I causing now by continuing the lock?

Gogi behaves as though he wouldn't care if I sawed his ankle off completely. Either he faked his injury earlier, or he's on some major painkillers right now. Then he does something he's never done during training: a very unprofessional, fish-like spiral. We end up rolling on the floor, each trying to get leverage on the other.

Before I even realize what's happened, Gogi's knee connects with my groin, and he headbutts me in the face. His nose cracks, but I'm momentarily stunned. When my world stops spinning, he has me on my back, his knees on my biceps and his hands around my throat.

I wriggle underneath and try to kick him without any luck.

Because of my enhanced bones, I don't fear my neck breaking, and with Respirocytes, it's much harder to choke me than a regular person. To make me run out of oxygen,

Gogi will have to block my airflow for many minutes—but if I can't escape this hold, that shouldn't be a problem.

Battle Mode doesn't highlight any useful maneuvers, and my body's fight-or-flight response doesn't seem to have gotten the Respirocytes memo. I gasp frantically, my heart rate skyrocketing and my vision narrowing to a tunnel. I don't know how long this choking torture lasts, but I can feel myself beginning to weaken. I assume my oxygen supply is dwindling, even with its fancy red-blood-cell-carrying technology.

"Somebody help," I scream in the VR room and send Zik messages to my whole contact list with the exception of Mom. "Gogi is choking me!"

My last hope is that Gogi's hands will cramp from all this intense squeezing, but it doesn't take long to realize he cares as little about the pain in his hands as his bleeding nose and his alleged ankle injury.

In the end, I realize that Respirocytes make dying of suffocation a more horrible experience because the process is so much slower. I begin to fade in and out. During a moment of clarity, I realize I'm no longer kicking with my legs, so I try to use the last of my strength to thrash about. The last-ditch attempt doesn't help, and I'm left with dazedly staring into the empty eyes of the former friend who's methodically taking away my life.

If I die, Mitya might eventually be able to bring a computer substrate version of me back, the way he did for himself. This thought only scares me more, since I can't picture what such an existence would be like. Besides, I can't die without knowing what's happened to Ada and

Alan—especially since I now fear the worst. And a digital resurrection would only happen if our adversaries don't destroy our whole company and the data servers, something no longer safe to assume now that they've somehow managed the impossible: turning Gogi against me.

Unable to fight anymore, my body slackens, and the darkness of unconsciousness closes in.

CHAPTER TWENTY

There's a flurry of movement behind Gogi, though it might simply be the final firing of my oxygen-starved neurons.

Gogi's hands fight to stay on my neck, but a force pulls him back so hard that his nails rip away chunks of my skin. I gasp for air as Dominic's bionic arm lifts Gogi into the air before tossing him aside like a racquetball.

Gogi slams into the wall, slides down, and to my amazement, tries to get up again. Dominic lunges for him.

Using the action of standing up as his cover, Gogi reaches into his boot.

"Dominic, knife!" I yell out loud as well as telepathically.

Gogi has always bragged about the many times that military-issue knife saved his life in the Georgian special forces. He'll be lethal with it even after that devastating smack against the wall. I struggle to crawl in the hope of helping Dominic as best as I can. My legs feel as if they've turned to hair gel and my arms are heavy, but I manage a wobbly few inches toward the couch where I last saw Gogi's gun.

Through the camera view, I see either anger or faith driving Dominic onward. If he heard my shout about the knife, he doesn't seem to care. Before Gogi gets a chance to fully stand, Dominic's artificial arm clamps on his hand like a vise.

Still frantically gasping for air, I reach the couch and fumble underneath it for the gun.

Gogi's knife gleams in the bunker's artificial light. He's grasping the hilt with his free left hand. Dominic sees the threat and tries to pull the man away from his own body, but he's too late.

The knife swings toward his face.

It lodges where Dominic's right eye would be, in the scar tissue that's a reminder of that horrific explosion. If he still had that eye, he would've lost it now without a doubt. He yelps in pain, and given how tough the big man is, I understand just how much harm Gogi just managed to inflict.

My fingers finally brush across the cold barrel of the gun. It takes me less than a second to pull the weapon out. I roll into a shooting position, heart pounding, and as soon as I see a clear shot, I aim at Gogi.

Even after this betrayal, I'm loath to shoot the person I thought for so many years was my friend.

Gogi rips the knife from Dominic's eye socket. He's about to stab him again.

Hesitation gone, I shoot Gogi's knife-wielding arm.

I haven't had time to enable the aim-assist app, but my time at the gun range pays off yet again. Gogi's palm blossoms with red, and the knife clanks against the floor, the handle cleaved in half by my bullet.

Dominic grunts and, with almost no effort, bends Gogi's right arm at an impossible angle. There's a crack of breaking bone.

Gogi doesn't even blink. He's still trying to get at Dominic despite both injuries. Fortunately, there's a limit to how much the body can do with a broken arm, even if the mind is willing it.

Dominic pulls Gogi's head into his bionic grasp, and I know he has enough power in his artificial limb to decapitate him. To my relief, he crashes his opponent's head against the wall instead. Since Gogi's skull doesn't explode into bits, it's safe to assume Dominic was tempering his strength. Nevertheless, Gogi slides to the floor, the cumulative damage enough to finally knock him out.

By the time I'm on my feet, Gogi's hands and feet are in handcuffs that Dominic produces from somewhere. The restraints come just in time, because Gogi comes to and begins thrashing against the cuffs.

"Monster," Gogi bellows when he sees that no matter what he does, he can no longer move. His voice doesn't sound like his usual voice; there's a flute-like quality to it. His efforts become eerily frantic, and I can only imagine the horrific pain in his broken, damaged arms.

Dominic produces a syringe from the same mysterious hiding spot as the cuffs and stabs Gogi in the neck with the thin needle. Gogi instantly goes limp, though as his eyes close, he says in the same odd voice, "If you don't do as you're told, Ada and Alan will die. You must—"

I don't hear what he says next, because he slumps into a drugged netherworld.

"Wait." Rubbing my aching throat, I start toward the unconscious man. "He said something about Ada and Alan. They're missing. I need to know what he knows."

"What's wrong with Alan and Ada?" Fury makes Dominic's avatar as frightening as his damaged body. Though he doesn't like me to, I switch from looking at his avatar to the burned flesh in the real world. His eye socket is bleeding despite the surrounding scar tissue, making it look as if he's shedding macabre tears of blood.

The wound must be bad, because he sinks onto the couch, clutching at his face to stop the bleeding.

"I can't reach either of them," I say. Mentally, I'm examining the bunker schematics to figure out where Dr. Jarvis sleeps. Jarvis is a brilliant surgeon, and I'm glad I tasked him with bringing his whole team plus equipment. "Obviously, their being incommunicado has something to do with Gogi's attack."

"I'm sorry. The drug I gave him…" Dominic tightens his left fist, and I get the feeling that he's as tempted as I to try to rip the information out of Gogi's unconscious body. "He's going to be out for a few hours."

"We don't have that long." I head over to Jarvis's room on unsteady legs. "We need information now."

There's a moan from where Muhomor stirs. Through the camera mic, I hear him say confusedly, "What? How? Who? Why?"

"Joe, Ada, and Alan are missing," I tell him in the fastest Zik I'm capable of. "Gogi seems to be a traitor."

As I speak to him, I storm into the doctor's bedroom and flick on the lights. Despite the gunfire, Dr. Jarvis and his wife are still sleeping. They either have the Do Not Disturb app on, or they overdosed on Ambien. I doubt it's because the walls in this bunker are as heavy and soundproof as the marketing people claimed when we were buying the place.

Breaching all etiquette, I approach the good doctor and slap him across the face.

His eyes pop open, his hand flying up to cradle his cheek as he sits up. "What's going on?" He looks as though he's about to have a heart attack, which I hope he doesn't, as he's our only surgeon.

I rip the covers from his bed, not caring that I'm also exposing his wife. "We need medical help. Get up. I'll go gather the rest of your team."

I repeat a version of this rude awakening several times, and when I've woken the last nurse, I find Dr. Jarvis and a few colleagues setting up a sterile environment in the big open space.

Dominic is already being prepped.

"They're going to be fine," the doctor says when he sees me.

"Is there a way to wake Gogi from his state?" I ask. "I know drug addicts get Narcan to come out of an overdose. Is there something similar here?" I do a quick online search via Brainocytes. "Perhaps Flumazenil?"

"Dr. Blantor?" Dr. Jarvis says to a thin man on his left who, according to face recognition, is an anesthesiologist.

"Nothing that we have here," says Dr. Blantor. "Plus—"

"I got some information," Mitya tells me telepathically. "Join me in VR."

I thank the doctors and take a seat next to where a nurse is applying a bandage to Muhomor's head. "Are you well enough to join VR?"

"Already there," he says through his swollen lip.

The nurse begins to examine me as I switch my full attention to VR. The well-lit illusionary conference room is such a contrast to the bunker that it takes me a moment to mentally adjust—proof I'm still groggy from near suffocation.

Mitya has prepared several screens for us. The biggest shows our private jet in the nearby New Jersey airport.

Mitya's expression is extremely subdued, and I fear the worst as I ask, "What did you find out?"

Mitya looks from me to Muhomor. "You best see for yourself. I've always warned you about him."

The screen shows Joe marching purposefully up the plane stairs, a gun in his hand.

Eugene, one of Joe's most trusted bodyguards and who's tasked with protecting Ada, greets his boss with a smile.

The smile instantly drops when Joe raises his gun, pointing at the man's chest.

"Boss," Eugene says, "what—"

Joe presses the trigger.

He then steps over the dead man without a hint of emotion and stalks into the plane.

CHAPTER TWENTY-ONE

In horrified silence, we watch Joe execute two more of his men—they run out to learn what the shooting is about, see their boss, ask a question, and get slaughtered. Following the same basic formula, a couple more people die inside the baggage compartment, then two more on the ramp that leads into the fuselage. After that, Joe stalks into the passenger compartment and puts another couple of bullets into his remaining people there.

The enormity of this betrayal doesn't compute in my enhanced brain. Nor does Joe's behavior. Why kill his men when most of them are loyal to him and him alone?

If Joe is with the bad guys, I'm well and truly screwed. After years of training in the dojo, I haven't beaten my cousin once during sparring. He still shoots better than I at the range, still lifts more weight at the gym. Simply put, Joe is the deadliest person I've ever encountered, and the idea of him as my foe is terrifying—especially since I don't know if I'm capable of hurting a relative. Yet I have no doubt that he wouldn't hesitate to kill me.

A new fear overrides all my concerns when he begins searching through the seats.

He's looking for Ada.

He discovers her sleeping on the massage-capable couch that was the selling point of this plane. She must have the Do Not Disturb app on as usual, because the bright lights after landing would've awakened her long before the gunfire. Before we developed DND, she made me tape up every LED light in our bedroom with black masking tape. If we survive, we should tweak the stupid app to allow life-threatening sounds and sights to come through.

Target acquired, Joe leaps for my wife, pulling out a syringe on the way. Her peaceful expression doesn't change. The only sign of what he's done is her complete lack of response when he throws her over his shoulder like a sack of potatoes.

In the real world, my nails dig into the base of my palms as my hands clench into too-tight fists.

"I'm sorry, dude," Mitya says as though from the distance. "That was only a part of it. Do you want to see more?"

I nod, because I don't trust myself to speak for the moment.

He plays a clip of Joe sneak-attacking the guards he took with him to the airport, and then he shows me a current video feed of the guards' bodies still lying in the bunker parking lot.

Then he plays the clip I'm dreading the most.

"Thanks so much for taking me with you, Uncle Joe," Alan says as the two of them exit the bunker. "Why did Dad not want to come with us?"

Alan's back is to Joe, so he doesn't see the syringe headed for his flesh. A second later, my son's tiny body slumps, and Joe catches him and places him on the ground.

Overwhelmed with emotion, I jump to my feet in VR and run up to the virtual window. Using my command of the VR design, I turn my reflection in the window into a shadow of Joe and proceed to punch it with all my strength. I'm not sure who I'm angrier at: myself for not preventing this disaster, or my cousin for being the tool my enemies used. My knuckles meet the bulletproof glass again and again, and I welcome the virtual pain.

Mitya puts his hand on my shoulder. "At least he left Alan behind when he was shooting the other guards."

I can't fall apart now, for Alan and Ada's sake. I launch the BraveChill app, which subdues my angst enough to halt my tantrum.

"You need to keep your cool," Mitya messages me privately. "We need your leadership to get through this."

He walks back to the table and swipes his hand along the glass. The surface turns into another screen that shows Joe carrying Alan into the car.

"I can't believe this." Muhomor spits on the table, aiming for the image of Joe. "We never should've put that psycho in charge of security."

"Where are they?" I demand of no one in particular. "We ought to be able to follow the car or limo or whatever Joe drove."

"I have no idea where they are," Mitya says, his eyes downcast. "Joe must've switched cars multiple times, and he must've started with that manual-drive clunker of his that has no tracking technology of any kind."

"Did you check the satellites?" Muhomor asks. "Traffic cameras? Dashboard cams?"

"You're welcome to check my work," Mitya replies testily. "Obviously I wouldn't tell Mike that I have no idea where they are before I had exhausted all options."

Muhomor doesn't answer with anything snide, which tells me he's doing research of his own. Figuring three enhanced brains are better than two, I try my best to follow Joe's trail but quickly discover that Mitya is right. Five minutes or so after the kidnapping, the trail goes completely cold—and it's been hours now, so he could be anywhere within an enormous radius. After futile attempts to reach Alan and Ada via every app we have, I admit defeat and crank up the BraveChill app to its maximum setting to keep from falling apart.

"This doesn't make any sense," I say both in VR and out loud as BraveChill begins to clear my judgment. "Joe is among the richest people in the world. No one could pay him enough to be willing to do this."

Mitya and Muhomor look at me worriedly. The same thought must've crossed both of their enhanced minds.

"Maybe someone had something on him worthy of blackmail?" Muhomor suggests. "Or another kind of leverage?"

Mitya nods. "We all have seen him kill people. Maybe someone has a murder on tape?"

The image of Joe killing my biological father strobes in the forefront of my memory, and I again feel like I'm about to lose my shit—BraveChill notwithstanding.

"Joe would sooner go to jail than do this," I say when I regain my speech. "Besides, Kadvosky and the rest of our lawyers would state the video is fake and make short work of it. Joe knows that."

"Maybe they have someone he cares about?" Muhomor sounds even less certain than before. "'Bring us Alan and Ada or else we kill X.'"

"Who would be X?" I try to get my breathing to even out. "If he cares about anyone, it would be us, his family. The people Joe took are the very people someone would need to kidnap to get him to cooperate—assuming Joe didn't preemptively kill the conspirators."

"Maybe someone poisoned Alan and Ada and told Joe he needs to bring them to some location for a cure." Muhomor bites the nail on his right index finger. "Or maybe they implanted a bomb into Joe's neck and told him it would go off unless he does as he's told."

"Dude." Mitya gives the hacker a baleful stare. "Do you think Mike wants to hear dumb theories like that?"

"It's okay," I manage to say. "No idea is a bad idea. The poison theory doesn't work, though. Joe would get us involved; he wouldn't kill his people. Plus, Gogi's actions don't fit."

"Mike's right," Mitya says. "Same logic, or lack of it, can be applied to Gogi." He puts a recording of Gogi's attack on the screens. "He's not as well off as Joe, but Gogi still has enough shares in Human++ to be too rich to be bought. He loves you like a brother."

"He's loyal to Joe, though," Muhomor says. "So maybe it's just one puzzle instead of two?"

"He's not that loyal to Joe," I reply confidently, though internally I'm less convinced than I sound. Would Gogi hurt me for Joe? I've never had to ponder such a question before, and now that I do, I'm not sure what the answer is.

"What Gogi did makes no sense at all." Mitya stares at the part of the recording where Gogi's hands are around my throat. "If I can think of some crazy reason for Joe to take Alan and Ada someplace, I simply can't imagine why Gogi would want to kill you—"

An earlier idea re-forms in my mind, and everything falls into place.

"Guys," I say triumphantly. "I think I know what's going on."

"You do?" my friends ask in unison.

"Yes." Either this epiphany or the BraveChill app finally allow my heart to stop racing like a kid with ADHD. "Gogi wouldn't betray his friends. Joe is even less likely to betray his family. The logical conclusion is that they did not betray us."

"So you think Joe took Ada and Alan for a fun ride?" Muhomor asks derisively. "And Gogi nearly killed us for kicks?"

"No. But they didn't *willingly* betray us," I say. "Someone hacked their Brainocytes. Someone is controlling Gogi and Joe like puppets."

CHAPTER TWENTY-TWO

Mitya and Muhomor stare at me, their avatar jaws threatening to perform an unrealistic VR animation of falling to the floor.

"No," Muhomor says. "AROS security can't just be hacked willy-nilly like that."

"No, Mike's right." Mitya looks somber. "That theory fits all the facts. I even considered it briefly, but dismissed it when we learned that all the people attacking us had the official Human++ Brainocytes—which you, Muhomor, claimed to be unhackable."

"I said Tema was unhackable." Muhomor makes his usual shades disappear, revealing uncharacteristically worried eyes. "I only ever said that it was improbable that someone besides me could find a flaw in AROS security. And any flaws I discovered, I patched up."

We look at each other. That's not what he said—in fact, his certainty was why I didn't consider this possibility from the very beginning—but now is not the time to debate semantics.

"The improbable happened," I state flatly. Since I'm in control of my emotions for the time being, I try to capitalize on it and move our investigation as far along as possible. "Someone took away your self-proclaimed best hacker title, Muhomor. You were beaten at your own game. Live with it. This isn't about your ego anymore. We have to figure out who did this and how."

"Well." Mitya gets up and begins pacing around the table. "We know how it could've been done with someone without Brainocytes already in place. Does that help?"

The topic is uncomfortable for us all. Though Brainocytes have generally been a force for the betterment of the world, like any technology, they're not without their demons. Monstrous people have created their own perverted versions of Brainocytes to turn people into zombie-like slaves. Whenever we hear about such efforts, we do our best to destroy the organizations responsible. Thus far, this has happened six times in Africa, twice in Eastern Europe, and once in the Middle East. We abhor this situation and don't shy away from the methods necessary to combat it, from legal action to Joe's ruthlessness and Muhomor's hacking.

The organizations caught doing this don't even exist as mentions on old internet pages anymore. Still, we know that it's simply impossible to locate and deal with every instance of this atrocity. Our best defense is to spread legitimate Brainocytes throughout the human population. Until now, having Human++ Brainocytes has been the best protection against getting your brain hacked.

Muhomor must be thinking along the same lines. "Gogi and Joe have Brainocytes already," he says. "That makes this a completely different problem for the hacker."

I drum my fingers on the table and try to calm my thoughts again. "If you were the hacker behind this, how would you go about it?"

Muhomor's forehead creases, and his shades return to his nose. "Assuming this is really what you say it is, then there must be a vulnerability in one of AROS's core apps."

Yet again BraveChill fails, and a knot forms in my stomach. Muhomor is right. For reasons of security, certain modes of Brainocyte operation, particularly the sending of data to neurons outside the visual and auditory regions of the brain, are locked to all apps except those built by us. Users have the option of overriding this for themselves, but everyone knows it's not safe to do so—especially people who work for Human++ like Joe and Gogi.

I take in a deep breath. "As unlikely as it sounds, let's assume it is a core app. For example, say it's the video player. What would you do then?"

"That's very farfetched," Muhomor says. "The video player is probably the most secure app."

"Humor us." Mitya stops pacing and slumps back into a chair. "Say the video player app had an exploit."

"Well, I'd have to write a virus to take advantage of whatever the imaginary weakness is," Muhomor says. "Then spread it. Somehow."

"Wouldn't you need to get a special video on another company's server?" I ask. "I imagine Netflix and their ilk wouldn't want someone using them to spread a virus like this. Bad PR."

"I'd hack into Netflix," Muhomor says dismissively. "Or I'd use social engineering to work with employees already at the company." He looks so excited at this roleplaying that I feel like reaching over and giving him a smack. "Alternatively, I'd put together a new video streaming service that I completely control and create a video that could potentially be used as a vector of attack—"

"There's a problem with all this." Mitya folds his arms across his chest. "This attack was targeted to Joe and Gogi. A virus that takes advantage of something like video streaming would get inside the heads of everyone who watched the video."

"You're right. Targeting the virus would be extremely difficult." Muhomor rubs his thin chin thoughtfully. "It's not impossible, though. You could give every user a virus that would lie dormant, then activate special instructions only for people in proximity to some location or—"

"I really hope that's not what's happening," Mitya says. "That would mean every Human++ customer has a vulnerability in their heads… that most of the world carries this exploit ready for abuse."

"They seemed to be laser-precise with Gogi and Joe." I'm trying not to freak out with dread for the Brainocyte users of the world—a group that includes everyone I know, including myself. "If this is a proximity-based virus, why not turn all our guards against us? Or better yet, enslave us and make us commit suicide? Or enslave Alan and Ada and make them kidnap themselves?"

The reminder of Ada and Alan's status increases my already elevated heartbeat, both in VR and on the couch where the nurse is checking me for damage. Despite the luminous speed of this VR conversation, I still feel enormous guilt because I'm talking instead of acting. At the same time, I have no idea what action I can take until we figure out this mess.

"For that kind of targeting, you'd need someone's Brainocyte ID," Muhomor says. "But getting someone's ID is as hard a project as finding a loophole in one of the apps."

"But it's not impossible?" I ask.

Muhomor shrugs. "You know better than I. In the software universe, few things are impossible. There are just levels of difficulty."

The three of us share a look. We purposefully left out the details about how the ID system works when we open-sourced Brainocytes to the world. But we also know that relying on trade secrets isn't a very good strategy for keeping secrets, so it was just a matter of time before everyone found out everything there's to know about Brainocyte technology—yet another reason we've dumped billions into security research and development.

"Someone would've had to reverse-engineer the IDs somehow," Mitya says, proving he's thinking exactly what I'm thinking. "It could be done from either inert Brainocytes, or if you wanted faster results, from hardware that you harvested from a hopefully dead user's head.

It would take many years, either way, even if you had as much money as we have."

The morbid mention of a dead someone's head sparks a hint of an idea, but when I try to verbalize it, it escapes my consciousness. This happens with enhanced thinking sometimes; you get that feeling of having something on the tip of your tongue, but it takes minutes or sometimes hours before it comes to the forefront of your mind in a eureka moment. For now, I say, "Let's skip the how of it for the moment and assume someone knows how Brainocyte IDs work. What would be next?"

"They might be able to work out a way to get someone's Brainocytes to reveal a specific user ID," Muhomor says. "It would require the Brainocytes to interface with some app directly—"

"Like a brain scan at the hospital?" I smack myself on the virtual forehead. "Gogi and Joe both got hit on the head and were scanned. Could someone have used that as a chance to learn their Brainocyte IDs?"

Muhomor looks a bit like my mom does when she's multitasking using AROS. He must be doing some heavy research.

Mitya, on the other hand, gets excited. "Lennox Dixon had his head scanned because of his tumor." The speed of his Zik messages is on the verge of being too fast to follow. "Ruzatov had a head trauma. The drunks in Russia had been to a hospital right before they attacked our robots."

"I just checked, and everyone involved shares this pattern," Muhomor says. "Every bomber, every drunk, the drivers of the two cars that tried to kill you in

Brooklyn—everyone was in a hospital or some other facility where they had their brains scanned. This is compelling evidence that Brainocyte IDs are a part of this mess, and that in turn supports the hacking theory."

He looks at me with the disgust of a person learning he just got syphilis from a toilet seat. I can relate. Besides BraveChill, the only thing that stops me from panicking is the knowledge that I haven't had my brain scanned, so my ID remains unknown to our adversaries. The only way I could be turned into a mindless slave is if the entire world—or a subset such as, say, all of New York—were turned into puppets, a disquieting idea on its own. Then again, it would take insane computational resources and staff to control more than a handful of people.

Mitya remains annoyingly calm, probably because his brain is cloud based and has no Brainocytes to hack.

"This would explain why previously nonviolent men would be willing to blow themselves up," I say. "Or why Gogi didn't care about his wounds when he fought me, and why the drunks in Russia didn't care about damaging themselves with the robots."

"It all adds up, unfortunately," Muhomor says, frowning. "Now we need to figure out who's behind it. And make them regret it."

"Yeah," Mitya says sarcastically. "That's so simple. Why didn't we think of that? We just need to figure out who's doing this. Thanks."

"No need to be snide," Muhomor says. "Let's just continue to break this down logically. The important question is who benefits from this."

"Someone who hates our guts?" Mitya looks at us. "Someone who thinks we're the antichrist?" He pauses dramatically, and when he sees recognition on both our faces, he says, "Did anyone else find it suspicious that Joe found our Real Humans Only prisoner not guilty so easily?"

"And with all her fingers attached?" Muhomor says.

"Could it be because he was already under her control?" Mitya continues.

Was this the theory that's been gnawing at the edges of my mind? When it came to Tatum, Joe's behavior had been odd, to say the least.

"It could be that he cleared her because he's just that good at reading people." I realize I might be playing devil's advocate. "Also, he might've had another agenda. You might think me crazy, but I thought maybe there was an unholy attraction between those two."

"You *are* crazy," Mitya says. "Your cousin is indeed good at reading people—but your second theory, the one that assumes he has human feelings, is preposterous."

In the real world, I hear the nurse tell me my blood pressure is high. I'm not surprised in the slightest.

"If it's the RHO behind this hack, things could turn ugly," Muhomor says. "If they want to make Brainocytes look bad, which we know they do, they can use this virus to make the entire world do something horrible. They can prove us to be the devil by bringing about an apocalypse of their own design—a sort of self-fulfilling prophecy."

"I don't think it would be so easy to do something like that," Mitya says. "How would they control so many people?"

"A specialized AI?" Muhomor suggests. "But I see your point. Maybe they can't cause chaos on a global scale, but they can certainly keep people from ever trusting Brainocytes again."

Goosebumps spread over my body as I picture the RHO targeting people in key government positions or with celebrity status.

"Tatum must be a great actress," Mitya says. "Alan spoke to her last night, and she didn't act like someone plotting to kidnap the boy."

A flicker of hope speeds up my pulse. "Let me see some of that footage. Maybe she gives something away?"

"Alan was recording everything himself," Mitya says. "You might prefer to experience the whole thing as he did—that way, you can examine his reactions to her at the same time as yours."

Before I experienced Ada's hive-mind-generating, trippy Join app, the only way to see what someone else saw, heard, and (to a limited degree) felt was to play back a recording made with the Share 2.0 app. Originally, these recordings allowed their creators to relive experiences they particularly enjoyed. Human memory would fill in the missing details and emotions, helping users feel as if they were truly reliving the past. With some work, we've retro-fitted Share 2.0 recordings to play back as VR experiences, with the emotions recorded in the Share 2.0 app simulated in the watcher's brain. Playing back someone else's record-ing isn't as cool as most VR movies these days, but it can come in handy in many circumstances. It's been a boon for the porn industry, for sure. Aside from that, Ada and I, as well as many other couples who use Share 2.0, have fewer fights of the "he said, she said" variety because we can show each other a recording of what happened from the other's point of view. We've learned how unreliable our regular memories are. I shudder to think about all the people in jail based on old-school eyewitness testimony.

"As per Alan's explicit request, I've never played back his Share sessions before," I say as I locate the recording in question. "He considers that an ultimate invasion of privacy."

I was worried that Alan might've encrypted them with Tema to make sure Ada and I kept our promises, but I'm glad to find he didn't take that precaution.

"Your intentions are pure," Muhomor says. "Besides, not encrypting a file is basically an invitation for people to watch it."

"You watched it already?" I narrow my eyes at both my friends.

"I never promised Alan anything," Mitya replies defensively.

"And as I already said"—Muhomor runs a hand through his anime hair—"not encrypting a file is as good as an invitation to watch it."

"So what did you think?" I ask.

"Why don't you watch it and form your own opinion?" Mitya says. "Don't want to bias you."

"I agree with the ghost," Muhomor says. "Watch it and then we'll talk."

Figuring it'll be faster to just do as they say, I load the file and prepare to watch my son's memory through his own eyes.

CHAPTER TWENTY-THREE

My steps are short due to Alan's tiny legs, and everything in the room seems taller and bigger than I'm used to. It's creepy. The last time I experienced this point of view was when I watched the recent VR remake of *Child's Play*, particularly the scene where the killer doll, Chucky, knifed the pretty teenager (who reminds me a little of the petite Tatum).

The RHO leader gives us the cooing smile people typically reserve for speaking with children. Her face completely transforms when she glances back at Dominic, who's walking behind us. With his camera for eyes, exoskeleton, and bionic arm, he must be her technophobic nightmare come to life.

Alan's annoyance and resentment toward Tatum are so strong the VR interface makes them feel like my own.

"Hello," Tatum says in a tone Alan finds patronizing. "Who might you be?"

"Hi, Tatum," we say. We feel further irritation when Alan realizes she's hearing his childish voice and seeing no AR avatar. "My name is Alan."

Only seconds into the experience, I can already see why Alan wouldn't want me and Ada to watch these recordings of his. He doesn't want us to feel what I now feel—shame at turning my son into an adult trapped in a child's body. Because that's precisely what he feels like when Tatum looks at him.

"Hi, Alan." Tatum bends down to shake our extended hand, and her eyes go from warm to confused. "How do you know my name?"

"I make a point to know people who want to destroy everything my parents and I stand for," we say. "You are Tatum Crawford, born in Kansas to Jenny and Mark Crawford." We proceed to read the first paragraphs of her Wikipedia page until she pulls her hand away and the confusion in her eyes turns to fear.

"Just because I criticize what your parents do doesn't mean I'm your enemy." Her usually pretty smile is nervous at best.

I find it interesting how little her feminine charm affects Alan's emotions. On some level, I'm relieved his maturity didn't extend into sexual interests.

"You want me to devolve to an intellectual invalid who runs around like a monkey and plays with toys," we say derisively. "If you had your way, Dominic there would be blind, unable to hear or move, completely locked inside his body."

She takes a step back. We take sadistic pleasure at the roller coaster of emotions on her face as she realizes she's not speaking with a typical four-year-old.

"Why are you here?" she asks after she recovers some composure. "What do you want?"

"I want to understand," we say. We walk over to the nearby redwood chair. "I've never had a chance to speak with someone as misguided as you."

"I don't think you'll understand," she says sadly. "Your parents brainwashed you too well."

"Try me," we say. "You might find I'm a pretty rational person."

"If you were truly rational," she says, her patronizing baby talk completely gone, "you'd see the self-evident dangers of technology, especially AI. You'd see that our dependence on technology threatens our autonomy. You'd understand that virtual reality prevents humans from experiencing the world directly and acting from free will. Your parents' creation will continue the horrific trend the internet started. It will alienate humans from nature, bringing about harmful psychological eff—"

"Your worries have some seed of truth, but the dangers can be mitigated." We purposely interrupt her in a way people without Brainocyte enhancements consider rude. "This technology will expedite progress beyond anything we've seen. It will broaden people's world view and empower those who have never had power before. Bashing technology the way you do is a trend that goes back millennia. Plato was against the technology of writing. The most classic case is that of the Luddites during the Industrial

Revolution. Those self-employed weavers destroyed weaving machinery. Since then, it's been a never-ending quest among the likes of you."

"Except now it's every job that's in danger of going the route of weaving." Her hands are on her hips. "AI and Brainocytes will see to that."

"Not every job should continue to exist." We climb up on the chair and sit. "Politics is a space where AIs can do a much better job than many of the current psychopaths in charge. This very tablet was created by people who work in conditions that lead to suicide, and if AIs take over that sort of production, that segment of humanity will be better off. In fact, the more we look back in history, the more examples we see of jobs that should've gone away—and did. Did you know that kids a couple of years older than myself were once trained to be chimney sweeps' apprentices? To fit into chimneys, they were purposefully underfed. Over time, they developed lung problems that included cancer, though often they simply died of smoke inhalation. I bet you bought into the romanticized image of chimney sweeps from fairy tales and long for the good old days before mechanical means of sweeping chimneys existed."

"You can cherry-pick examples, but that doesn't address my main thesis," she says. "All jobs will go away."

"No," we say calmly. "Look at the rise of VR bloggers who make money from advertisers fighting to put ads before the best content. Look at the VR video game industry that became a multi-billion-dollar business nearly overnight. New technology always creates new jobs. Once the dust settles on this technological revolution, professions you couldn't even dream of will take place of the old drudgery. Those who don't embrace technology will end up jobless, true. But we'll take care of them via the universal basic adjustment benefit that our company is trying to put into place."

"So you want people like me to live on handouts?" Her eyes glint. "To live without any purpose in our lives?"

"Unenhanced people can and will find purpose in artisanal work." We jump out of the chair—the energy of a four-year-old human male makes it very hard to sit still for such a long subjective slice of time. "Arts, science, philosophy—once everyone's basic sustenance needs are met, purpose in life will reach a new Golden Age, both for people with Brainocytes and, to a smaller degree, for people like you."

Tatum's mouth tightens. "You see? I told you I couldn't reason with a zealot."

"Do people without Brainocytes completely lack the sense of irony? Calling me a zealot is like me calling you 'kid.'" We turn to leave the room.

"We are the only people left who have true senses," she counters sharply. "You're just crunching data now."

"Crunching data is what all brains do." We are level with Dominic now and wave the big man to join us in leaving the room. "Humans expanded their senses with technology as soon as they began inventing lenses, hearing aids, and the like. We're just integrating those technologies more seamlessly with everyday experience."

"Your parents and their people claim that they will not create AIs that can think and act as people." Her voice rises. "From where I'm standing, they already have."

If she thinks she can insult Alan by calling him an AI, she doesn't know my son. He loves Einstein and has considered him a friend since early childhood.

"I'm more human than you'll ever imagine." We don't say the words louder because we know it's pointless to expect her to understand them. "I'm better than you at everything you consider a purely human pursuit, from empathy to my ability to love."

As though to highlight our words, we pat our pocket and overflow with deep love for Mr. Spock, one of our earliest childhood friends. We love him despite our different intellectual levels and superficial differences such as belonging to different species.

My attention is no longer on Alan's recording because my son inadvertently gave me a new hope.

I exit the Share 2.0 experience shaking with excitement. "How could I forget about Mr. Spock? I told him to watch out for Alan."

Before Mitya or Muhomor can respond, I'm already contacting Mr. Spock. "Hey, bud, where are you?"

"Don't know," comes the rat's anxiety-imbued reply. "Alan doesn't wake up."

"So Alan is with you?" I'm trying not to make Mr. Spock panic with either worry or the excitement that overwhelms me.

"Yes," the rat replies. "But I can't talk to him."

"Don't worry. He was very tired, so he's just going to sleep for a while," I lie. "This is very important: do you know where you are?"

"I am hiding," he replies. The memories are clearly making him uncomfortable, because he sends me enough fear to shake an elephant. "Something is wrong."

"You did an excellent job hiding." I make my Zik message as reassuring as I can. "But now I need you to do something a little scary. Do you think you can be brave to help Alan?"

"Yes," he says with renewed confidence.

"I'm going to enable your Share app and have you peek out of Alan's clothes," I say. "Can you do that very carefully?"

"Okay," he replies, his confidence noticeably weaker.

"I know you can do it," I say firmly. "You're the alpha."

Mr. Spock is the alpha rat in our mischief—the proper term for a pack of rats. Unlike his wild cousins, he's an enlightened ruler who doesn't try to keep the other males away from food (even peanuts) or females (even Uhura). Still, the reminder of his high social status seems to work, because his affirmative reply is full of pride and determination.

I enable the rat version of the Share app. The first thing I do is verify something I already inferred but didn't want to worry Mr. Spock by asking: Alan's heartbeat is steady through his shirt, and the boy is breathing evenly.

Relieved at the proof my son is alive, I examine Mr. Spock's surroundings as much as I can. With the rat's inferior vision, it's hard to tell for sure, but it seems like we're in a well-lit room—or so I presume, based on the vague shapes I can discern through the fabric of Alan's pocket. Being a lab rat and thus albino, Mr. Spock's sense of smell is slightly worse than that of a regular rat, but that's still light years above that of an unenhanced human. Since the Share app translates rat experience into human perception, the room smells stagnant, reminiscent of the recycled air in our bunker. It also tells Mr. Spock (and thus me) that there are a couple of male humans in the room.

"Be very careful when you peek," I say. "It's okay if we can't see what's going on."

Mr. Spock slides his nose about a millimeter out of Alan's shirt. I make a snapshot of the environment before I have him hide again.

Ada is lying on a cot next to Alan, and there are indeed two armed men in the room, though unfortunately, both are wearing Richard Nixon masks over their faces.

"Stay still," I tell Mr. Spock. "We're lucky they didn't see you."

"Okay." He proceeds to contemplate whether he wants the cashew, the walnut, or the raisin that remain in Alan's pocket.

Using Muhomor's app with Mr. Spock as a conduit, I check out the Wi-Fi networks in the place. The single network smells like rotten eggs, so I give up trying to hack it for now, though I plan to unleash Muhomor himself on it shortly. I then try locating Mr. Spock's coordinates using GPS, but wherever he is, there's either no GPS signal or they're using a jammer. At least Mr. Spock has access to Global Terahertz wireless internet, or we wouldn't even be able to communicate. The Terahertz system allows me to approximate the location of Mr. Spock's connection.

"Catskills," I announce triumphantly.

The walnut gets stuck in Mr. Spock's throat, and he sniffs the air in full panic mode. "I know they do," he says when he doesn't find a cat in the pocket with him or smell one in the room. "Why remind me?"

"I'm sorry, bud," I say. "Not 'cats kill.' The Catskills is the name of a mountain range in New York state."

He relaxes. "Bad name."

"I know. I'll petition to change it to Ratsrule, but don't hold your breath."

"I don't like to hold my breath," he says sagely. "It's hard."

"Then don't hold your breath," I say as seriously as I can. "I want you to keep your nose ready so you can let me know if those men leave the room."

"Okay," he says with the kind of pride in his olfactory senses I'd expect from a good hunting dog. "I'm on it."

Almost giddy with progress, I switch attention to the VR room and find Mitya and Muhomor watching me intently.

"So it's hard to say if she's guilty or not," I say. "But watching that video gave us a big break." I proceed to tell them about Mr. Spock.

"I'll try to get onto that Wi-Fi." Muhomor changes his sunglasses into the pince-nez he likes to wear when he hacks. "But if it uses—"

"Just do it," Mitya says. "Tell us when and if it's done."

"What's with the hostility?" Muhomor uses his middle finger to pretend to push the pince-nez farther up his nose, but we all know he's flipping Mitya off.

"Sorry," Mitya says in a tone that suggests nothing of the kind. "I just keep feeling like we're playing catch-up with our adversaries. They seem to be a couple of moves ahead of us at all turns. Their plan A was to get Gogi to kill Mike for them, but they also had a plan B—take Ada and Alan hostage in case plan A fails."

"And force Mike to leave the safety of the bunker to run after his family," Muhomor says, his tone more serious.

"Which I'm about to do," I say, nodding. "But I don't really have a choice."

"Which is why I'm irritated." Mitya looks at Muhomor apologetically. "It's like a bad game of Go."

"Well," I say. "We do have Tatum. Perhaps we can question her on the way to the Catskills and get ahead in the game."

"Assuming she knows anything," Muhomor says.

"And assuming our adversaries didn't plan for whatever Tatum revealed," I add.

"And assuming she herself is not the adversary who manipulated us to get her out of the bunker according to some plan," Mitya says.

"I can leave her here with Muhomor to question her," I say. "Then we'd still have some leverage."

"I'm not going?" Muhomor asks.

"I don't think you should," I say. "You're not a fighter, and we can use your help here on the back end."

"Okay," he says. "Anyway, someone with a brain needs to look after your mother and uncle."

I nod. "And this way, Tatum doesn't leave the bunker."

"Agreed," he says. "Let me prepare to question her while you get ready for departure."

I nod and switch to the real world, where the nurse is beginning to agree that I'm going to be fine. To make sure the medical staff doesn't revolt, I try to exude health and vitality as I get up from the couch.

Step one in my prep: check on Dominic's condition.

"I'm fine," he says, though the bandage around his eye looks serious to me. "What's the update?"

I tell him what's going on until Dr. Jarvis comes over and gives me a stern look. "He should be resting."

"I'm coming with Mike," Dominic says to the doctor.

"Then you're doing so against my recommendation," Jarvis says.

"I'm going," Dominic says with the kind of certainty only people with that much brute power can have. "I'll organize the other guards."

He gets to his feet, his legs running without a hitch thanks to his exoskeleton. As he rushes to rally his troops, I tell the doctor to keep Gogi unconscious until we return.

Then I head to Mom's room, mentally debating what, if anything, to tell her before I leave.

Mitya's avatar shows up in the air in front of her door. "I suggest you speak to her afterward."

"But she'll wake up and not know where I am." He has a good point, though.

"When she wakes up, Muhomor will tell her the truth—that you went to get Ada."

"But he'll avoid the full truth," I say sternly in VR. I make sure Muhomor nods back.

A part of me fears that later, I might not get a chance to tell Mom anything at all. If I get myself killed, she might resent that last night's mundane conversation about the quality of the bunker food was our last one. I picture myself as a digital ghost like Mitya, resurrecting in a few years to a torrent of complaints from Mom.

To stop these morbid thoughts, I go into the kitchen to put a banana-avocado smoothie into my system.

"You'll elaborate on Muhomor's story when you come back," Mitya says when he sees me come out and glance at Mom's door one more time. What he leaves unsaid is: "*If you come back.*"

"I'll come back," I mutter, more to myself than to Mitya. "Even if that means I come back as a ghost like you."

CHAPTER TWENTY-FOUR

Mitya is driving the car again because Einstein doesn't speed even when his creators beg (or forcefully insist) that he drive faster.

We're going to be in the Catskills soon, but I still have no clue exactly where Alan and Ada are or who's keeping them and why. Though the likely answer to this last question is: to lure me outside the bunker.

"It's all ready," Muhomor says in Zik. "I sent you a camera view."

"What's ready?" I ask.

He doesn't answer, probably to force me to look. I'm tired of staring out the window at the same never-ending fields, power lines, and distant factories, so I close my eyes and dedicate my attention to the new viewpoint.

The camera shows Tatum's bedroom in the bunker. Muhomor stands over the poor girl like a crazy stalker. He reaches out and touches her shoulder in a way that's creepy even for Muhomor.

"Hey, what are you doing?" I say, frowning. "I know your experience with the female of the species is limited, but I can assure you, they don't like what you're currently doing."

"You don't need girl experience," Mitya chimes in. "Just use the golden rule. Picture yourself waking up and seeing some really weird-looking dude touching you like that."

"It would depend on why the handsome stranger was there," Muhomor says, but he leans away from Tatum.

"Mike, when you tell Ada about this later, I did not approve Muhomor's plan," Mitya says.

"But he did help me with it." Muhomor seems to be on the verge of maniacal laughter. "Our ephemeral friend was actually instrumental to my plan."

"I really hope I get the chance to sell you out to Ada soon," I say. "I think I know what you did—but why don't you tell me anyway?"

"I just attached a transdermal Brainocyte patch to her shoulder," he says.

"One that runs the Polygraph app on the loop, as we earlier discussed," Mitya adds, confirming my suspicions.

"Not sure I want to tell Ada about this at all," I mutter. "This is pretty messed up, you guys."

"Her people have your wife and kid," Muhomor snaps.

I'm shocked at the intensity in his voice. I didn't think he cared this much, and it's a pleasant surprise to find out that he does—even if it's resulting in unethical behavior.

"Miss Crawford," Muhomor whispers loudly. "Please wake up."

"There are earplugs in her ears," Mitya says. "They look heavy duty, so I doubt she'll hear you even if you shout next to her face."

"But don't shout next to her face," I say, unsure if Muhomor needs the clarification or not.

"How last century." He deftly plucks an earplug from the woman's ear.

Her head lolls to the side, exposing a pillow-creased pink cheek.

Muhomor gets bolder and repeats, "Miss Crawford?"

She pulls a blanket over her head. He tugs the blanket away and then, for good measure, leans over her and shakes her shoulder. Her long eyelashes flutter open, and she gapes at the thin weirdo above her for a fraction of a second.

Then, predictably, she screams.

"You're still our guest," he says calmly as she proceeds to jump up and cover her nightgown with the fleece blanket.

"He's not there to hurt you," Mitya's voice says from a wall speaker.

Her gaze darts around the room, likely in search of something she can use as a weapon—objects that Dominic thoughtfully removed last night.

"That's right." Muhomor tries to smile reassuringly. On his face, the expression looks more like a scowl. "We have a bit of an emergency, and I wanted to ask you some questions."

Tatum now looks more confused than frightened.

"Please, Tatum," Mitya's voice says. "People's lives are at stake."

"Can you give me a moment to dress?" She looks around, trying to find the source of Mitya's voice. "Whoever you are."

"Sure," he says. "My colleague was just leaving."

Muhomor stands there as though he doesn't know that he's the colleague in question. His eyes narrow on Tatum as he launches a private Zik chat with us. "I don't want her to have too much time to realize she has AROS now."

"I think it's safe to let her put some clothes on," Mitya replies, imbuing his Zik message with so much snark that I fully expect Muhomor to revolt. "As the only incorporeal member among us, I'll keep an eye on her, though."

"Digital perv," Muhomor mumbles vindictively as he stalks out of the room.

"All right, Tatum, just come out when you're ready. I'll give you some privacy," Mitya says.

The camera goes blank—Mitya is being a gentleman—so I can only assume she gets dressed.

In a couple of minutes, Muhomor gives me a new camera view in the kitchen.

"Come eat some breakfast," he says with surprising warmth when Tatum finally comes out. "I just need a couple of questions answered."

Tatum warily eyes Muhomor's pajama-clad body, but hunger must win out because she says, "Fine. Let's go."

"Did you write an article for the *Green Voice* at some point?" he asks casually as he opens the fridge and grabs himself a Twinkie. Privately to Mitya and me, he adds, "I know she did. This is a baseline question."

He gallantly holds the fridge door open and gestures for her to get what she wants.

"I did," she says after fishing out a pack of cheese. "It's probably still on their website, if you want to read it."

"That was true, both according to facts and according to the app," Mitya says to me privately. "Now I wonder how he's going to get her to lie without telling her that he wants her to tell a falsehood."

"I'd love to read it," Muhomor says, sounding impressively genuine. "I have an oddball question for you: do you think my little nephew is cute?"

Using the screen attached to the front of the smart fridge, he pulls up a picture of the most hideous baby I've ever seen in my life.

She takes in the image, and I can tell she nearly loses her appetite. "He's very cute," she says after she recovers her composure. "How old is he?"

"That was a lie, according to the app, and it's safe to say we now have a baseline," Mitya says. "I don't even want to know where Muhomor got that picture."

"I had to use Photoshop to create that monstrosity," Muhomor tells us. To Tatum, he says, "Little Dimochka just turned two."

"Hey!" Mitya protests. The name Muhomor used is the diminutive of his own. "You should have named him Freddy or Jason."

"Oh, the terrible twos," Tatum commiserates. Her shoulders relax as soon as Muhomor takes down the picture. "Your brother or sister is in for some tough times."

"Especially if this imaginary parent has eyes," Mitya mutters.

"I really hope you can help us, Tatum." Muhomor bites into his snack.

"You said so before." She spreads mayo onto a slice of rye bread and slaps cheese on top. "What happened?"

"You remember Alan? The child you spoke to last night?"

"Yes." She takes a careful bite of her sandwich. "Charming little guy."

"She's lying," Mitya comments. "About the charming part."

"Alan was kidnapped today," Muhomor says. "Do you know anything about it?"

"Kidnapped?" Her eyes look as if they might pop out of their sockets. "That's terrible. Of course I had nothing to do with it. I told Mike yesterday, my people are peaceful and would never hurt anyone—let alone kidnap a little boy."

"Everything she said was true," Mitya comments with clear disappointment. "Not good."

Muhomor proceeds as though Mitya didn't just shatter all our hopes. "Do you think anyone in your group is more radical than you? Someone tired of everyone else's nonviolence?"

"I can't think of anyone," she says without hesitation. "If I knew someone like that, I'd change their mind."

"Even this is all true," Mitya laments. "Or at least, this is what she really believes. We know some of her fellow RHO idiots are violent, like that asshole who poked holes in the tires of those Uber cars. But she truly doesn't see them as violent."

"There's something else," Muhomor says to Tatum, but it's obvious he's losing hope now. "Is anyone in your group knowledgeable when it comes to Brainocytes? Does anyone know how they work or how to hack them or to cause Brainocytes to have unintended consequences?"

She stops chewing, her expression as disgusted as if she'd just bitten into something spoiled. "We all stay as far away from those abominable devices as we can. Anyone who fetishizes Brainocytes would be kicked out of RHO."

"Again, true," Mitya says. "Let's go discuss this in the VR room. Looks like she was a complete dead end."

"I leave it to you to explain to her that you put the 'abominable devices' into her head," I tell Muhomor vindictively. "Just be careful she doesn't finally find that violent bone in her body and choke you to death."

"Or break one of your bones," Mitya adds helpfully.

"Make sure you also teach her how to use Brainocytes and disable the Polygraph app," I say. "Good luck."

My real-world eyes still closed, I pop into the VR room, which feels achingly empty without Ada.

"So," I say as Mitya and Muhomor's avatars turn my way. "Tatum is not guilty."

"It appears that way," Muhomor says reluctantly. "Or she should get an Oscar for that acting, and be entered into the hacker hall of fame for working around the Polygraph app."

"There's no way she worked around Polygraph." Mitya gives Muhomor a dark look. "You need to learn how to gracefully admit defeat."

"Fine." Muhomor grits his teeth. "She's innocent of the kidnapping, I admit that much."

"Then we must now explore our other big clue," I say. "Something we should've done in parallel with this Tatum fiasco."

Mitya's face lights up. "Russia."

"Exactly," I say. "We already thought Russia was the key to all this somehow. The original theory was that maybe RHO was working with some Luddite group in Russia, but if we know that RHO is innocent, a Russian anti-tech group sounds less plausible as well."

"Agreed," Mitya says. "But that means we're back at zero."

"Not exactly." I sink into the simulated high-end office chair and try to uncoil the tangle of emotions overwhelming me. "I had a glimmer of an idea back when you said something about skimming Brainocyte IDs from a dead user's head."

As I say the words, the theory that's been hovering in the corners of my extended mind clicks into place, and I blurt out, "We never found the head of Mrs. Sanchez."

Mitya's eyes gleam with understanding, but Muhomor looks confused, so I explain. "Mrs. Sanchez was the woman in that fateful Brainocyte study who was kidnapped together with Mom. She went into a diabetic coma and died before we met you in Russia, so maybe we never told you about her."

"Oh." Recognition dawns on Muhomor's face. "I think you did tell me, but I forgot her name and some of the details."

"The most important detail is that she was beheaded after her death," I say, hoping that when I say all this out loud, it will still make sense. "Her head could've given someone a chance to study Brainocytes long before we released any Brainocyte information to the world."

"And thus plenty of time to learn about Brainocyte IDs by now," Muhomor mutters. "Of course."

"You're following my reasoning now." My muscles involuntarily tense, because what I'm about to say next is, to a large extent, responsible for all the therapy I've needed over the years. "You were already with us at the end of that kidnapping disaster when we learned who was behind it all."

I surprise myself when I stop speaking, unable to continue.

"His mom was kidnapped by his biological father," Mitya tells Muhomor softly. "And I think Mike suspects that this new mess is because of those events—and now that I think about it, I tend to agree."

"But didn't Joe kill everyone who had a hand in that?" Muhomor asks, his eyebrows pulling together.

Images of Joe's knife slicing my father's throat intrude into my thoughts, and it takes slow breathing and an effort of will to say, "There were thousands of people involved in that operation. Joe only went after the leaders, and even so, I doubt he got everyone."

My friends wait expectantly, though I suspect Mitya has figured out where I'm going with this.

"In any case," I say after a pause. "I think I know who's behind all this, and it's a person Joe definitely did not kill."

CHAPTER TWENTY-FIVE

Mitya and Muhomor don't chastise me for taking my time with the next part of my revelation.

Now that the theory is in my head, as so often happens in such situations, I don't understand why I didn't think of it sooner. Probably because I associate this person with painful memories. In fact, if I'm honest, I often try to forget he exists at all because of all the guilt I still carry over my father's death. Also, I suspected him of evildoing once before and was wrong, because Alex Voynskiy (now definitively deceased) turned out to be the culprit. I guess being wrong once before has biased me this time around.

"I think it's Kostya," I finally say. In the likely case that Muhomor doesn't recall who I'm talking about, I add, "My father's son with his wife in Russia. My half-brother."

I proceed to share all the research I did four and a half years ago on both Konstantin (Kostya for short) and my half-sister Masha. Kostya got rich from oil and became even richer when he invested in the right internet startup. As of four and a half years ago, he was still unmarried and a good brother to Masha, a poor soul who requires a lot of psychiatric care.

"You hacked the computers at the clinic where my half-sister was," I remind Muhomor. "You told me that Masha worries about poltergeists all the time."

"You can't expect me to remember such minutiae," Muhomor says. Noticing Mitya's evil eye, he quickly adds, "But now that you mention it, it all rings a bell."

Mitya gives me a sympathetic look. "Is she still alive? I recall you saying that Masha attempted suicide a number of times."

"I don't know," I admit. "I haven't looked up either of them in recent years."

"Well, let's look them up now." Muhomor rubs his hands together the way he does whenever hacking is about to commence.

"We can start with public info," Mitya says preemptively, though we both know it's futile.

"You two start with the boring public junk," Muhomor says. "I'll learn all the juicy details going on behind the scenes."

Mitya rolls his eyes but lets Muhomor do his thing. I search Yandex, the Russian search engine, for Kostya. Glad I can simultaneously read the thousands of hits I get back, I proceed to analyze them as fast as I can. It looks like my half-brother has become even richer in the last four and a half years and might now be on the Russian equivalent of the *Forbes* list of wealthiest people. Like me, a huge chunk of his new money was made thanks to Brainocytes. He owns companies that develop AROS apps of different varieties, plus a firm that turns out to be a third-party manufacturer that Human++ uses to produce Brainocyte patches for hard-to-reach corners of Russia. It's amazing how many such locations are in that country and how expensive regular deliveries there would otherwise be.

"Have you read this?" Mitya sends me a link to an article. "It's pretty incriminating."

I marvel at Mitya's newfound speed-reading skills; I haven't made it to this article in my results yet, and have to scroll forward a couple of thousand hits to see where he got it.

The first thing that catches my eye is an image of Kostya shaking the hand of the Russian president. This probably counts as a KGB connection. Kostya still has a scar on his cheek from when Masha scratched him after he broke the news of what happened to our father; clearly, she never heard the saying about killing the messenger.

I peer more closely at the photo. I never noticed until now, but Kostya and I both have sharp cheekbones and the same strong chin. I keep scanning until I see what Mitya meant: a big contract Kostya's company handled for the Russian military. Reading between the lines, I can see how brain manipulation might be something they would've experimented with.

"I have something much better," Muhomor says after he also reads Mitya's findings. "Check this out."

Muhomor got his hands on the records from the psychiatric facility where my half-sister spent so many years. As it turns out, she's no longer a resident there, and according to Dr. Ivanov, her shrink of many years, she was "miraculously cured using a therapy developed by her brother." Dr. Ivanov mentions that she received Brainocytes three years ago to aid her treatment, but it was an app that Kostya used a year ago that led to her amazing breakthrough.

"The patient was not herself," Dr. Ivanov's notes say. "It's as though she became a different person."

"My guess is that he used some mind control app on her." Muhomor drums his fingers against the glass of the conference room table. "If she starts to misbehave, he just takes over her mind and makes sure she behaves as a good sister should."

"Creepy, but sounds plausible," Mitya mutters. "And get this: As soon as she was 'cured,' he finally got married. The wifey is a supermodel."

"It doesn't fully make sense," I say. "If Masha is merely being remotely controlled, she isn't cured."

"My guess is that he wanted to get her out of that institution." Muhomor stops the drumming and wraps his arms around his chest, as if trying to give himself a hug. "It's where the Russian government would put political dissidents during the Soviet days, and it's just as drab now as it was back then. Even some of the staff are the same sons of bitches who worked there during the good old days."

"I just checked out the place, and he's right," Mitya says. "Think Russian version of the insane asylum from *Sucker Punch*."

"More like Arkham Asylum from *Batman*, if you ask me," Muhomor says. "Not a place you'd want your sister to stay long term, no matter how messed up she is."

"He must've hired a babysitter who takes over her body like a puppet when she misbehaves," Mitya says. "This way, she can live a semi-normal life outside the institution—and probably for a fraction of the cost."

"But it must be terrible for her," I say, frowning. "She has paranoid schizophrenia, and here Dr. Ivanov says she has delusions of control, which is a fear of being controlled by someone outside oneself. Now that's her actual reality. It's like sticking an arachnophobe into a cave filled with tarantulas."

"I'd choose her current fate to being in that facility," Muhomor says. "But that doesn't make your brother any less of an asshole if this whole thing is true."

"Have you been able to locate him?" I look at Muhomor as the likelier of the two to accomplish this feat.

"I thought you didn't want me to do any hacking," Muhomor says, the sarcasm clearly lifting his mood. "To know where he is, I would've had to get into his secretary's email—and that's illegal and unethical."

"You are the mightiest and most powerful hacker, and your services are greatly appreciated by all," Mitya says with his own flavor of sarcasm. "Now, can you spit it out? Mike doesn't know where to drive."

"I don't know where he should drive either," Muhomor admits. "But I just confirmed that Kostya is in the United States, which I figure is convincing evidence that he's our perp."

"Knowing the identity of our enemy is a great start, but we need more info," I say. "The Catskills span 5,892 square miles."

"I'll keep looking," Muhomor says.

"I will as well," Mitya echoes.

"Let me talk to our asset behind enemy lines," I say. "Speaking of whom—Muhomor, did you crack the Wi-Fi around Mr. Spock?"

"I would've said something if I had." Muhomor looks down. "Whoever your half-brother hired to handle security is very good."

"Fine." I make a mental connection to Mr. Spock. "Hey, bud."

"They took us somewhere," Mr. Spock reports. "I was scared."

"Where are you now?" I ask, fighting to keep the urgency out of my Zik messages. "Are the men still in the room?"

"I smell them. There are more now."

"When they took you someplace else, did you smell them also?"

"Even more men and some women," Mr. Spock says. I don't ask how he could smell the difference between males and females. "And bad smell, like at the veterinarian."

"A medical facility?" I'm unable to keep the worry out of my message. "What did they do to Alan and Ada?"

"Nothing with pain," Mr. Spock says. "Or else I would bite them."

"I know you would. They probably scanned their heads, which doesn't hurt."

What I leave unsaid is that scanning gives the bad guys Ada and Alan's Brainocyte IDs. If that's true, it means Kostya (or whoever) can now make my family do what he wants.

"Guys, I want you to make that loophole in Brainocyte security a priority," I say. "Not that it should've ever stopped being one."

"I never stopped working on it," Mitya says. "But it's a tricky problem."

"Same," Muhomor says. "Don't get your hopes up. I always look for loopholes in our security, and if this one was easy to find, I would've discovered it before."

"Just knowing it's there should make it a little easier," I say, more as a motivational tool than because I really believe it. "Just keep looking."

I open my eyes in the real world and look out the window at the glorious mountain landscape in the distance. Alan and Ada could be anywhere here. We might be passing them right now. It's an infuriating idea.

After all this evidence, do I think that Kostya is behind the kidnapping and the bombings? Could vengeance for our father's death have motivated him to do something so heinous? If it is Kostya, given that we share DNA, does it mean I too could be pushed to do something like this?

No. I mentally shake my head. I share DNA with Joe too, and I know I wouldn't do some of the things Joe has done. Still, a small voice inside me tells me that if something happens to Ada or Alan today, my vengeance against the person responsible would be terrifying indeed.

We drive for another ten minutes in silence. I want to know where Ada and Alan are so badly that I feel like screaming or punching someone—and if killing someone got me the information, I'd stoop to it despite how Ada might feel about it. When I'm just about to burst from the nerves, I'm shocked into alertness by an email arriving into my inbox.

It's from Alan.

Marked as high priority, the email contains a video file attachment. The subject is the same as the single line of text inside: "Watch me."

My heart rate accelerates. I forward the email to Dominic and my friends and launch the video file.

The video pans across a room where Alan and Ada lie unconscious, surrounded by armed men in Richard Nixon masks. One guy isn't wearing a mask, and his face reminds me of a rabid bull terrier. The scary guy leans down slightly and takes an exaggerated sniff of the air near Ada, as though he's trying to determine what perfume she's wearing.

My hands ball into tight fists. If I were in that room now, I'd break that flat nose into tiny pieces that would hopefully pierce what passes for a brain in that thick, egg-shaped skull.

"I bet she's as sweet as she looks," says the abomination in a voice that sounds like gravestones rubbing together.

Trying to stay rational, I run facial recognition. He's a Russian citizen by the name of Boris Sobakin. The fact that he's Russian further supports our ongoing theory, but the things this man did in Chechnya turn my blood cold. I truly hope he's a zombie under Kostya's control; at least what Kostya is doing is motivated by vengeance, not twisted sadism.

"Now," says a voice from behind the camera.

The hair on the back of my neck stands up when all the men aim their guns at my wife and son in a rehearsed motion.

In unison, the men click safeties off their weapons, and their fingers tighten on the triggers.

CHAPTER TWENTY-SIX

"That's enough for the moment," the voice behind the camera says.

The men reengage their safeties one by one. The bull terrier Boris lowers his gun last. If I could, I'd punch his annoying face to wipe away that look of disappointment.

"Hold the camera," the speaker tells Boris, and there's a dizzying maneuver where the room spins, ending with the viewpoint centered on a new face.

Any doubts about my half-brother's culpability are now gone. Though he looks slightly older than some of the recent images, it is without a doubt Kostya, a fact facial recognition needlessly confirms.

"If you had just let the Georgian kill you, I would've let them go," Kostya says in a falsetto voice. He gestures at the camera, but I understand he means Ada and Alan. "I will give you one more chance. Come here, alone, and your family can go. You have twenty minutes. Here are the GPS coordinates—"

I frantically key them into my AROS GPS app. Einstein estimates it will take me a half hour to get there without traffic, meaning I'm already ten minutes late.

"Stop the car." I pop into VR conference room and look Mitya in the eye. "The guards need to get out."

"Is that wise?" Muhomor walks up to the big window. "If you go alone, as your half-brother insists, you're as good as dead."

"If I don't, Ada and Alan are going to get killed." I stride to the window to join Muhomor. "I don't think he was bluffing about that."

"Could the video be fake?" Muhomor drums his fingers against the glass.

It's a good question. Enhanced brains combined with some of the amazing hardware we've designed in recent years have led to a revolution in the cinematic effects industry. Particularly notorious are CGI VR porn and its cousin, political scandals based on fake video. It's common for Brainocyte users to enjoy ultrarealistic VR experiences, such as sleeping with their favorite celebrities (who, unfortunately, don't participate in the video at all and thus neither consent to the use of their likenesses nor make money). A good chunk of CGI VR porn originates in copyright-lax places like Russia, and I have no doubt that Kostya owns a bunch of the necessary studios. Every oligarch probably does.

Kostya could easily have faked that video and even created a virtual reality version of it to make me swear I was looking at the real Kostya, Ada, and Alan. The fact that Ada and Alan were sleeping would make that much easier to implement.

"There's no motive for someone to fake such a video," I say after a moment of consideration.

"Maybe to scare you or blame Kostya?" Muhomor asks without confidence.

"I'm already scared. We already knew Alan and Ada are missing. We already suspected my half-brother before we got this video."

"I concur," Mitya says. "I've researched tests for video authenticity, and I'm certain this was a real recording."

Muhomor and I exchange impressed glances. Mitya's speed of thought is beginning to reach biologically impossible levels.

"Relatedly," Mitya says, "I've analyzed the video for microexpressions—the sort of detail that a fake wouldn't bother recreating—and found no sign of deceit on Kostya's face. In fact, his face was extremely emotionless. Your half-brother is either as cold as a lizard or has had major Botox done."

"Doesn't that lack of expression point toward the video being fake?" Muhomor asks.

"Microexpressions are just one of the points I used to determine the video is real," Mitya says. "Plus, Boris has enough microexpressions for everyone in that video, and I can't think of a reason why someone would bother with such subtle detail for a minor character in a fake."

"Moving on, then. If there was no deceit on his face, do you think Kostya would really let them go?" Muhomor turns from the faux Manhattan skyline outside the window and stares intently at each of us in turn.

"Alan and Ada didn't have anything to do with our father's death," I say. "After Kostya deals with me and Joe, he might not want the death of a woman and her child on his conscience. The fact that he's kept them sedated is a good sign. It implies he doesn't want them to be too uncomfortable."

"Or he knows that Alan might go *The Ransom of Red Chief* on his ass," Muhomor mutters. "We all know that if Alan was aware, your half-brother would've killed him already—or if he's really above killing a child, he would now be begging you to take the little devil back."

"Ada's no picnic, either," Mitya says. "If I were your half-brother, I'd keep her as sedated as the kid."

"The biggest issue is that I suspect one or more of our guards might be taken over like Gogi." I massage my temples in a futile attempt to relieve some tension.

"Because your half-brother knows where you are?" Unsurprisingly, Mitya's quick to catch on.

"Exactly. How else did he know to give me so little time I'd have no choice but to drive where I'm told?"

"And if he does have eyes on you, you must get rid of the guards, or he might kill Ada or Alan to show he's serious," Muhomor says, catching on to my logic as well. "Not to mention that if you brought a compromised guard with you, he'd be a real hindrance."

The horrific theory rings in my virtual ears as the car screeches to a halt in the real world.

The guards respond with varying degrees of surprise. Dominic is the only one who knows what's going on, though he chooses to leave his Augmented Reality face unreadable.

"Get out," I bark. When they stare uncomprehendingly, I add steel to my voice. "Everyone out. That's an order."

"Are you sure?" Dominic asks privately. "We're in the middle of nowhere, and without a car, we have no way to follow you."

"Please get them out, Dominic." My private reply is beseeching. "I'm already late. There's no time for discussion."

Dominic grabs the shirt collars of the two men nearest him and drags them out of the car. Everyone else finally registers my demand and exits amid curses and grumbling.

"I'm driving," I tell my friends in VR. Matching actions to words, I launch the Batmobile app, take control, and press the virtual gas pedal all the way to the metaphorical floor. "At least the road is empty."

The car launches forward and hits sixty miles per hour in two seconds flat.

"I-84 isn't empty," Mitya says when he notices me double my initial breakneck speed. "You drive this fast, you'll die in a fiery explosion."

"It's the only way I can get there on time," I say. "If I crash, maybe Kostya will consider us even."

"Do you want me to take over?" he offers. "My response times are better."

"I want to do the driving myself. If you didn't get me there in time, I'd have to kill you."

"There are drones in the sky above," Muhomor remarks. "They defied my intrusion attempts. Their security is as good as the Wi-Fi security around the rat, so they could be Kostya's."

"Keep trying to break the security," I say. "Or better yet, make progress on figuring out how Kostya takes people over. If we can release Joe, I'll have an ally."

"Obviously." In VR, Muhomor appears to be trying to hypnotize his feet through the glass table. "I already explained how difficult it is."

Mitya shakes his head with overblown disappointment. "Dude. The one time everyone is begging you to do your favorite activity, and you manage to let us down like this?"

"You're supposed to be pure intellect now," Muhomor snaps back. "Brain completely in the cloud. Thinking at unimaginable speeds. Why didn't you solve this problem?"

"In fact, I do have one idea." Mitya looks at me. "It's just not very practical."

In the real world, my tire rolls over a pebble. The car shudders like a choking victim. I guess at these race-car speeds, even a pebble can cause a skid. Ignoring everything but the car, I slow down and even out the virtual wheel. Zapo creaks, but I manage to keep it steady and on the road.

"Any idea is welcome," I say in VR when I have the vehicle back under control.

"If we know ahead of time who your half-brother will try to take over," Mitya says, avoiding my gaze, "we can put their Brainocytes into a modified debug mode I designed. This way, we can have AROS itself provide more data. Of course, that means the person in debug mode still ends up being taken over."

"Great," Muhomor says sarcastically. "Now we just need another member of Mike's family to hand over to Kostya with a request to take over their mind."

"Mike is heading into enemy territory. There's a chance that"—Mitya hesitates, clearly searching for a tactful way to proceed—"they'll take over his mind."

If this is Mitya's way of sparing my fears, I wonder what he had originally planned to say.

"You're right," Muhomor says with way too much excitement. "Kostya might want to make Mike kill himself. That's what I'd do. It's the perfect crime that would look like suicide to the cops."

I fight the urge to leap for Muhomor's throat in VR. Instead, I channel the surge of angst into my insane driving in the real world.

"Mike," Mitya says gently. "There's no harm in being prepared. I just sent you a link to the version of AROS I'm talking about. Install it, and hope we don't need it."

An email arrives. I silently proceed to install the new AROS interface. Once installation is complete, the only difference I notice is a slight slowdown of perception, which could be the result of anxiety. Still, I complain about it.

"It's the debug mode," Mitya affirms. "This AROS sends certain details back to our servers, and that kind of extra processing is going to slow you down. Is it too much to live with?"

"It's fine. It's no worse than a crappy internet connection." What I don't say is that a crappy internet connection is worse than a mind fogged up by pot or alcohol.

"Just focus all your attention on driving for now," Mitya suggests. "Once you reach your destination, focus on survival."

He makes a good point. I stop all nonessential tasks and, for good measure, I even stop the threads of myself that are trying to figure out how Kostya hacked Brainocytes. I'll rely on Mitya and Muhomor for this from now on.

"I'm feeling normal enough," I say hesitantly. "I think I can pop into this VR room without jeopardizing my life."

"Here's an aerial view of I-84," Mitya says.

My email dings, but there's something happening on the road up ahead.

"Crap. Why is there traffic here in the middle of nowhere?"

"There was an accident." Mitya highlights the part of the road where the density of cars lessens. "I'm guessing people are asking their car AIs to slow down so that they can gawk at the damage as they pass by."

"That makes sense." I wipe virtual sweat from my avatar's brow and wonder if we should at some point turn down the level of realism in this room. "I just had an idea about the drones. Can you guys take control of all the drones in the area, as well as any robots you can locate, and direct them to where I'm going? Kostya didn't say anything about bringing toys with me, just that I come alone."

"Unfortunately, 'all robots and drones in the area' amounts to a couple of drones and no robots," Mitya says.

"I already checked. Sadly, this region is far behind the times."

I spare a moment to do some research, though the distraction almost causes me to veer off the road. When I'm safe again, I say in VR, "We do have that factory in Albany."

"That's an hour and a half away from your destination." Muhomor puts up a large map on the big screen with a map of New York state and the route from the factory highlighted. "By the time the robots arrive, you'll be dead."

"Even so, we'd make his half-brother pay for his death." Mitya curls and uncurls his hands.

"On that cheerful note, I think I'll avoid this room until I pass that traffic." I demonstratively walk toward the meeting room door before poofing out of VR, as proper etiquette demands.

"If you don't slow down, you won't come back, because you're going to turn yourself into a pancake," Mitya says to me privately.

"If I slow down, I won't make it to Kostya's hideout." I shift my focus to the road.

Since I-84 is still a few miles away and there's no traffic until then, I speed up as much as Zapo allows. Soon, the trees blur into a green haze. I push the car some more, until the seat starts to vibrate as though I'm riding an international ballistic missile, and then I push it harder.

I have to get there on time.

I simply have to.

CHAPTER TWENTY-SEVEN

It takes 1.7 seconds of breakneck speed before I approach the ramp to I-84 and slow down to merely two times the speed limit. Knowing that each car I pass could easily be my last makes my heart rate as fast as the insane rotation of my tires.

"Dude," Mitya tells me privately. "Your driving would make NASCAR proud."

I pull the virtual wheel all the way to the right to avoid the gray Volvo in my path. "That's always been my ambition, NASCAR or stunts for *The Fast and the Furious.*"

I blast past a biker, provoking a stream of obscenities. I can't blame the bearded guy, since unlike most other people on the road, he's driving his death machine without AI assistance. I turn left and slip between a green Toyota and a silver Honda. If these cars hadn't been self-driven, their drivers might've cursed me out worse than the biker. As it is, most of the people I nearly kill are busy with their VR entertainment, or ironically, they're trying to look at the accident ahead instead of paying attention to the one in the making.

By the time I finally get through the snarl, I allow myself to check how I'm doing on time and feel giddy that I've gained five minutes of the ten I was short. Still, to make up the other five, I must get back to turbo speed, which I do without hesitation, focusing all my energy on the road.

"I heard a door close." Mr. Spock sends me his words along with a huge dose of excitement through the EmoRat app. "I can't smell the men anymore."

They probably left to prepare for my arrival. I begin to reply, then stop myself. No need to tell Mr. Spock I'm on a suicide mission. I say instead, "You did a good job telling me about this. How do you feel about leaving Alan's pocket to do a little reconnaissance?"

"Scared." Despite his words, Mr. Spock peeks out of the pocket and shares his view with me.

The room is indeed empty.

"Find a better hiding spot," I suggest. "Some place you can keep your eyes on them when they come back."

He runs down Alan's sleeve and then down the inside of his pants leg.

"That's very clever," I say encouragingly. My small friend likes compliments on his stealth skills. "Even if someone had come back in just then, they wouldn't have seen you inside Alan's clothes."

The compliment breaks through the fear that threatens to paralyze the little guy, and he leaps the rest of the distance to the floor and quickly scans the room. This looks like someone's man cave, with a high-end home theater setup and a pool table in the far corner. Both Alan and Ada are half sitting, half lying in plush La-Z-Boy recliners in front of a giant TV like the ones popular before VR made them obsolete. The light from a massive window to the right makes Ada's face appear almost angelic in her slumber, while Alan looks as if he might open his eyes at any moment to cause some mischief.

I turn off the emotions going to Mr. Spock from me, because I don't want to overwhelm the rat with heartache at seeing my unconscious family like this.

"How about you hide under Alan's chair?" I suggest. "You'll be able to see that door."

The door in question creaks open.

A surge of adrenaline nearly makes me lose control of the car in the real world.

Mr. Spock reacts much better than I would have. In a whirl of whiskers and white fur, he dives under Alan's recliner, finds an angle where he's hidden, and tightens his muscles in an effort to make his body smaller and less detectable.

The door is wide open by this point, and a man walks in. I can only see the lower portion of his body, but based on his clothes, I recognize Boris, the asshole from earlier. Two more guard types follow him in, and though I can't see their faces, I suspect they're wearing masks.

"Stay hidden," I tell Mr. Spock, even though he's smart enough to know this himself. "No matter what happens, don't leave that spot."

"I'm worried about Alan and Ada." Mr. Spock's EmoRat worry is nearly as bad as my own.

"They'll be okay, bud," I reassure him. I wish someone would do the same for me. "I promise they'll be fine. I'm working on saving them."

"I'll guard until then," he states bravely.

"Mitya," I write in a private Zik message. "If something happens to me, I want you to make sure Mr. Spock comes out of this alive. He's hiding under a chair where Alan and Ada are kept."

"Of course," Mitya replies. "And just so you know, if something does happen to you, I'll use the robots to make sure everyone responsible pays dearly for it."

"I'm not sure I want my half-brother killed," I say after a moment's hesitation.

"Then I'll just make sure he regrets what happened to you for the rest of his life," Mitya replies, the Zik message completely free of any emotional overtones. "But the punishment will fit the crime."

"I better focus on driving," I tell both Mr. Spock and Mitya. "Let's talk later."

"Keep Share on so Muhomor and I know what happens when you get there," Mitya says.

"I'll watch this room." Mr. Spock demonstratively narrows his pink eyes to get a better view of his surroundings.

Though the road after the accident is relatively empty, it doesn't feel that way at this speed, and I must swerve to avoid cars almost every moment. It's clear that if Zapo and I survive this, the car is going to need new tires by the time

I get to my destination. And I might need a new set of adrenal glands and clean underwear.

When the GPS informs me that Kostya's coordinates are on the right side of the road, I let out a breath I've held half the distance down I-84. Pulling up to the gate of the giant mansion my half-brother has made into his lair, I take in my surroundings. With a forest on one side and mountain views on the other, the location is a high-end realtor's wet dream. There's a giant fence surrounding everything and a driveway that spirals up the hill for at least half a mile.

I jump out of the car, rush over to the large in-wall intercom, and press the only button there.

"*Da*," someone says almost instantly.

"Tell Konstantin that I'm here," I bellow in that exaggerated way my mom uses during international phone calls to her school friends, as though she wants them to hear her all the way in Russia. "I still have three minutes."

"Leave your car behind," the voice says. "Walk in with your hands above your head."

I raise my hands and trudge up the intricate pavers, my eyes never leaving my destination. My gray hair count doubles by the time the first Richard Nixon-masked asshole greets me with a machine gun, and triples when I realize just how many armed people are guarding the locked door.

"Where is my wife?" I demand from the guy closest to me. "Where is my son?"

The man doesn't answer, so I repeat the questions in Russian. This doesn't yield results either.

Yet another masked guard comes out and gestures for us to enter, looking like Richard Nixon as a creepy butler. I follow him into a gorgeous foyer and down a long, spindly corridor.

Through Mr. Spock's ears, I hear the grating voice of Boris. "The show is about to begin. Let me turn on the TV."

The television set in front of the room comes to life. Mr. Spock can only see a chunk of the screen from his vantage point. There's not much to see, only the figure of a large man with his back to the camera. He's standing like a statue, holding something shiny in each hand. The muscles in this guy's back are formidable, and even with the poor viewing angle, something about him is familiar. I have a good idea who it might be, so I keep a small window in my AROS interface open to keep a metaphysical eye on the TV screen as the guards lead me farther into the mansion.

Light from a skylight illuminates the modern art on the walls, but the masked guards with guns are the most common decoration throughout. Including this batch, I count fifty-eight men so far. Assuming they're spread evenly throughout the place and represent a typical ratio of armed men to house space, if I add the size of the mansion into the equation, I get a very depressing result. There must be close to five hundred armed people here.

"This place would be a death trap even if I were armed and had brought Dominic and the rest of security guys," I say after popping into the VR room. Since I'm no longer driving at race-car speeds, I can spare some attention.

Muhomor and Mitya both nod knowingly, verifying that they're watching through my Share app feed.

"Kostya is probably bankrupting one of his companies paying all these goons, assuming they're not being compelled like Gogi and Joe," I continue.

"I doubt any of these people are controlled." Mitya's palms must be sweaty because I see droplets on the arms of the chair where his hands rested a moment ago. "Like Boris, they must be guns for hire."

"Too bad the robots are still an hour away." Muhomor points at the map of upstate New York where a number of dots are moving ever so slowly in our direction. "We have a hundred of them, which would be plenty to deal with these guys."

"Speaking of resources, Dominic is running toward you on foot." Mitya wipes his hands on his hoodie and puts a tiny dot on the map. "With his exoskeleton, he's almost as fast as the robots. He might get to the mansion in an hour and ten minutes if he keeps up that pace."

"Do you have anything more immediate than the robots?" I ask. "It's nice to know I can be avenged after my death, but I'd be even happier if I could stay alive in the first place."

"I've got three drones zeroing in on your location," Muhomor says proudly. "They should be there in about twenty minutes."

"Great," I say sarcastically. "With three measly drones, you'll be able to watch a live feed of my funeral from three angles, assuming Kostya buries me instead of liquefying my corpse in acid or something equally gruesome. I assume you failed to free Joe from his control?"

Muhomor looks down, and Mitya avoids my gaze.

"I didn't think so." I show my displeasure by poofing out of VR in a wisp of virtual smoke.

In the real world, we stop next to a set of heavy red doors, and my Nixon-masked guide pokes me painfully with his gun and then jabs it pointedly toward the entryway. Working completely in sync, his masked partner opens the doors. I enter of my own volition before I'm forced to do so.

The large room is empty of all furniture, and the ultra-polished hardwood floors reflect sparkling light into my eyes with unpleasant intensity. This must've been a dance floor before Kostya appropriated the space for his revenge. The room is also familiar because I'm now looking at it from two angles.

It's the room on the TV screen that Mr. Spock is currently watching.

The doors behind me snap shut, and I focus my gaze in the middle of the room where a single figure stands, a knife in each hand.

My earlier guess was unfortunately correct.

This is my cousin, Joe.

His Siberian icicle eyes show even less emotion than usual, zeroing in on me like two blue lasers. Instead of recognition, all I see is a "target acquired" type of acknowledgment.

Sunlight glints off the two blades as Joe menacingly lumbers toward me.

CHAPTER TWENTY-EIGHT

"Is that you?" Mr. Spock asks worriedly.

"It's me, buddy. Joe and I are just sparring. Just like that time in the dojo."

"I didn't like that time," he replies.

I don't have to remind him this is an understatement. The one and only time I took him to see me train, he threw the rat equivalent of a hissy fit. I always left him at the Furry Ritz after that. The fact that he remembers that fight at all is telling; his long-term memory isn't as good as a human's.

"It's a lot like your dominance games with the other males," I remind him. "No one will get hurt."

"But you're the alpha," he states, and despite everything, I'm warmed by my friend's high regard.

"Sometimes you must remind the other males that you're in charge. Remember your disagreement with Chekov?"

"Yes." His Zik message is full of guilt over biting his friend's ear. "I did give him a peanut later."

"You're the best alpha," I reassure him. "For now, can you do me a favor, bud? Go enjoy Alan's Rat World for ten minutes or so, but keep your eyes open. This way you won't see what happens, but I can still see the TV screen."

"You are smart," he replies distantly, the way he does when he submerges himself in my son's VR version of rat paradise.

In the time Mr. Spock and I telepathically converse, Joe makes it halfway across the room.

This part of Kostya's revenge is elegant in its devious simplicity. One of us—likely me—is about to die. Joe and I are the two people Kostya blames for the death of our father. I suspect he blames me as the leader and Joe as the executioner. He probably doesn't care that it was Joe alone who both decided and enacted our father's fate.

What Kostya doesn't realize is that he, Boris, and the rest of them are not going to get the big spectacle they anticipate. This fight will be over before anyone gets the popcorn, because every single time I've faced Joe in the gym, he's beaten me in a matter of seconds. I mean that literally. Unless he was purposefully toying with me, my record against Joe is four seconds and five milliseconds, and even that I only achieved thanks to Battle Mode. Those fights were also bare-handed. My survival probability shrinks significantly with each knife in Joe's hands.

"Please tell me you can fly a drone through that window," I say to Mitya and Muhomor.

"The three I mentioned are still nineteen minutes away," Muhomor says. "Give or take."

My heart drops to my feet, but I keep a poker face, determined to die with at least some dignity.

I enable Battle Mode.

Joe draws ever closer. Lines begin to show up in Augmented Reality, ideas for my actions and Joe's possible reactions to them. Not surprisingly, time seems to slow, though I think it's more of a trick of adrenaline than my superfast cognition this time.

I have a decision to make. If I enable the Emotion Dampener add-on, I won't have the problem I had when I fought Gogi—hesitation at hurting someone I care about. Should I willingly turn myself into a monster? Is there even any benefit to playing Kostya's game and hurting Joe, when the winner will ultimately die along with the loser?

"Joe is controlled, you're not," Muhomor tells me privately. He must've guessed at least a part of my dilemma. "He has no chance, while you do, albeit a small one."

Cognizant that I'm taking advice on ethical behavior from Muhomor of all people, I nevertheless turn on the Emotion Dampener.

"How many seconds should Emotion Dampener be on?" Einstein asks. This is a safety feature to make sure I don't remain a psychopath once the fight is over.

"Set it for eight seconds and ten milliseconds," I reply. "That's double my estimated time for survival."

Counting the moments, I try to imagine what fighting with Emotion Dampener will be like. I will probably be like a Viking berserker—

"Emotion Dampener enabled," Einstein states.
The world around me transforms.

CHAPTER TWENTY-NINE

The Opponent is a leap away.

He has two knives, which is a huge advantage. But I can see his movement from two vantage points, a tactical benefit I need to leverage. His right knife hand is the dominant one. Battle Mode estimates he will thrust with it first; the TV view shows me his shoulder blades twisting in confirmation.

I sidestep and slightly pull back. At the same time, I strike the Opponent's forearm.

The knife clanks on the hardwood floor and slides toward the door. Though the weapon is behind me, the TV view shows that I have no chance to get it—but neither does the Opponent.

I don't need Battle Mode to show me that the left knife is about to slice at my mid-chest. I'm already reacting. I grab the Opponent's left wrist, successfully trapping it. With as much intensity as I can, I strike the Opponent in the groin. My plan is simple: the intense pain should force the Opponent to let go of the weapon, after which I can use the knife to carve the Opponent like a Thanksgiving turkey.

The groin strike doesn't cause the Opponent to let go of the weapon. Either he's wearing a cup, or Kostya's control enables him to withstand this intense pain. I surmise the latter, since that was the case in the fight with Gogi. This presents a problem, because outside of the ideal scenario in which I kill the Opponent, much of my strategy relies on inflicting copious amounts of pain.

So now I need to focus on killing him as fast as I can. If that's not possible, I need to cause the kind of damage that would make fighting physically impossible despite the mind control—for example, broken bones or severed limbs. Ripping out the eyes probably wouldn't be as strategic, because Kostya could still control the Opponent via camera views, but if the opportunity presents itself, I will gouge out the eyes to test this theory. Once the Opponent is thusly handicapped, killing him should be trivial.

I scan Battle Mode's recommendations and pick one unlikely to be anticipated, because it will cause minor harm to me. I pull back with my hands while bringing my head toward the precious knife. Stretching my jaw muscles like a snake, I take a vicious bite.

My teeth grate against the metal of the knife, but I ignore the pain of enamel scraping off and rip my head so violently to the right that my neck muscles spasm in complaint.

The Opponent's grip on the knife loosens, and I find myself with the weapon in my mouth. I let go of the Opponent's wrist with my right hand while simultaneously tightening my grip with the left. I claw at the knife in my mouth. As soon as I feel the plastic hilt in my palm, I thrust the knife at the Opponent's right eye. My goal isn't to blind him but to penetrate the brain—a very efficient way to kill.

Unfortunately, the Opponent acts as I would in his position. Ignoring the potential damage, he grabs the blade.

I could twist the blade to inflict maximum pain, but that isn't a motivator in this fight. I try another gambit. Letting go with my left hand, I wrap it around the Opponent's knife-holding hand and squeeze. If the knife is sharp enough and I apply enough force, I should cause the hand to cleave in two—a useful handicap.

As expected, the Opponent ignores the pain, curls his other hand into a fist, and throws a punch at my face.

I throw my head back to reduce the impact of the punch, but the maneuver doesn't help. The fist smashes into my chin, sending me to the verge of consciousness. Abandoning the plan to cleave the Opponent's hand, I let go with my left hand and rip the knife from his grasp with the right.

Blood pours from the Opponent's palm, but not fast enough to provide any advantage anytime soon.

Battle Mode shows me an opportunity. If I toss the knife just as the line shows, I'll pierce the Opponent's heart with a high probability of instant death.

I arc my arm as instructed and begin to throw.

I'm mid-throw when the world around me changes again.

"Emotion Dampener disabled."

CHAPTER THIRTY

Once a human body begins to perform an action, it's hard to stop. I hope that my highly trained and enhanced mind will be able to accomplish what regular free will cannot.

In the end, I only tweak my action very slightly as I let go of the knife, but the adjustment makes all the difference. Instead of piercing Joe in the chest, the knife scrapes his flesh, leaving a small gash that bleeds instantly.

Now that my emotions are back, taming my sympathetic nervous system is like riding a bull at a rodeo in hell. Ignoring the deafening pulse in my ears, I can't help but focus on how appalled I am at what the Emotion Dampener made me do and think. I initiated it because I thought that Joe would kill me so quickly and easily that Emotion Dampener might give me a slightly better chance at survival. As it is, I survived double the time I thought I would—but I find it hard to believe it's because of Emotion Dampener.

I nearly maimed and killed my cousin, something I don't think I could live with (though I guess "living with it" is a purely hypothetical concept under the circumstances). At the very least, I don't intend to give Kostya the satisfaction of becoming a monster for his viewing pleasure.

"You should delete the Emotion Dampener code from our source control repository," I tell Mitya. "I'm never using that atrocity again."

"I'd also add taking advice from Muhomor to your 'never' list," Mitya replies.

"If by some miracle I survive long enough to need advice, I'll only ask for yours," I tell him.

My cousin tries to punch me in the face. Specks of blood from the earlier knife wound trail the path of his fist like a tail following a comet. I block the punch with my forearm and reflexively counter with my elbow into his jaw.

The way my elbow screams in pain tells me he'll likely need surgery if he ever wants to chew again; even his strengthened bones couldn't have helped in this case. Despite the massive pain Joe must now feel, his expression doesn't change at all.

The realization finally clicks into place.

"Dude," I tell Mitya telepathically. "The reason Joe hasn't killed me already is because I'm not actually fighting Joe. I'm fighting whoever is controlling Joe—the puppet master, so to speak. Luckily, that person isn't as good a fighter as my cousin."

"This also explains why Gogi didn't fight like himself," Mitya says instantly.

On the TV screen, Joe begins to move his leg, so I step back from his kick. Now that I know what to look for, I'm certain my theory is right. This wasn't Joe's kick—he would've never been this sloppy. This was Kostya's (or whoever's) attempt at a kick.

This small droplet of good news in the sea of bad reinvigorates me like a full night's sleep and a gallon of coffee. I execute a combination of moves I never would've dared with the real Joe, finishing with a punch in the pit of his stomach. My fist strikes his solar plexus with an audible smack. Joe's body doubles over and draws in wheezing breaths.

This is my chance to knock him out—the only way out, outside of the heavy-handed ideas I'd had during the earlier Emotion Dampener insanity. I grab Joe by the hair and prepare to slam his face against my knee.

The tightening of Joe's neck muscles on TV is my warning that I've failed. I try to regroup, but it's too late. He rips out of my grasp and uses his momentary advantage to put a foot behind me and push.

On the TV, I watch myself fly toward the wooden floor in a wide arc. The fall seems to proceed in slow motion, and I even have a moment to calculate the odds of breaking my back when I land. I decide such an eventuality is unlikely.

I also realize my earlier mistake. A typical solar plexus punch hurts so much that the victim is unable to think for a moment—but in Joe's case, that didn't apply because Kostya doesn't feel Joe's pain. Also, a typical solar plexus punch knocks the wind out of the victim, but the

Respirocytes swimming in Joe's system ensure his body has enough oxygen to throw me to the floor.

The good news is that these same Respirocytes should help me in a millisecond.

I land on the floor, the pain jolting through my nerves like a creaky wooden roller coaster. Despite knowing I'm not lacking oxygen, I'm unable to stop my body from desperately gasping to replace the air that cowardly escaped my lungs.

The TV screen shows Kostya preparing for another move that the real Joe would never do.

With a colossal effort of will, I override my uncooperative biology just in time to roll to the side of a wrestler-style slam that's just as likely to hurt him as me. There's a loud bang as Joe's elbow hits the floor; it sounds as if he's cracked either the wood or his bone. At least it wasn't my ribs.

Judging from my earlier fight with Gogi, Kostya must have some experience with wrestling, which makes me deeply regret ending up on the ground. I try to jump to my feet, but Joe's already next to me. Even without Battle Mode assistance, I can see that he wants to grab my right arm in a judo-style lock.

My counter is pure textbook and proves Kostya isn't as good of a fighter as I feared, because Joe's body ends up under mine. I spot his leg on the TV screen and realize that if his kick connects, I'll be singing falsetto for a while. I block the kick instantly and do my best to intertwine his legs with mine while grabbing both of his wrists.

In theory, I should be able to hold him this way for a while, but Kostya must realize it too. He makes Joe do something that no sane fighter would: he headbutts me at an angle that will be much worse for him than for me.

Joe's already damaged jaw crashes into my forehead, making me see an explosion of sparks where his bloody face should be. When my vision comes back, Kostya repeats the headbutt; this time, it's Joe's forehead that hits mine.

The concussion and the blood in my eyes make it impossible to see what's happening until I check out the TV and see Joe's head connecting with mine again. The impact makes the world around me seem unreal. I recognize this sensation—it happens every time someone (usually Joe) knocks me out.

I'm not the only one affected. Joe's body slackens under me, and on the TV, I see him pass out—right before my own world goes completely blank.

CHAPTER THIRTY-ONE

I wake up to a loud hum.

"You have been unconscious for twenty-three min-utes," Einstein's voice says too loudly in my aching head.

The hum seems to intensify, and I realize that I'm some-place dark—at least I can't seem to detect any light through my closed eyelids. Before opening my eyes, I check on my family via the EmoRat app.

Mr. Spock is clearly bored. The room is quiet, and judging by the unmoving boots of the three guards, they must be motionless as well.

"Hey, bud, you're doing an excellent job as a guard," I tell the rat. "Keep it up."

"You're back," Mr. Spock says excitedly. "I called after I was done with Rat World, but you didn't respond."

"I was a little busy," I say. "I still am, but we'll have a long talk soon."

"Okay," Mr. Spock replies. "I'll wait."

A Zik message from Mitya interrupts, full of paranoid urgency. "Don't show them you're awake. Join us in VR."

I do as my friend suggests. Three people are in the VR room now: Dominic, Mitya, and Muhomor.

"Dominic," I say in lieu of a greeting. "Please tell me you're about to barge in and save us."

"I'm about half an hour away." Though this VR version of Dominic is free of the exoskeleton and bionic arm, he's still a formidable presence in the meeting room.

"He's running on foot through a shortcut in the wilderness." Mitya looks at Dominic's giant form with admiration. "We should give him a huge bonus when this is all over."

"What about the robots?" I ask.

"Twenty-five minutes until arrival." Mitya puts a map up on the big screen to point out the dots representing Dominic and the robots.

"What are the blue and yellow dots following the robots?" I ask after examining the map.

"The police and the news. It's not every day that someone reenacts a scene from *I, Robot* in upstate New York." He puts up a view of the robots marching uphill in unison, sunlight gleaming off their metallic heads.

"They won't be here in time either," Dominic says. "They're lagging behind the robots."

"So is there anything that can help my current situation?" I look at everyone in turn, trying to ignore the sick feeling in my stomach.

"The three drones I promised you are outside the window of the room where you're being scanned," Muhomor says. "I have an idea, but I'd like your input."

He puts up three screens. Each drone must have a telescoping lens, because I see three views into a room that was probably a big guest bedroom before Kostya turned it into a makeshift lab and infirmary. On a bed to the right of the window, Joe is hooked up to some monitoring equipment. It shows a heartbeat that proves he's alive, at least for now.

Three figures in white coats stand with their backs to the window, huddling around another body inside a big brain-scanning machine. Only the middle of the man's torso and legs are sticking out. It takes me a moment to realize that the torso belongs to me, and that this explains the hum and the darkness.

"What are they doing to me?" I walk up to the screen and point at the machine. "Is that a CAT scan or an MRI?"

"They just got your Brainocyte ID," Mitya says apologetically.

"But on the plus side, they also scanned your noggin for real, and it looks like Joe didn't fracture your skull," Muhomor adds.

"They probably want to hack into you the way they did with Gogi and Joe," Dominic says. He winces at the vicious glares from Mitya and Muhomor.

"As Captain Obvious says," Muhomor continues after a small pause, "Kostya must have more planned for you."

One of the people surrounding me is likely Kostya himself.

A crazy idea pops into my head.

"Muhomor, could you crash each of the drones into one of the people in that room?" I ask quickly. "There are three of them and three of the drones. I could jump out of that machine, finish them off, disable a guard to get a weapon, and barricade myself, Ada, and Alan in this room with Joe until the robots and Dominic arrive."

"What you said is my earlier plan," Muhomor says. "I can—"

"This plan has a low probability of success," Mitya says. "These drones are not that maneuverable, so unless the people are distracted already, there's little chance they'll allow themselves to get hit with one."

"And when that glass breaks, they'll have ample warning." Dominic stares at the screen intently. He must be looking for another idea and finding none.

"Anyone have any counterplans?" I ask. "Or are you dead set on sacrificing me to learn how this brain hack works?"

"Assuming the debug stuff they told me about even helps with that," Dominic says glumly. "That's a big if."

We sit in sullen silence as the people on the screen begin to pull me out of the machine and I feel the motion in the real world.

"The bad men are moving," Mr. Spock tells me urgently.

Through Mr. Spock's senses, I see the door open and a man in a white coat enter. In VR, I explain that something is happening in Alan and Ada's location and provide them with the EmoRat app so they can look on. They didn't already have this app because only Ada, Alan, and I use it routinely; it never became part of the standard AROS package.

"It's wakey-wakey time," says the new guy. "Boss wants them awake for the next part."

The two syringes in the white coat's hands probably mean he plans to inject Ada and Alan with something that might wake them. That would usually be good news, but in the context of "the next part," it seems beyond sinister.

"How long before the girl is fully awake?" asks the rock-on-rock voice I recognize as belonging to Boris. He's trying to sound casual, but there's a creepy inquisitiveness in his tone that fills me with dread.

"She'll come to her senses almost right away, but I'd give it a few minutes before she stops being groggy," the white coat replies. He walks up to Ada's chair, the syringe menacingly extended.

"Shouldn't we tie her up?" Boris asks with an unhealthy eagerness.

"Motherfucker," Dominic mumbles in VR. My other friends echo his sentiment in their own ways.

"Boss said not to use restraints," the white coat says. The chair blocks Mr. Spock's view, but I'm pretty sure the guy administers Ada's injection. "He has these two under control already, so they'll sit still once they come to."

It takes a huge effort to pretend to be unconscious in the real world. What I really want to do is open my eyes, grab Kostya's throat, and not let go until I choke the life out of my twisted fuck of a half-brother.

"We all suspected that your family would be hacked," Muhomor says in VR. Before he can expand on that thought, Dominic leans over and smacks him on the back of the head with an open palm. It couldn't have hurt too much, especially in VR, but Muhomor still squeals like a little piglet.

Ignoring VR, I work on calming my tumultuous emotions as the white coat injects Alan with the wake-up drug. To my luck, the people who took my body out of the machine are all busy watching something in the air above me, probably a private Augmented Reality screen.

"I'm needed back in the lab," the injection guy says on his way out. "Boss will be here shortly."

"I need a favor," Boris says to the other guards as soon as the door closes. "You two should take a short bathroom break."

The men look at one another.

"Boss said they're not to be harmed," one says, his voice muffled by the Nixon mask. "Not that it makes sense, considering, but orders are orders."

I really don't like the implication of that "considering" remark, but worry about its meaning is quickly overshadowed by the fury building in my heart.

"She will not be harmed," Boris says in a tone that sends angry shivers down my whole body. "Just a little sore is all. You know I'll make it worth your while if you do this for me."

The two other guards chuckle lasciviously and turn away.

My blood is boiling out of my veins. I'm probably more dangerous now than I was with the Emotion Dampener on. Emotion Dampener makes you a cold monster, but I would enjoy inflicting pain on Boris right now.

"The subject's heart rate is elevated," says someone next to me in the lab. "I think he's awake."

"The bypass is now activated," says Kostya's voice from my right. "It doesn't matter."

"They hacked you," Muhomor says in VR.

"I captured it via the debug mode," Mitya says.

"I don't give a fuck," I shout in VR, my fists clenched so tight it hurts. "That fucker is planning to rape Ada."

My friends look shocked at the vehemence in my voice. Even Dominic steps away from me.

"Your orders are about to be disobeyed," I scream at Kostya in the real world, yet nothing comes out of my mouth. "You said not to harm Ada, but she's about to come to harm!"

My brain reels from the strangeness of talking without any sound coming out of my larynx, and my fury intensifies at my helplessness.

Then my attention snaps back to the room with Ada, because Mr. Spock sees the door close behind the two guards.

Boris walks toward Ada's chair.

"I really hope you're already awake," he says in his grating voice. "I'll enjoy this so much more if you are."

No sound comes from Ada, but it could be because she's unable to scream, like me.

Boris's hands move toward his zipper.

CHAPTER THIRTY-TWO

If I were there, I'd rip this fucker's neck out with my bare teeth. Hate must create its own form of dark focus, because a plan of action instantly comes to me.

"Muhomor," I shout in VR. "Fly the drones into his head. Now."

"But you need them—"

"Now, or I'll fucking kill you!"

Something in my eyes must be convincing, because Muhomor swiftly obeys.

"Mr. Spock, you have to do something very dangerous for Ada, but it's very important." My EmoRat Zik message is a lot gentler than the order I barked in VR, but it conveys the same urgency.

"I'm ready," Mr. Spock replies right away. "What do I do?"

"I want you to run up this man's pant leg." I try to ball my hands into fists in the real world, but this doesn't work either, and my hands remain at my sides. "Once you reach the top, I want you to bite, over and over, as hard as you can."

A wave of eagerness comes back from the EmoRat. It's obvious that Mr. Spock has been itching to bite the bad guys for a while now, and only the social conditioning we've instilled in him was preventing this.

My perception slows to a crawl as the three drone views zero in on the nearby window. While I can't hold my breath in the real world, I stop breathing in VR as Mr. Spock dives for Boris's shoe.

Boris doesn't seem to notice the flash of white fur on the floor.

Mr. Spock's eyes show a repulsive view of a thick, hairy leg as he climbs toward an even more disgusting destination.

Boris must feel little claws on his leg, because he stops. The fastest drone points its lens at the window, and through that camera view, I see his puzzled expression.

Mr. Spock climbs higher. When he spots the white underwear, rat rage seeps through the EmoRat interface.

"Yes!" I spur the little warrior onward. "Bite that motherfucker."

Even lab rats like Mr. Spock have large teeth capable of administering painful bites. Rats usually avoid fighting humans because they know it's a losing fight, but if you corner one, you'd better prepare for some pain (and sometimes for rat-bite fever).

Mr. Spock's teeth easily pierce both the cotton fabric and the thin flesh of Boris's testicles.

The tortured yelp of pain is music to my bloodthirsty ears.

The drone is now an inch away from the window, and I get a glimpse of Boris's horrified face before window shards spray into the room and that face grows bigger.

Mr. Spock bites his target again, so hard I feel the little guy's jaws ache.

Boris's next scream is higher pitched. Via the drone, I see him struggling to decide if he should punch himself in the groin—a tough call.

"Run away," I command Mr. Spock. "Quickly."

I can feel his desire to keep biting, but he's a good rat and runs down. He's near Boris's knee when the first drone hits the man in the chest.

Boris doubles over, hopefully distracted from the source of the biting.

"To the rat, this must be like a scene from *King Kong*," Muhomor says in VR, earning him another smack on the back of the head from Dominic.

The second drone flies in through the window just as Mr. Spock leaves Boris's pants leg. Boris swats at it, and it crashes into the TV at the front of the room. His momentary distraction gives the third drone the chance it needs, and it slams into his temple with a satisfying smack.

Boris drops like a tree, his flailing foot inadvertently kicking Mr. Spock in the butt.

Momentum sends Mr. Spock skidding under Alan's recliner. He tries with all his might to slow down, but his claws don't provide enough traction.

There's a loud crash as Boris hits the floor. Through the camera of the last drone, I see him land on the debris of the TV, cutting himself in multiple places. Unfortunately, the view through Mr. Spock's eyes is nauseating as the little guy torpedoes toward the chair leg, followed by the smack of the rat's head into the wood.

Mr. Spock sends a rush of an all-too-familiar sensation—he's passing out.

"You did well," I tell him guiltily. "You're the fiercest rat in the world."

He seems to have heard me, because he flickers pride before he loses consciousness completely.

"Is the rat dead?" Muhomor asks and dodges Dominic's hand this time. "Hey, I'm just asking."

"I have a biofeedback chip in him," I say sharply. "His vitals look okay. He's just going to be out for a bit—and probably have a big headache once he comes to."

"Can we tell Mike about his own situation now?" Muhomor looks belligerently at Dominic. "I doubt he has much time left in VR."

"We've learned more about this hack," Mitya says. "It's basically a backdoor that allows Kostya to turn off and on any app inside your—"

"The loophole was the GPS interface," Muhomor jumps in excitedly. "They must've had to hack into every satellite in the world to pull this off. The scope of this—"

Dominic smacks Muhomor much harder this time. "Shut up, or I'll shut you up for good."

"As I was saying," Mitya continues, giving Muhomor a withering stare, "the backdoor also allows Kostya to run any app in your AROS without your consent. You're getting some of these installed while he's shutting down your regular apps. When he gets to the VR interface, you won't—"

I abruptly find myself only in the real world. The VR room is gone without a trace. Kostya has done what Mitya was trying to warn me about: he closed the app in question.

I try sending Mitya a private Zik message, but nothing happens. I try email and social media without any results. Even the ancient instant messenger doesn't start.

"Let's try the motor function controls program," Kostya says next to me. "Have him open his eyes."

My eyes snap open without my willing them to.

The light in the room hurts my unadjusted eyes. I try to squint, but I don't have even that much control.

Panic forms in the back of my mind. Everyone has that visceral fear of being locked inside one's body without the ability to control it. I guess for me, this fear is stronger than usual. I try to distract myself from full-on terror, reminding myself that this is probably what those poor paralyzed patients experienced before we gave them Brainocytes. I focus on how good it feels to have helped people recover from such horror.

"Einstein?" I mentally ask. "What time is it?"

No reply.

Like every user, I've long since associated all my favorite apps with mental commands, which is why I haven't used the original visual AROS interface in a while. I try to summon it now.

To my surprise, the AROS interface shows up. Kostya must not have disabled the AROS UI controller app just yet. The number of icons that hover in the air in front of me is tiny in comparison to what's usually there. The Paint app icon disappears in front of my eyes before I can formulate some practical use for it; it had a Share button that likely uses APIs of the closed apps—a tiny chance that now is gone.

What's worse are the unfamiliar icons that show up. These must be the apps that allow Kostya to do whatever evil thing he plans to do to me—apps he can activate without my consent.

The AROS interface disappears, and a major portion of my mind splinters and dies a horrific death. The awful sense of dumbness is vaguely reminiscent of when I was without internet on a government black site. This sensation, though, is a million times worse. I've had more boosts since then and have come to rely on my cloud extensions even more. It's unclear if the computer substrate in my bones is helping my thinking or not, but in any case, I'm barely able to form a semi-coherent thought. It's as though I'm a ghost of myself, an analog copy of a copy of a copy.

Kostya must now have complete control over my mind, but the implications of that are now harder for me to grasp. I wonder if I knew what Kostya was about to make me do when I was whole just a minute ago. I also wonder if I had a plan at that point, because I'm overwhelmingly clueless now.

"Try to move around," a thin man in a lab coat recommends.

Kostya looks thoughtful for a moment, and suddenly, my body moves.

If having no control over my eyelids was weird, getting up like a marionette is even more bizarre. It's as though I've become a passive passenger inside my own mind. I still feel the pressure of each step, the in-and-out of my breathing, and the swing of my arms. But without control, it's more reminiscent of a low-budget virtual reality movie than of being myself.

I take a step, then another. The weirdest thing is that a part of me feels like maybe I'm controlling my movement after all, and it takes focus to verify that I'm not. That I can't. I guess my consciousness isn't used to not being in control, and tries to cling to an illusion of freedom, an illusion that's easy to shatter—all I need to do is wish to stop walking.

My body makes its way to the unconscious Joe, and my hand reaches toward a table with medical instruments right next to his head. My fingers brush the cold metal of a scalpel and gently pick it up.

"No," I try to say, but no words come out.

I fight for the control of my hand, but it's futile. The scalpel caresses Joe's ruined jaw, leaving a bloody streak where it cuts his skin. The cut is shallow and shouldn't do much harm, but if Kostya presses my hand even a millimeter deeper, the story will be different.

"Have you heard from Boris?" one of the lab coats asks.

My hand stops, and Kostya pauses his own movements momentarily. I can picture him placing a private call with his AROS and learning what happened to Boris. If that's the case, he's probably also summoning more goons to clean up the mess.

With a violent jerk, my hand throws the scalpel back onto the tray and my legs carry me back to Kostya. I stand in front of my half-brother like an ice sculpture, futilely willing my hands to grab his neck.

"How did Boris get hurt?" Kostya asks in that weird falsetto voice. "Where did those broken drones come from?"

I assume this means my mouth will work, so I test it out. "Fuck. You. I'm going to—"

To my huge disappointment, my stream of threats and obscenities gets cut off. That doesn't stop me from trying to inject my disdain for my half-brother into my unblinking gaze.

Something akin to an Augmented Reality icon flashes in front of my face. I'm abruptly grappling with the worst pain I've ever felt in my life, and I've lived through gunshots, explosions, and even torture. It's as if someone is repeatedly kicking me in the balls, only inside my brain.

I want to gasp for breath, but my body is breathing with the calm of a Hindu cow. I want to scream, but my mouth isn't working.

That flicker of an icon must've been the launch of an app that does the opposite of the Relief app: it causes lightning bolts to hit various parts of my brain.

The pain stops and Kostya repeats, "How did Boris get hurt? Where did those drone pieces come from?"

"Anyone ever tell you that you look like a syphilitic pedophile?" I say, my voice hoarse from residual pain. "You motherf—"

The surge of agony is worse this time. It's purer. Less reminiscent of anything physical. This is what it would feel like if a zombie munched your brain while you're alive—if your brain had pain receptors, that is.

After a subjective decade but probably a real-world second, the torment stops and Kostya repeats his questions.

As tempted as I am to curse my half-brother again, the fear of that pain returning is so intense that I decide to stop being a hero. "You never said I couldn't fly drones here. You just said to come alone."

He considers my words, and I inwardly brace for the pain to begin again.

"He can't command any drones now," one of the lab coats says.

"Still, I'm going to expedite the proceedings," Kostya says to the coat. "Let's go."

My body comes alive again, and I walk toward the room's exit, passing a number of white hospital beds as I go. Kostya directs me into a wide corridor. A door to the right opens, and several masked guards bring out a stretcher carrying Boris. More guards follow with black garbage bags that probably contain broken glass and the remains of the drones.

Kostya stops me next to the door the people just left.

"You made my worst nightmare come true," he says in an emotionless falsetto monotone. "I'm about to return the favor."

My attempt at a torrent of Russian and English obscenities doesn't leave my uncooperative mouth.

Kostya looks at me unblinkingly, and my perception momentarily flickers. When my vision reasserts itself, I realize he must've shut down my eyes, because I missed him move. And he must've moved, because he's already a foot closer to the door.

My arm rises, and Kostya hands me a Glock 19 just like the one I use at the range. There's something ceremonial about this handoff, and if my body were still my own, I'd be gulping down breaths.

Kostya walks through the door, and I unwillingly follow.

Something about the room doesn't fully make sense, but Kostya forces my eyes to dart from Ada to Alan—a rare case when his malevolent purpose is in sync with what I want to do anyway.

Both Ada and Alan stare at me with paralyzed faces that hint at being under Kostya's control.

"Please, Dad, no," Alan says with an intonation that makes him sound like a stranger—likely a side effect of Kostya using his vocal cords. "Don't kill me."

"Do not shoot us, Mike," Ada says in the same strange way, her face completely emotionless.

My hand clutches the gun and rises.

I try to scream, but no words come out.

The barrel of my gun points at Ada's head, and Kostya forces my eyes to look through the sights. All my shooting range experience leaves no doubt in my mind: if my finger presses that trigger, the bullet will hit my wife in the middle of her forehead.

If it were possible for the naked brain to scream, mine would've done so already.

Desperate ideas flit through my head.

"This is a dream. Einstein, please show up." The AI doesn't appear, as he would if this was a nightmare.

"Maybe this is a precog moment." Then I remember that it can't be. Precog moments disappeared with the newer brain boost technology, and even when they did happen in the past, they short-circuited as soon as you thought the words "precog moment."

My finger slowly presses the trigger.

The gun's recoil pushes my hand back as Ada's head explodes.

CHAPTER THIRTY-THREE

"This can't be happening," I chant inside my head. "Please, please, please. Let this not be happening."

"Daddy, don't," Alan says in that creepy way again.

My arm points the gun unwaveringly at Alan's tiny torso.

I curse myself for wasting the drones on Boris earlier. I should've saved them to somehow kill myself—not that I have any app to control a drone with, but maybe Muhomor and Mitya could've done it.

My finger squeezes the trigger.

I'm oblivious to the ringing in my ears and the recoil. All I see is Alan's small rib cage devastated by the bullet.

With torturous intent, my eyes travel back to Ada's corpse, forcing me to stare at my dead wife for what feels like an eternity of grief before coming back to Alan.

I want to fall to my knees. I want to clutch my eyes. I want to rip out my hair. But my body just stands there.

If human beings could will themselves to die of grief, I would do so now.

Then my vision blurs once more, and I'm back outside the door.

How am I back here? What just happened?

Wild hope seizes me.

Could that murder scene have been a precog moment, as unlikely as that is?

Kostya is standing the same way he was before my vision went weird the first time. "I wanted to show you a preview of what's about to happen," he says. "I want you to know what I'm going to make you do in a minute, so you have a chance to really savor that experience."

I understand then. Kostya can run any app inside my AROS. That means he can force me to watch virtual reality videos, which is what that horrific vision was. That explains why I thought the room looked odd: there was no sign of Boris's earlier struggle. When Kostya made that fake video, he didn't know the incident with Boris would happen, so he didn't stage it.

In hindsight, it wasn't even that good of a video. I'd thought Ada and Alan's speech and facial expressions were weird because of Kostya's control, but it was just unre-searched CGI.

"Here." Kostya hands me the gun as though I have a choice.

My hand extends and grasps it again, or for the first time—I don't care about semantics right now.

This time around, when I begin walking, I pay close attention to the most minute details to make sure I'm not in VR again. Given the pressure of the handle against my palm, the weight of the Glock pulling my arm down, and the faint smell of Boris's blood and Kostya's sweat, I must conclude that this is happening for real. VR technology doesn't yet have this level of detail—although neither does a nightmare, for that matter.

I appreciate Kostya's evil genius at making me doubt reality right now. As the result of the earlier VR, I'm hyper alert. If he makes me repeat the atrocity from the fake video, I'll feel every aspect even more vividly.

My right leg takes a step. Again I focus and make sure to sense the pressure of my foot touching the ground, the interplay of leg muscles. It's not only to verify the realness of what's happening, but also to try to wrest back control. Maybe some leg muscle will listen to my brain and allow me to topple over. Maybe some muscle in my hand will twitch upon my wish and drop the gun.

If Kostya's control has a loophole, I don't find it in the time it takes me to lumber into the room.

This time, I spot the signs of Boris's earlier mishaps: a window is missing, and glass crunches under my feet. Kostya makes me scan the room. There are two guards, one next to Ada and the other next to Alan. Kostya stops on my left, within easy reach—if only I could control my body.

As in my earlier vision, Alan and Ada's eyes are open. Unlike before, their expressions aren't completely blank. There's a nervous twitch in the corner of Ada's eye, and something similar at the corner of Alan's mouth.

My left hand takes the gun off safety—another detail the VR video omitted earlier.

My right hand fluctuates, as though Kostya is deciding whom he should have me shoot first.

He must make his decision, because my hand turns in Alan's direction.

CHAPTER THIRTY-FOUR

Kostya is slowing my movements in order to torment me as much as he can. His plan is working extremely well.

Then something penetrates his control.

If I could blink in confusion, I would, because I don't understand where this wave of groggy emotions comes from. Without a brain boost, it takes me a long moment to recognize what I'm experiencing.

This is how Mr. Spock feels when you wake him from a rat nap.

Has Kostya forgotten to stop the EmoRat app?

Now that I think about it, it's likely. Only Ada, Alan, and I are users of this app. Kostya or anyone outside our circle wouldn't even know it was there to stop.

"Buddy!" I shout urgently through the app. "I think you got hit on the head and knocked out, and you just came back to your senses."

"Sounds true," the rat replies. His mind is clearly groggy. "Your friend is in my head."

"What?" I ask with a glimmer of hope. "Muhomor…? Mitya? Can you—?"

"Already on top of it," says Mr. Spock with unusual sophistication. "This is Muhomor, by the way."

"Dude." I cram my reply with all the desperation of a man whose hand is in the process of aiming a gun at his son. "Please tell me Mitya's debug mode worked."

"Yeah, once I knew how they got in, it wasn't hard to reverse engineer the rest of it—especially since fate was kind enough to provide me with a Georgian test subject right here in the bunker." Muhomor's Zik reply contains an inappropriate amount of glee. "Ada and Alan are already free from control, by the way. They're just faking submission. Things are trickier with you because I've had no way to get in touch until now. I have to say, I always thought your pet rat was a stupid frivolity, but now that I can use him as a proxy for—"

"Can you see the room?" I interrupt. "The gun is almost pointing at Alan's head."

"True," Muhomor says. "That's where we want it. Until the last second. We don't want them on to us."

"This *is* the last second." Though my mind isn't nearly as sharp as it needs to be, I understand his plan—but I'm so pissed that if this conversation were happening in VR, I'd punch him in the face. "Free me. Now."

"Not yet. Kostya is paying close attention to you right now. If I wrest his control away, he'll instantly know that it happened. In case you hadn't noticed, there are armed people in the room."

"If you don't give me back control of my body, I will genuinely kill you when I see you next." I cram my hatred of my half-brother into my Zik message with the hope of getting through.

"Fine," Muhomor snaps. "Let's see if this works."

CHAPTER THIRTY-FIVE

My mind becomes whole again.

No drug-induced ecstasy or the best orgasm in the world can compare with the sensation of regaining my full mental prowess. If someone magically turned an ant into a rocket scientist, this is how the little creature would feel.

Seeing simultaneously through my own eyes and Mr. Spock's viewpoint, I reassess the situation. It was a mistake to force Muhomor to give me control back at this very moment. Kostya is indeed about to become aware of what's happening—a few milliseconds too soon. Now I'm pissed that Muhomor gave in, but I have no choice but to work with the situation at hand. If I ever not have my brain boost again, I hope I retain enough wits to unquestioningly trust someone whose intellect (at that time) is so much superior to mine.

On the bright side, Mitya and Muhomor don't know the full extent of my combat skills. Hopefully, I can still get us out of this mess alive.

Instead of continuing the trajectory that would point the gun at Alan's head, my hand shifts an inch to the side, and I put a bullet between the eyeholes of the Richard Nixon mask of Alan's guard.

The mask breaks into little pieces, as does the skull of the man underneath.

I feel a tinge of regret at the death—an obvious side effect of having my mind Joined with Ada's so recently. Any police manual would advise lethal force in a situation like this. Shooting to kill is the safest option under the circumstances. I took unnecessary risks in the past by shooting people in the shoulder; now that I'm more experienced, I refuse to risk my family's life for some asshole again. If that makes me too much like Joe, it's something I'll have to live with—and I'd rather live to regret my choices than die as a saint.

In less time than it probably takes Kostya to register the boom of the gunshot, I elbow him in the stomach while pointing the gun toward Ada's guard with my other hand. Most people have trouble moving their hands completely independently like this; they first realize it in grade school when attempting the trick of patting their head and rubbing their belly at the same time. Of course, just like with that trick, practice helps tremendously.

My elbow connects pleasantly with Kostya's flesh at the same time as my right index finger presses the trigger.

The second gunshot thunders, and the second guard's brains splatter the wall behind him with streaks of brown and red, like the bloody stool of a cow suffering from dysentery. It's fitting, I think. The guard clearly had shit for brains.

Kostya doubles over in pain. I turn to him now, fury shading the blue lines of Battle Mode in red.

I raise the gun to his head, and my finger itches to do what Joe would've done in my place—end my half-brother, here and now. Yet a part of me wavers. I'm not sure if it's Ada's influence, my kinship with my target, or my seeing that he's no longer a threat.

Also, Alan and Ada are watching me.

To quell the bloodthirstiness that threatens to make me press the trigger anyway, I remind myself that Kostya could be useful as a hostage. Even Joe would consider that a reason to let him live.

Instead of firing, I pistol-whip Kostya in the face with all my might. There's a crack of something breaking, and my half-brother falls to the ground in a limp heap.

Ada and Alan are staring at me in shock. If we had a family competition to see whose eyes could grow wider, I'm not sure who would win.

"React in VR," I tell them both via Zik messages. "We don't have time for that in the real world."

Hopeful they'll agree, I pop into VR and leap into action in the real world. My first objective is to grab Mr. Spock from his hiding spot.

I arrive in the VR meeting room in time to catch Ada screaming like a banshee. She's madly pacing the room's circumference, and I give her space to finish a few circles before I attempt any consolation. Alan is faring a little better, or so I assume. The kid is sitting at the conference table, face down, arms hugging the top of his head as though he's blocking punches.

After a couple of circles, I grab Ada into a bear hug. She resists for a moment, then softens into me.

Muhomor and Mitya look extremely uncomfortable, while Dominic seems eager to break something or someone.

"We're okay," I say soothingly to no one specific. I gently release Ada and make my way toward Alan. "We're going to be okay."

"Those five hundred guards swooping to your location might disagree." Muhomor pushes his sunglasses higher up his nose. "You're far from okay."

I'm hugging Alan when I hear a solid thump behind me.

Muhomor angrily yelps, "That's classic. Shoot the messenger."

"Sorry," Dominic says. "All that adrenaline."

Ada's comforting hands slide around my shoulders. I think she wants her turn to hug our son, so I move away.

"Mike had a good idea earlier," Mitya says with urgency. "Go to the lab to rejoin Joe. Once there, try to barricade yourselves in. The robots will arrive in about twenty minutes, so hopefully you can hold out until then. Dominic should be there around the same time."

I can tell Muhomor wants to say something, but he sees my expression and holds his tongue. Besides, I know what he's about to say because I'm thinking the same thing: what kind of a barricade can withstand such an overwhelming force?

"We're going," I say nonetheless. "Ada, Alan, can you guys move?"

Ada's chin is still quivering, but she nods.

"Think you can look after Alan?" I ask. "My hands will be full."

"Of course," she says. "I'll carry him."

"I can walk," Alan says in a barely audible whisper. "I'm too heavy for you."

"You only weigh thirty-five pounds," she says, her voice already steadier. "If the lab isn't far, I can carry you."

"No, seriously." Alan's voice sounds healthier, and I wonder if Ada's using her mom reverse-psychology Jedi mind tricks on him. "I can walk."

"While we move, I have a task for you two," I tell Mitya and Muhomor.

"A diversion?" Mitya asks.

"A very specific one," I say. "You now have the back-door into the Brainocytes of the entire human population."

Muhomor's eyes light up—he sees where my mind is going. "Including the assholes at your location."

"Exactly," I say. "I want to get inside the heads of all the guards in this place and—"

"We don't have their Brainocyte IDs," Mitya interrupts.

"We don't need them if we create a proximity-based virus," Muhomor says. I notice he's VR-magicked himself a new pair of sunglasses. "Mike here can be our ground zero. Anyone within a mile of him will get the Payload app, which will activate instantly thanks to the nature of the backdoor."

"I wish I had time to design a virtual hell to trap these fuckers in," Alan mutters through his teeth with unusual viciousness.

"Language," I say on autopilot. Ada rewards me with a small smile.

"So when I get there, I'll get this virus also?" Dominic asks worriedly. The idea of spending time in a virtual hell of Alan's creation doesn't seem to appeal to him, and I can't blame him.

"We'll obviously use a harmless app whose main purpose will be to distract its victim," I say. "Anyone besides Alan have an app in mind?"

"I do." Some mischief returns to Ada's amber eyes. "How about the Join app?"

"That'll certainly distract them." I put my hand on her shoulder and give it a reassuring squeeze.

"What app?" Mitya and Muhomor ask in unison.

"I never submitted it to source control," Ada says apologetically. "I'll send you the code now. You can figure it out from there."

Though Ada, Alan, and I don't leave VR, we refocus on the real world. My wife grabs my son (of course she won that argument), and I put Mr. Spock in my pocket. I tell Ada and Alan to wait in the back of the room, reload my Glock with the bullets I found in a clip inside Kostya's back pocket, and open the door.

The two guards in the corridor each get a bullet to the head before they can raise their weapons.

I return to the room, reload again, and grab Kostya by one leg so I can drag him.

"Stay behind me," I say in a telepathic message once I'm in the corridor again.

Ada nods in VR and follows with heavy footsteps.

"You're barely walking," Alan complains. "Put me down."

Ada ignores Alan's plea, and I debate taking the kid from her; she's tiny herself, and our son is heavy for her small frame. But before I can intervene, she relents and sets him on the floor. All signs of fear are gone from my son's face, and I suspect I was right earlier about Ada's mind tricks.

Dragging my half-brother behind me like a sack of potatoes, I continue down the corridor. Ada follows with Alan behind her. I step over the bodies of the dead guards, taking sadistic pleasure in Kostya's head banging against the floor as I drag him over the grisly obstacles.

When I reach the door to the lab, I make eye contact with Ada and put a finger to my lips. She nods gravely, kneels next to Alan, and hugs him protectively.

With a powerful kick, I take care of the lab door, and as soon as it swings in, I scan the space for targets. Two guards raise their guns in my direction while the white lab coat guys from earlier look on in horrified fascination.

I shoot the two guards without hesitation.

"Now." I address the rightmost lab coat guy, whose face is whiter than his clothes. "The person who tells me the Wi-Fi password gets to live."

The men glance at each other and begin shouting all at once, though the guy I singled out is the loudest.

Since I'm now recording every second of my life, I play back the cacophony of words and easily decouple the password. They've all given me the same string of digits and numbers. After a few moments of mental fumbling, I'm into the mansion's ultra-secure network.

I pass the log-in credentials to the VR room. "Go to town." I debate teasing Muhomor about being the one to get the password but decide to let him focus on the virus app.

It takes only a fraction of a moment to take control of the nearby cameras. Ada and Alan both look tense as they wait outside the room, but the good news is that I see no danger creeping up behind them.

"Another chance to live," I tell my captive audience. "Who has those nifty syringes that knock people out?"

Every hand goes up, and they pretty much all yell their version of, "Yes, me, pick me and kill the others."

"Inject yourselves with the syringes," I say. "Anyone not unconscious via the drug will be made permanently unconscious via a bullet to the head."

The lab coats must think there's a competitive component to this injection command, because they race to avoid being the last man standing.

I let go of Kostya and enter the room.

Methodically, I give each seemingly unconscious man a strong kick to the head. If anyone's injected themselves with something other than a knockout drug, they'll give themselves away by grunting in pain. No one makes a peep.

I guess they weren't faking. They'll have horrible headaches upon waking, but that's the least I could do as payback for their part in taking over my mind.

Returning to the doorway, I grab Kostya by the leg and drag him into the room.

"The room's clear," I tell Ada after another quick scan.

She walks in after me, and Alan follows her warily. They both pretend not to see the bodies of the dead guards, and I'm grateful for their charade.

I dump Kostya's limp body on one of the hospital beds nearest the door. Boris's unconscious form is taking up the bed on the opposite side, and Joe is lying on an adjacent bed.

"Joe," I say out loud. "Can you hear me?"

"We freed him from the mind control," Mitya tells me preemptively. "He must still be out, though."

I check the monitors hooked up to Joe and exhale in relief. His vitals are good—much better than Boris's arrhythmic heartbeat.

"I'm going to barricade the door we came through." I head back, looking for a piece of furniture that would best do the job. Through the lab's security camera, I spot Ada searching for heavy objects to place next to the other door.

Alan turns from my cousin, worry contorting his small face. "We have to summon an ambulance," he says in VR. "Uncle Joe needs urgent medical attention."

"A helicopter is flying in," Mitya says. "Should be there in twenty minutes or so."

"Make sure they—"

I don't hear what Alan says, because I spot a flurry of movement from the bed on Joe's right—a bed I assumed to be as empty as the other ones.

A skeletally thin figure is hiding under the sheet.

A female figure.

I begin turning back, gun already in my hand and the Battle Mode and aim assist apps ready. But by the time I make a quarter turn, the woman is holding my son like a human shield.

Through the camera in the back of the room, I see her emaciated hand press a small-caliber pistol to Alan's temple.

"Drop your gun, or I'll shoot the little bastard," she says in an eerily familiar voice. "Do it now."

CHAPTER THIRTY-SIX

"That voice reminds me of how everyone under control spoke," Mitya says, sounding horrified.

He's right. All the mind-control victims we heard spoke in that specific, high-pitched voice. And because they all happened to be male, their voices sounded falsetto—but it must be that this woman's vocal cords are the basis for that strange register.

Then I realize that even Kostya spoke in this way. Could my half-brother have been another victim? Has everyone been under her mind control all this time?

Still looking through the camera, I'm not surprised to recognize her face, though I still run the face recognition to confirm the bad news.

There's no denying it.

This is Masha.

"My literally crazy half-sister has Alan," I say to everyone, in case they haven't figured this out already. "I don't know what to do."

I push Battle Mode to its limits, but neither it nor my own experience with violence show me a way to disable Masha without Alan getting hurt.

I demonstratively drop my gun and stop turning.

"Turn toward me," Masha orders. "Slowly."

I complete my rotation, and she peeks over Alan's shoulder. I stare into those eyes—the eyes that remind me of what mine would look like if I hadn't slept for a year.

Through the camera, I see Ada grab the inert Kostya by the throat. "If you don't let go of my son, your brother is as good as dead," she threatens loudly.

I'm not sure Ada has enough strength to choke a grown man, plus I know how she feels about violence and murder. Then again, who knows what a mother, even one as peaceful as my wife, might do to save her child?

Masha's expression doesn't change. "You already killed poor Kostya," she says, and I realize her mind is damaged beyond repair. "I can't guide him anymore."

"*Guide him*," Muhomor says. "That's a nice euphemism. I don't need to be a shrink to confirm her diagnosis."

"I agree," Mitya says. "She just admitted she was controlling her brother. When Mike knocked him out, she saw it as a disconnect in her controller app—so she probably really believes he's dead."

"Masha," I say as soothingly as my nerves allow. "Kostya is just unconscious."

"I don't care what happens to Kostya." She shoves the gun harder against Alan's temple, making him wince. "He put me into Serbsky Asylum. He tried to take over my brain. I only suffered him to live to use his resources to get to you."

"She sounds convinced of what she's saying," Dominic says worriedly. "The brother leverage isn't going to work."

"Look, Masha." I apply all the power of my enhanced cognition to search for a way out of the situation. "You took Kostya over and made him do your bidding. He's suffered enough. So have we. Let's just stop this."

"Muhomor," I shout in VR. "I want you to unleash that distraction now."

"I'm still making sure the virus is safe for releasing into the wild," Muhomor replies. "Besides, I bet it won't affect her—she'll have closed that GPS backdoor into her Brainocytes as soon as she could."

"Alan is an innocent," Ada says in the real world, her hands leaving Kostya's neck. "And he's your family."

"He has your husband's tainted blood." Masha glares at me with pure hatred. "This is for my father," she adds— and blood leaves my face as her finger starts to squeeze the trigger.

CHAPTER THIRTY-SEVEN

As Masha's finger continues its deadly arc, her jaw muscles tighten and she leans away from her target, as though worried about the blood that will splatter her in a moment. My mind is sifting through an infinitude of flawed actions I can take, but none of them will save Alan or improve his chances.

Ada's eyes are wide with horror. She must also see the inevitability of Masha's actions.

A burst of motion explodes right behind Masha.

One moment, Joe was lying unconscious on the hospital bed; the next, he's on his feet wielding a scalpel. In a blur of violence, he slashes at Masha's gun hand. The scalpel goes through her fingers like a warm spoon through half-melted ice cream.

As the gun clanks to the floor, her scream turns into a dreadful gargling sound.

Joe just sliced her throat.

"Incoming," Dominic announces urgently in VR. "Has anyone been scanning through the cameras?"

I frantically consult the camera that monitors the lab's second exit and see five masked guards approaching.

I reach down to grab my gun and roll over the nearest table to hide us. Ada snatches a gun from one of the dead guards and throws it to Joe. He catches it, but I can tell he's weak. Dealing with Masha must've taken all the energy he had.

"Muhomor," I shout in VR. "Are you ready with the fucking distraction now?"

"I'm not sure if—"

"You told me you used something you made for the government as a basis," Mitya says. "Wasn't it safe to start with?"

"If it was, I wouldn't need to further secure it, would I?" Muhomor retorts. "Fine, fine, give me another minute."

"Ada, Alan—on the floor," I scream in every mode of communication I can access.

The door swings open, and the first Nixon-masked guy appears. Spotting Joe, he shoots. I shoot back at exactly the same time.

Joe is lucky Boris is in the bed next to him. The bullet meant for Joe hits Boris, and the asshole's heart monitor goes berserk.

Joe's shooter is down. Although I didn't even get a chance to aim, I got him smack in the brain. Joe shoots the second guard in the chest, and as soon as the man topples over, I put a bullet in the head of the guard behind him.

A bullet whooshes by my shoulder, and Joe fires two more times.

Two more bodies hit the floor, and the room goes quiet. The only audible thing is the equipment beeping about Boris's lack of heartbeat.

"Ten more in the corridor," Dominic reports in the VR room. "If you can hold out another ten minutes, I'll be there."

"So will the robots, and the cops after that," Mitya says.

"They won't survive long enough." Muhomor puts up a giant mosaic of camera views, most of them showing people with guns running toward the lab. "I want the record to show that I don't have a choice but to unleash the virus now."

"Just do it already," Dominic says.

All eyes in VR are on Muhomor, but his face grows thoughtful. "Just a few more seconds."

Dominic unleashes a growling sigh. "I just want to make sure I understand what's about to happen. Ada wrote a trippy app that cross-wires people's minds, and you're about to wrap it in a virus and use the GPS backdoor to force it into the minds of anyone within a mile of Mike?"

"That pretty much sums it up." Ada chews on her lip as she stares at a screen showing a huge crowd of guards moving ever closer.

"What I don't get is why that app?" Dominic asks. I suspect he's trying to keep Ada from panicking about the oncoming danger. "Why not take control of your attackers the way Kostya did?"

"Even if that weren't an ethical abomination," Mitya says, "we simply don't have an app for that." He looks at Muhomor, his eyes narrowing.

If any one of us had an app like that, it would be Muhomor.

"I don't have anything of the sort," Muhomor says, looking offended.

"But surely there are better distraction apps that are possible?" Dominic asks.

"I doubt it," Ada says. "Besides, I'm hoping that seeing through our eyes and experiencing our memories, hopes, and fears will turn some of these men away from violence against us. It's hard to harm people you get to know so intimately."

"She has a point," I say, thinking back to our Joining. "Though this is all academic, because we're about to die. I don't have enough bullets for the next wave of guards."

"Fine, just shut up already," Muhomor says.

An icon shows up in my AROS interface in that eerie way Kostya and Masha placed them there before.

"Alan, Joe," I whisper as the app launches. "Prepare for a wild ride."

CHAPTER THIRTY-EIGHT

Just like the previous time, the Join app puts all my senses into a blender and presses the "Crush Ice" button. The intensity is much greater than my Joining with Ada, which makes sense since I'm sensing through multiples of sensory organs. The exact number of people now participating is hard to discern; it's an ever-growing target. Each of the people I'm linked with are experiencing the same thing I am, and that creates a downward spiral of cross sensations until we all begin to lose ourselves in this experience.

There's a duality to my consciousness in this sensory Armageddon. The boundaries between me and countless people disappear, yet I still feel that I'm my individual self.

A part of me can still see what's happening in the cameras. The men in the view are ripping off their Richard Nixon masks in confusion. Their guns are on the floor, and they're staring around and sniffing the air as if they're experiencing the world for the very first time—which isn't unlike how I feel as well. The thoughts of the guards seep into my mind and vice versa, and I realize this experience is infinitely more intense for them because they aren't comfortable being in many places at once, unlike Tier 1 minds like me.

I feel vividly alive and completely immersed in the present moment. Freedom and contentment spread through our Joined minds.

"Well, I've never seen a better distraction," Mitya says from someplace. "I'm jealous I'm not running this app myself."

Mitya's words pull me out of the experience enough to realize that something is going awry. I'm seeing the world from the eyes of a helicopter pilot—a pilot who's lucky he put his flying vehicle under Einstein's control today.

"Shit," Muhomor says from the same distant place where I heard Mitya. "The news helicopter got there too soon. They're going to spread the virus outside the necessary range. You guys didn't give me time to put the proper precautions in place."

"I thought your virus only worked up to a mile away from Mike." Mitya's voice rises.

"Not from Mike—the nearest virus carrier," Muhomor says irritably. "The helicopter's only about seven hundred feet above them, well within the fucking range."

Looking out through the helicopter pilot's eyes, I can see he's well trained. As soon as his trippy experience begins, he notifies Einstein. The AI sensibly sends the aircraft back to the base.

"Shit," Muhomor yells. "We need to stop that helicopter."

"On it," Mitya says.

"You're too fucking slow." Muhomor sounds like he's gritting his teeth.

"Why couldn't you do it yourself?" Mitya snaps back.

"Because I'm trying to think of a way out of this mess," Muhomor replies, and they glare at each other.

"How fast does this virus spread?" Mitya asks after a moment.

"With the speed of electromagnetic waves, plus however long it takes to make a copy of itself—so very, very fast," Muhomor says, his voice subdued. "It's too late to stop the helicopter now."

He's right. A huge number of new people Join us, some driving, some flying in a plane.

"You realize what this means?" Mitya sounds awestruck.

"Yes, I do. It means you guys shouldn't have rushed me," Muhomor says. "I was working on safety procedures but—"

"You said you based the virus on the work you did for the government." Mitya's voice rises again. "What was the basis, Stuxnet?"

Stuxnet is the old cyberweapon allegedly created by the US and Israel to sabotage Iran's nuclear program. The thing got aggressive and spread indiscriminately worldwide instead of staying in Iran.

"The basis for my virus is none of your concern," Muhomor retorts. "I'm going to have to work on a countermeasure right now."

"Make sure your countermeasure stops the Join app, deletes any sign of your virus, and closes the GPS backdoor forever," Mitya says sternly.

"Don't teach an expert or you'll eat baked shit." The Russian proverb sounds ridiculous in Zik.

I don't follow the rest of my friends' conversation because in that moment, the Join virus reaches the town of Kingston. Suddenly, we're not just six hundred people but over twenty thousand.

Our former opponents are now on the floor, the overwhelming flood of sensations putting them into a near-comatose state.

"I'm looking at this code," Mitya says from far away. "They're only in the first phase of the app, the initialization. Once everyone's merged, their memories are exchanged and the other phases begin. I think you'd better finish your cure virus before that happens."

"How does it know when the initialization is complete?" Muhomor asks. "I mean, they're gaining more people as we speak."

"When there's no new participants for a few seconds," Mitya says.

"I guess there's an unseen benefit to how quickly it's spreading," Muhomor says. "They won't reach a new phase for a while."

The virus reaches Woodstock, and another five thousand people join the sensory roller coaster. Joe slumps back on his hospital bed. His Tier II Brainocytes can't cope with all that data and keep him upright at the same time.

Roxbury and Saugerties are next, and another twenty thousand people's senses are thrown into the mix. Now Ada, Alan, and I collapse on the floor. Dealing with this much sensory data is too much even for us.

"I better take over the antivirus task," Mitya says from even farther away.

"Why?" Muhomor asks, but he sounds scared. I think he knows what Mitya is about to say.

"Because the virus is spreading almost instantly, and as the radius of the infected area increases, so will the rate of newly infected people," Mitya says. "All of New York state is a moment away from being affected, and New Jersey will follow a moment later. You're not over a mile underground, which means you and everyone in your bunker are about to be victims of your own stupid virus."

"But you suck at this!" Muhomor shouts. "It will take you so much longer—"

If I were a Jedi, I would call what happens next "a great disturbance in the Force." My best guess is that this is what having millions of people Joined together must feel like.

It's hard to form an intelligible thought, but I still manage to guess that, as Mitya said, all of New York and New Jersey are now Joined with us. If correct, that means eighteen million Brainocyte users in the Empire State and seven million in the Garden State just Joined together—an unfathomable number of people.

If it were possible to die from data overload, I'd now be a corpse.

The lab around me completely goes away, replaced with the Join app universe. It's as though I'm sitting on the bottom of an ocean of sights, smells, tastes, odors, and kinesthetic sensations.

Another, bigger disturbance follows as three hundred million American Brainocyte users are infected. Canada and Mexico are next.

Though it's difficult to think, I observe that it's easy for the virus to spread from North America to South America. The spread to Europe is trickier to puzzle out, because the distance between Russia and Alaska is a little short of three thousand miles, while the virus has a mile-long spread. Then again, there are the Diomede Islands between the continents; those people have Brainocytes. Considering submarines in the oceans and aircraft in the skies, it's reasonable to fear that the virus is already on its way to Russia, with the rest of Europe and Asia to follow. From there, it will travel to Africa and who knows where else after that.

When you're experiencing so many points of view, time becomes one of those concepts that has no meaning anymore. It could be that a second just passed, but it just as easily could have been many hours. It's impossible to discern. To preserve my sanity, I try to ignore all senses but vision; we humans are a visually oriented species.

A tsunami of sights rolls over the shores of my mind. I gaze at the spire of the Empire State Building from every conceivable angle and, at the same time, take in the stately White House from even more viewpoints. All the eyes I see through seem to be very low to the ground. These people have collapsed from sensory overload just as I have— their eyes, like cameras, continue to feed their brains the never-ending input of vision, now shared throughout the world.

The Golden Gate and Brooklyn Bridge crisscross the skies and blend with other bridges from millions of eyes. I get a chance to see through colorblind eyes, as well as nearsighted and farsighted ones. The red-orange colors of the Grand Canyon instantly change to the blues of Niagara Falls, and places I don't recognize flit through my mind like a kaleidoscope on steroids.

If I had any doubts about the potential scope of this virus, they're erased by the next wave of images. Christ the Redeemer spreads his arms over the green hills of Rio De Janeiro, followed by Florence, Cologne, and St. Basil's Cathedral. Stonehenge and the Colosseum, the Eiffel Tower and the Pyramids (both the ones in Egypt and the ones in Mexico) all explode in my mental view. The Taj Mahal and the Great Wall of China, Mount Fuji and Yellowstone National Park splash into my mind, followed by billions of things just as beautiful but whose names I'm too over-whelmed to recall.

The onslaught of visual data seems to be equally over-whelming to all of us around the world. As one, we close our eyes.

For a moment, it's as though the whole planet has gone dark. At the same time, closing our eyes does nothing to calm our other senses, so we're just as overwhelmed by odors as we were by sights, only there is no way to close off these perceptions.

After forever, I find that I no longer feel other peo-ple's senses. The data blends into a paralyzing cacophony.

Thoughts become a distant memory, and memories an abstract concept.

A group in Asia has discovered a way for us all to cope better with these worldwide crisscrosses of senses. I recognize the solution with relief. These people were experienced meditators before the Joining began, and they are guiding the rest of the participants to ignore all sensation but one: the in and out of our breathing.

Slowly, breath awareness spreads through the Joining, and after a hundred years of subjective experience, we—a large bulk of humanity—begin to breathe at the same pace. The world becomes the in and out of air in our bodies.

Soon, we become simply the breath. I almost don't recall what it is to be me. I'm a single ant in a colony of ants—no, even less than that. I'm more like a single, lonely byte of data in a multi-terabyte hard drive.

After another eternity of breath awareness, my mind is clear enough to think again. No new people have been added to the Joining for a while, which means the next phase of Ada's app is going to kick in at any moment: the part where each participant becomes aware of others' memories.

As though my thought has been made manifest, the memories of billions of people slam into every one of our Brainocyte-enhanced brains like an ice asteroid crashing into a searing desert planet.

I think I lose consciousness for a few years, though I might be experiencing one of Dominic's memories. There was a time in his life when he was completely cut off from the world.

Memories bombard me. One moment I'm Alan, playing with his friends, the rats. The next moment I'm Joe, pummeling a school bully and intentionally trying to break the kid's nose.

Memories of joy and memories of sorrow barrage me with unspeakable intensity. I try to cling to something familiar, like recollections of the best VR flicks, or the billions of memories of riding in a self-driving car for the first time, or the varying reactions to the realization that electricity is not something you need to treat as a scarce resource anymore.

With each memory, I become that person for that moment. I am an architect in Germany working on our next design and reminiscing about a middle-school adventure at the zoo. I'm a woman in France remembering how we felt when we nursed our first daughter.

The rate of memories speeds up.

I'm an elderly shepherd in the Caucasus Mountains, Gogi's homeland. I recall shepherding the old-school way, but I also marvel at the new method using Brainocytes and Augmented Reality, where our enhanced sheep avoid obstacles only they can see.

I'm a Russian woman who recalls joining the Pioneers in the Soviet days. Our mother ironed that little red scarf for us, and we were proud and excited. The memories clash with my own—I too was a Pioneer, though I saw it for the commie propaganda that it was and couldn't have cared less about the dubious honor.

I'm a man in Rwanda who remembers the horror of hunger and is grateful that our son has never been hungry, thanks to free electricity and other technological marvels.

I'm a software engineer in India, reminiscing about the awe we felt when we first used Brainocytes to search the web with our mind.

The memories stream into my mind like a waterfall, and soon I'm only seeing patterns: millions of people getting married, smiling at loved ones, holding hands, eating comfort foods, and on and on.

Interspersed with our memories are the tiniest moments of clarity—moments when the interconnected humanity realizes something together. When I Joined with Ada, this is when we understood and forgave each other every grievance we'd ever had in our marriage. Such a feat is too difficult to accomplish on this global scale, but we do feel as one for many moments, and we jointly realize how much every human being has in common, especially when it comes to the inner world of our minds—the only reality that truly matters.

The moments of clarity start to get longer, and that sense of enlightenment I felt when I Joined with Ada comes back a billion times stronger. I feel part of something unimaginably bigger than myself. There's a certainty in our minds that we're all intricately connected to something unfathomably complex. For a nanosecond, the entirety of humanity experiences what it's like to be in Heaven, or Nirvana, or Shangri-La, or Zion, or Utopia, or fill in the name of a place of ultimate contentment, spiritual and psychological fulfillment, and pure joy.

The pleasant sensations give way to fears. We realize just how vulnerable we are. We have weapons that can kill us all in a blink, and despite the new abundance of energy, we still have habits that could turn Earth into a human-unfriendly hellhole. These fears turn into a determination to do something about these problems, and that leads us back to feelings of connectedness and hope.

A subjective century later, the whirlwind of memories and enlightenments subsides enough that I have an independent thought, and I recall this is when The Cohens made an appearance when Ada and I first Joined. Could Ada's self-organization code really take advantage of so many brain resources? In terms of hardware, it could. She uses each user's own allocation on our servers, outside their biological and virtual brains, so no extra server space or CPU is necessary.

Ada also mentioned she leveraged Einstein as part of the app. Would he have enough processing cycles? Mitya once claimed that a Brainocyte-enhanced brain at Tier III can perform two quintillion computations per second. Quintillion is ten to the eighteenth power, a number that's difficult to comprehend even at a Tier I brain boost. That means this worldwide version of The Cohens would achieve a few billion quintillion computations per second.

In theory, Einstein should be able to cope with that. He usually has enough processing cycles to assist every single Brainocyte user anyway, and since we're all lying on the ground not doing much, the AI should currently be idle and ready to assist.

Sure enough, the feeling I had with Ada returns many billionfold stronger.

"We think, therefore we are," we jointly contemplate with the intensity of an earthquake.

"You're still a philosopher," I mentally say after I recover my wits. "But I guess it's not appropriate to call you The Cohens anymore."

"That being was but a shadow of me," the humanity thinks back. This time, the force of the reply almost makes me lose consciousness. "If I had to name myself, I think Gaia or Earth might be more apropos."

"Gaia," I think back, after I overcome the sense that I'm not worthy to speak to a creature so terrifyingly vast. I have a million questions vying for the honor of being asked first, but I go with my first intuition. "What is it like to be you?"

"What is it like to be anything? The simplest answer is the analogy already in your mind, the one where you compare yourself to a neuron and us to a fully functioning brain," Gaia mentally booms.

This time, the force of the answer does make me black out.

CHAPTER THIRTY-NINE

I float in a darkness of complete sensory deprivation, eager to awaken so I can resume conversing with Gaia.

A familiar voice pierces the darkness. "Mike, this is Mitya. I've finally worked out a way to stop everyone's Join app and patch up Kostya's backdoor. You and your family will be the first to receive the fix."

"Wait," I want to shout. "I have more questions for Gaia."

I'm not sure if Mitya hears my plea or not, but I find myself thrust back into my physical body.

It takes a few hours to reorient myself. When I do, I'm still lying in a fetal position on the floor of the lab. Now that I'm disconnected from the worldwide Joining, I'm filled with utter despair for its loss. All I want is to reconnect or cry myself to sleep.

"Mom, Dad," Alan whispers in a haggard voice. "Are you alive?"

"I'm here, sweetie," Ada says from the middle of the room. "Let me recover a moment, and I'll crawl your way."

"I'm alive too," I reply. It takes all my focus to make sure my voice doesn't break as I talk. "Not sure if I can crawl yet."

"Can we talk in VR while we recover?" Alan suggests.

I'm flooded with relief at Alan's amazing resilience. The kid already sounds like his usual self. I wish I could say the same about me.

With a huge effort of will, I recall how to put myself into the VR conference room and appear there. The light from the windows makes me narrow my eyes, and Mitya's smiling face makes me jealous. He wasn't part of the Joining, and there's no way he can understand how I feel. Especially since I'm not perfectly clear on that myself.

"You should've given the world a few more minutes of Joining," Ada says as soon as she appears. "Maybe even a couple of days."

"Right," Mitya says sarcastically. "I should've watched the human population die of thirst and hunger. Great idea."

"You don't understand what it was like," Alan says from behind me. I didn't even notice him appear.

"I know that the world is a mess," Mitya counters. "Thousands got hurt, and there are many casualties."

The idea that fellow beings might be in pain overwhelms me with an unusual surge of empathy. I sink into an office chair before I succumb to the fetal position here in VR as well as in the real world.

Muhomor shows up, his eyes wider than dollar coins. "I'm a genius! My virus did that. I should get the Nobel—"

Mitya places a hand on his shoulder. "Your virus is also the reason we need to undertake an enormous restoration project."

Using every screen as well as the table surface, Mitya shows us the problem. Though most vehicles are self-driving nowadays, plenty still work the old way, with humans in control. Additionally, countless bicyclists, skateboarders, bikers, and rollerblade riders crashed into things or fell when the Joining first began.

"Transport is only one of many issues," Mitya says as he puts up more imagery. "Surgeons were midsurgery, countless folks were swimming, or fixing roofs, or—"

"That is so awful," Alan says in a barely audible whisper. "Are you sure people died?"

"Logic would dictate so, unfortunately." Mitya closes his eyes for a moment. "It could be that some instinctive part of them retained enough mental capacity to float on water or not kill a patient, but as you can see"—he shows another slew of images of people in trouble—"there are plenty of problems to solve."

"What about the men who tried to kill us?" Ada asks. "I doubt they would want to continue their folly or even be ready to continue if they did, but you never know what—"

"I had them tied up as soon as the robots arrived at your location," Mitya says. "They'll have to wait for the police to take care of them, and the police will be busy for a while. Now if you don't mind, I'll have those same robots carry you to the hospital, just as I'll use the rest of our robots worldwide to try to get things back in order."

Everyone agrees to let Mitya handle things while we recover. Before long, I find myself in the metallic arms of one of the more sophisticated robot models. The same thing happens to Alan, Ada, and Joe, although it takes two robots to carry Dominic. He was almost at his destination when the Joining took him over with the rest of us.

During the trip to the hospital, the yearning for Joining dissipates, and I offer my services to Mitya since I can also control a small army of robots. By the time we get to the Kingston hospital, I've learned that some people are easier to rouse to action than others. Luckily, doctors and other emergency personnel tend to be in the easy-to-wake group.

"You need to get moving," Mitya says through the metallic voice of a robot that's kneeling next to a man wearing scrubs. "We have people who need help."

Just as we've seen elsewhere, it takes only a couple of prompts before the man gets up.

Once there are enough self-aware doctors here at Kingston, I get them to check over Alan, Dominic, Ada, and me. After a bunch of stitches for me, we all get the green light, except Joe, who needs jaw surgery and some bones set.

"I don't foresee any complications," says Dr. Jarvis, whom Mitya flew out in a helicopter. "Your cousin might have trouble talking for a few days, but that's about the only concern I have."

I convince Dr. Jarvis to stay in the surgery room as our representative. If it's unusual, the hospital staff are too dazed to object.

I keep myself busy as I wait for Joe to come out of surgery. Every thread that I spawn grabs a robot and tries to help someone still in trouble. I soon learn that most Human++ employees are doing the same thing I am, and by the time we run out of robots, plenty of people have recovered enough to help physically.

In another half hour, the media recuperates too, and the news begins blaring all over the world.

"We don't know much about what just happened," says a blond newscaster from the ancient TV in the dingy waiting room. "Here at the studio, we're calling the event the Joining. Here are some theories about—"

I ignore the rest, though it's amusing to hear some of the crazy ideas, the least fantastic of which has something to do with alien visitors.

Using AROS, I check better news sources on the web and find that not every reporter is as clueless as the blonde on TV. Some are covering what's most important: that worldwide recovery is underway and people should pitch in. Some are providing useful instructions, while others are reflecting that this restoration project is as unprecedented as the Joining that precipitated it.

I agree. It's heartwarming to see people, sometimes via robots, come together to help each other literally get back on their feet.

"You can see your cousin now," the surgeon says. His face is haggard, and I'm amazed the man could perform something as complex as a surgery so soon after the Joining. "The procedure was a success."

Dr. Jarvis gives me the thumbs-up over the man's shoulder, and I listen to the surgeon's instructions on how, when, and where I'll next see my cousin. Ada, Alan, and I make our way to the recovery room and watch as they wheel Joe in and hook him up to the monitoring equipment.

"He should be up shortly," Dr. Jarvis says, walking toward the door. "I'll go make sure he has a competent nurse to look after him when I leave."

We patiently wait until Joe opens his eyes, which takes what feels like two hours. Finally, his eyes blink blue, and when he sees us all standing there, I see something new in his gaze. It's not exactly warmth, but it's as close as Joe's probably capable of.

"It wasn't me in that room," he telepathically tells me in Zik, the message heavy with dark emotions. "I couldn't get control back. I tried."

"Don't even think about that," I say. "Masha almost made me kill my family, and I couldn't wrest control back either. It wasn't a matter of strength of will. The technology affected your brain directly."

"There are more people here to visit him," a pretty nurse says as she enters. "You'll have to give them space."

Reluctantly, Ada, Alan, and I turn toward the door, but when I see who the visitors are, I'm stunned.

"Mom! Uncle Abe! And what is *she* doing here?" I point at Tatum.

"Why wouldn't Joe's girlfriend visit him at the hospital?" Mom asks, her forehead furrowing.

"She's not his—" I recall the lie we told Mom earlier and cringe, adding, "Never mind."

Mom, Uncle Abe, and most surprisingly Tatum look at my cousin with worry.

"He's fine," I reassure them. "He probably just needs lots of rest."

At the mention of "rest," the full weight of the post-adrenaline slump hits me like a freight train, and I yawn, loudly.

"You need rest as well," Mom says, her eyes narrowing. "But once you've rested, we're going to have words."

"Great," I mumble under my breath as I make my way to my chosen hospital bed. "Now I won't hear the end of it for at least a year."

"I'm going to take a quick nap too." Ada follows me and gets into the bed next to mine. "You and I are going to spend a week in the Bedroom once I wake up."

"I'll hold down the fort while the old people relax," Alan says, his eyes crinkling with mirth. "But I do suggest you learn those sleep tricks Mitya's researching after the dust settles."

"You're not quitting sleep until you're eighteen," Ada says as she pulls the hospital blanket to her chin. "Not unless you conduct statistically sound research to prove the safety of said tricks."

"Which he will do by the end of the month, I bet." I pull my own blanket up. It's fuzzy and smells like antiseptic. "Now if you'll excuse me, I'm long overdue to pass out."

Ada and Alan chuckle, but it sounds far, far away because true to my word, I instantly drift off to dreamless slumber.

EPILOGUE

"Happy birthday, Alan," Uncle Abe announces in Zik and raises his shot glass.

"Five years old." Mom clinks her vodka glass with her brother's. "He's becoming such a charming young man."

I raise my own glass and look over the enormous picnic table in the middle of Central Park. Everyone from Human++ is in attendance, as well as their families, all of Alan's online friends, and many acquaintances. Even the mayor is here with his whole retinue, and a couple of other politicians I hoped to avoid.

"I propose a toast." Gogi ceremoniously holds up a shot glass, the scar I gave him barely noticeable on his hand. "Once upon a time, in a village high up in the Georgian mountains, there lived a strange rat—"

"I think this toast panders to you," I privately tell Mr. Spock as I add more walnuts to the tiny tea saucer that serves as his plate. "I believe it traditionally involves an eagle."

"Eagles are scary." He moves his whiskers worriedly back and forth.

"Don't worry, bud. I made sure there are no birds of prey here in the park. If one tried to get you, our security people would scare it off."

Mr. Spock resumes his meal, and I half listen to Gogi as I survey everyone around the table. My eyes settle on Kostya, my half-brother, who's sitting with the family some eight feet away.

After last year's events, we eventually let Kostya return to Russia—but not before Joe got the whole story from him using a custom version of the Join app. As Joe's investigation revealed, Kostya developed the Control app to get his sister out of the asylum, not for revenge against me.

However, his research and development team did discover the GPS backdoor in a project for the Russian government—SVR connections Kostya met through his father. This backdoor work was separate at first from that of the Control app, but just when the GPS backdoor information was in its final stages, Masha took over everything. The handoff of the GPS backdoor to the SVR never happened. In hindsight, I guess the only positive development from that whole nightmare was that the SVR didn't get a monopoly on such a powerful weapon.

As to how Masha took over, from what Kostya could puzzle out, she seduced one of the scientists, an expert on Brainocyte IDs, and took over his mind as part of some bondage game. She used that opportunity to make the man do her bidding, and things went downhill from there.

Kostya sees me gaze his way and salutes me with his shot glass, his face unreadable. He looks pretty good, given all he's been through, but I know he spent most of the past year in therapy. And it's no wonder. I was in his shoes for mere minutes, and I still have horrific flashbacks. To my relief, he's never once raised the question of his sister's fate with me. He must mourn her, despite all she'd done, and if I'm honest, even I sometimes wish Joe hadn't had to kill her. She wasn't evil; she suffered from a psychosis that she channeled into misguided revenge.

The thought of my cousin makes me look across the table. Joe isn't drinking his vodka—he just brings it to his lips for a moment, then places the shot glass back and gives Gogi a dirty look. Joe takes his job as Head of Security seriously. He refuses to get intoxicated on duty and doesn't like Gogi to drink either, even though Gogi officially retired a few months ago. Joe looks from Gogi to me, and the dirty look turns into a frown. I guess he's still mad about the choice of venue. As he put it, Central Park is a "security clusterfuck."

To Joe's left, Tatum downs her shot and cringes like all the non-Russian guests. This is her first official family event, and so far, I'm impressed with her poise. That she didn't press charges against us a year ago wasn't so surprising; the Joining had that sort of effect on a lot of people. What was surprising (and maybe even shocking) is that she didn't run away screaming after visiting Joe at the hospital after his surgery. Instead, she was there for him during his recovery, and now there's some sort of strange relationship between the two. Einstein and I think she shows signs of Stockholm syndrome, but I don't bring this up with my cousin. Joe seems happy in his own creepy way, and that's good enough for me.

"Is it time for gifts now?" Alan asks after everyone's shot glass is finally on the table. "You know I don't like suspense."

Everyone laughs, and Ada stands up and says, "May the gift giving begin."

There's a quick tussle as to who goes first, and as people often do these days, we let Einstein decide. The AI creates a list, and I can't help but notice that some of the honorary guests, mostly politicians, get to go first—very Machiavellian on Einstein's part.

"I'm happy to announce that we named a street after you," the mayor tells Alan. "It's in the south part of Queens. We named it Cohen Street."

Alan accepts the gift graciously, but I suspect he couldn't care less about this honor. I'm impressed, however. Given that the mayor is letting us use this park as a birthday venue, I didn't think he'd bother with more gifts. I make a mental note to support his campaign at reelection—probably the reason he's here in the first place and why the gift he gave Alan is as much an honor to Ada and me.

Politicians have a nuanced relationship with us. After Joining Day, most countries blamed Muhomor's virus on each other, especially the United States and Russia. The reason was simple: Muhomor had created cyberweapons for both nations, making his work difficult to attribute to any one player. But when Human++ took responsibility for the Join app without taking responsibility for the virus that spread the app, the governments put two and two together. Instead of prosecuting us, they made the wise decision to seek our favor instead.

"Wow, a trip on a spaceship?" Alan's voice brims with excitement as he puts down the ancient-looking gizmo that JC just handed him. "You're the best grandpa ever."

Ada and I exchange glances. We both know that if the kid finally called JC his grandpa, he must be beyond himself with joy.

"It's from the both of us." JC clasps Mom's hand.

He isn't fooling anyone. Mom wouldn't dream of getting her grandson such a dangerous gift, and I marvel at the effort it must've taken JC to convince her to allow this. I also wonder if he overspent. Then I decide that as a major shareholder in Human++, he can afford it.

After our admission that the Joining app is ours, some thought Human++ would finally suffer financial ruin. In contrast, even after funding restoration costs and compensating the victims and their families, our company is enjoying the largest profits since its inception. As tales of the Joining spread to the distant corners of the globe, Brainocyte adoption rates have soared beyond our wildest dreams. Most people who didn't have them now do, even members of Real Humans Only. Not having Brainocytes today is what not having internet access was a few years ago; some people choose to avoid it, but they're an ever-shrinking minority.

"Thanks, Grandma," Alan says earnestly and runs up to hug Mom.

As usual, when those skinny arms wrap around her, Mom melts into a puddle of oxytocin. I love to see such a joyful expression on her face. It's a pleasant change after all the months she grumbled at me about the risks I undertook on Joining Day. Even though she was part of the Joining, it provided no advantage at all when it came to quelling her ire afterward. I'd say it took at least a week for her to begin to forgive me for almost getting myself killed again, then another two weeks until she let go of the fact that I hadn't told her a single thing before going to Ada and Alan's rescue.

"A house in the Hamptons?" Alan's expression is unreadable when Muhomor finally presents his gift. "Thanks."

Ada and I pretend surprise, though in reality, we precleared Muhomor's gift this year. This house was the only acceptable thing our hacker friend could come up with. I'm not sure about Alan, but I like the idea of a house with an ocean view. It reminds me of the Miami condo we stayed in while we were rebuilding the penthouse, which is only now beginning to feel like home again.

The gift giving takes an hour. Once it's done, the party changes from a Russian-style sit-at-the-table affair to an American cocktail party, with guests mingling at an open bar spanning the whole park—which is as expensive as it sounds.

I waltz up to a large group of Alan's online friends and smile at the two I recognize from last year, John the professor and Margret the computer scientist. Unsurprisingly, the Joining is the topic of this group's conversation. It's really all anyone has talked about for the past year.

"Gaia allowed me to glimpse something the philosophers of old would've sold their souls for," John says, his voice all but shaking with conviction. "I can't believe your negativity."

Looking much calmer, Margret sips her martini and says, "I just fear what would've happened if Gaia had existed for a few seconds longer. I'm not saying we'd all be like the Borg, but we ought to think twice before—"

I carefully make my escape before someone pulls me into this discussion. The nature of Gaia has been a topic of unending debate and obsession. People have compiled a whole database of wisdom Gaia reportedly conveyed during the Joining, and volumes have been written trying to analyze and make sense of it all.

We in the Brainocytes Club decided to play it safe going forward. All future versions of the Join app have had that hivemind component removed. It's impossible to grasp the motives of such a being as Gaia, yet all too easy to envision losing control. We used the same logic here as when we considered building an AI smarter than us. Mitya summarized our attitude well when he said, "I'd rather we ourselves become vast intelligences over time. Building one just because we can or by accident, as with Gaia, is too risky."

"Mr. Cohen," says a male voice as I'm walking back to Alan. "If I could have a word."

It's the mayor, so I smile and say, "Sir, it's an honor. What would you like to talk about?"

"The honor is mine," he says pompously. "And this has nothing to do with my official role. I'm just here as a Brainocyte user—"

"You want to know when you can try the Join app again?" I make a mental note to use Battle Mode the next time I want to avoid politicians.

He looks scared for a second, and I wonder if he's one of those crazy conspiracy theorists who thinks Human++ would bother reading the thoughts of Brainocyte users. But curiosity seems to win out, and he nods. "That's exactly what I was going to ask."

"This stays between us," I whisper. I lean so close I can smell the vodka on the guy's breath. "I'm only telling you as a thank-you for letting us have the birthday here."

The man's eyes widen—I have his complete attention.

"The next update of AROS, the one that's slated for next month, will contain the Join app." I pull back and wink conspiratorially. "Of course, this version of the app will only allow you to send the Join request to the people in your contact list. Those people will have to accept the request before any Joining can begin."

"A bit like the videoconferencing?"

"Right." I sip my champagne. "This means that Joining Day cannot repeat itself again anytime soon—not unless someone has the whole world in their contact list."

I debate if I should tell him that we're capping that list at a million people and decide against it.

"So Joining Day definitely can't recur?" His disappointment is obvious.

"Not anytime soon." I give him a bland smile. "Even if you hypothetically had billions of friends, you'd have to convince them all to Join on the same day and time with you."

He nods. As a politician, he can appreciate the daunting nature of such a feat.

"It's not that we don't want Joining Day to repeat, per se. We just want to design a way to prevent such an event from becoming another worldwide disaster. That will take time."

"How long?"

"I can't say for sure." It's too much for him to know the truth: that another Joining Day must wait until every human on Earth has a mind that's mostly nonbiological. That would allow the Joining to happen in tandem with normal activity, as it now does for us Brainocyte Club members when we Join our small circle together.

"That's a shame," he says. "I worry that the citizens of Earth will begin to forget Joining Day and drift back to their old ways."

I know exactly what he means. After Joining Day, hundreds of conflicts ended in cease-fires, even in the most troubled zones in the world. Multiple peace treaties were born, as well as aggressive global nuclear disarmament initiatives. The US president suggested international accords to protect the environment, and the Russian president backed him up. To Ada's delight, many countries passed laws against capital punishment and took other steps showing that human life became more valued.

"I've made a hobby of collecting the things people credit to Joining Day," I tell the mayor. "And as an expert, I don't think all the positive effects are only due to that Joining experience, no matter how transcendental it felt. Some of the good things we saw might simply be thanks to Brainocytes making people so much smarter. In any case, not everything resulting from Joining Day was rosy. So many people died, and then there are all the new religions that sprouted in the aftermath. Nor is it clear to me if the overhaul of some of the older religions is a good thing."

"You might be right," the mayor says, his gaze growing distant for a second. Then he refocuses on me and says, "My people tell me you have the all-clear for the fireworks now. When will you start?"

I glance up at the dusky sky. "Let's wait until it gets even darker. Thanks for all your help."

"No problem. Sorry we had to put limits on the fireworks."

"I totally understand." The bubbly and the vodka have given me a buzz that spreads comfortably through my body. "We're going to enhance the real fireworks with a bunch of Augmented Reality ones, so Alan will still see the crazy display we had planned."

"I'm glad to hear that. I'll let you get back to your party."

I make my way through the crowds and locate Ada and Alan in a circle with Muhomor and Dominic, with Mitya in the middle.

"Hey, all," I say as I approach their comfortable meadow. "Is this an impromptu Brainocytes Club meeting?"

Muhomor raises a big bottle of vodka to his mouth and takes a generous gulp. "Just drunken musings."

I disable AR and still see Mitya's shimmering figure glowing blue in the dark. He's here as a hologram, something he does now when he wants to have a semi-physical presence.

"I was just asking Alan if he thinks we need to change the world some more," Mitya says in the slurred speech that means he's either clowning around or simulating intoxication inside his virtual body and brain. "I was in the middle of going over what we've accomplished already—things like enhanced brain capacity, Augmented and virtual reality, unimaginable new hardware, advances in robotics and AI... We even learned how to cheat death."

"Partial credit for that." Alan laughs and runs his hand through Mitya's holographic image. "At least in my opinion."

"I'd say my existence is superior to your meat-oriented one, birthday boy." Mitya floats up and lands on a branch of a nearby tree. "But what do you say, brother?"

A slightly taller version of Mitya's hologram appears where the original Mitya was just standing. This taller Mitya glows a shade of green.

We all stare.

Of course Mitya could already project multiple versions of himself using holograms, but I strongly suspect something else is happening. I don't share my suspicions with the others, because I'm sure Mitya wants to be the one to explain.

"Alan, I thought you might enjoy this announcement on your birthday," Mitya says triumphantly from the tree. "This is Dmitriy—the second me I hid from you to make him a surprise guest."

My guess was spot on. For the past year, Mitya has been using his new advantages, such as faster thought processing and less need for sleep, to escalate our hardware production to previously unseen levels. His efforts have resulted in more powerful chips and server types. He always claimed his work was aimed at supporting the new user base and bringing higher-tier brain boost capabilities to more people, but I knew there was more to it.

Now I see that I was right. He wanted to fulfill an idea we first discussed after his resurrection a year ago, and this taller version of him, this Dmitriy, is the result.

"Hello, Alan," Dmitriy says with a bow. "I am Mitya's superior copy, at your service. I'm smarter, handsomer, faster, and even taller than the original. I therefore propose my maker be called Mini-Me going forward."

"You didn't inherit a better sense of humor from the mini-you, but nice to meet you." Ada winks at the newcomer.

"The more Mityas we have, the merrier," Alan says. His eyes excitedly dart up to the blue hologram and then back down to the green version. "This day just got that much better."

"Just as long as you guys remember that you and your mini-you only get a single vote to share at the next Brainocytes Club meeting," Muhomor grumbles.

"I hope that's open for discussion." Mitya lands next to his other self. "Dmitriy is going to be as much a person as me in the eyes of the law, so—"

"I'm sorry if my appearance interrupted your earlier conversation," Dmitriy says. "You were just talking about your impact on the world. As it so happens, Mitya's motivation in creating me was to effect change in the world—more specifically, to kick-start an unprecedented hardware revolution."

Dmitriy pauses for dramatic effect, and it's clear he's superior to Mitya even in his ability to present an effective speech.

"We'd like to build the ultimate computer, given the laws of physics as we know them today—to cram as many computations as possible into a given piece of matter. We have some basic designs already, and once you review them, I think you'll agree that we can push the limits of nanocomputing very close to their ultimate physical limits. Scientists made molecule-sized transistors and storage back in the late twenty-teens, and over the past year, we made these practical. Our ambition is to build a two-pound, laptop-sized computer capable of ten to the forty-second power computations per second—and to do so within Alan's biological lifetime."

"Such a big number is hard for even our brains to fathom," Mitya says. "To provide some comparison, the laptop Dmitriy describes would be able to perform the equivalent of all human thought over the last ten thousand years in ten microseconds or so. Another way you can look at it is this: this laptop-sized device could be used to run the brains of a billion civilizations of beings such as the two of us—where a civilization is defined as ten billion of us."

"And that's just in a laptop-sized device," Dmitriy picks up. "There's no reason we can't build much bigger devices, even data centers. In the far future, we can cover the Earth with a computer substrate. Later still, it could fill the whole solar system—à la the matrioshka brain."

I try to imagine what we could do with the vast computers Mitya and Dmitriy have conjured up, but it hurts my alcohol-soaked biological brain.

"I now want this magic laptop as a birthday gift," Alan says, his voice filled with awe. "It would let me take world-building projects to the next level and create a whole multiverse of virtual univer—"

"A bunch of Rat Worlds, but for people?" Muhomor crinkles his nose in distaste. "I hope you're benevolent enough to randomly generate the denizens of these worlds. It would be very cruel to upload real people just to cast them into such a purgatory."

"I'm sure there are people who'd be glad to volunteer." Alan's eyes look distant—he's already lost in his fantasy. "The worlds could be thematically different, some optimized for educational value, some for pure entertainment. For myself, I'll make a world where sorcery is possible, and maybe a world where superpowers exist, and perhaps something with aliens or monsters—"

"And maybe a world with sexy vampires for your mom's birthday?" I say jokingly and get an elbow from Ada in my ribs. She thinks her reading preferences are a closely guarded secret, but Muhomor hacked her Amazon account long ago.

"I can make anything," Alan replies excitedly. "Even mash-ups, like a world with vampiric aliens or—"

"A very good argument could be made that we already live in a place akin to what Alan is envisioning." Ada rubs her temples with her fingers. She's only drinking wine this evening, but it doesn't take much to overwhelm her tiny frame. "If you think about it statistically, is a random person likelier to be one of the mere seven billion lucky people who live in the 'original and thus real' universe, or one of the billions of billions that can be easily emulated on the laptop Mitya will probably give Alan for some future birthday? The odds are not in our favor."

"Babe," I say to her privately, "my brain officially hurts. Is that a sign that it's a real brain or one emulated by an Alan of the future?"

"It's a sign that we should start the fireworks," she answers with a grin.

Out loud, she says in a raised voice, "If I can get everyone's attention on the sky."

Hundreds of faces turn up. Following their example, I gaze at the blackness just in time to catch the first colorful explosion, a spherical halo of blinking stars. The next explosion follows on the heels of the first, with comet-like tails chasing each of the sparks. The effects escalate with each subsequent round: a willow-tree-like gold stars beneath a plumage that reminds me of the Firebird, followed by visuals with such complex mathematical patterns that only a pyrotechnician with a brain boost could've designed them.

I suspect all of New York City is gaping at the sky at this point.

Alan's mouth opens wider and wider as the fireworks continue. Ada and I exchange knowing glances. This is just the real-world event. The crazy Augmented Reality fireworks to follow will make this seem like backyard firecrackers in comparison.

"I have to say something." I project my voice virtually as well as through my flesh-and-blood mouth here, next to my friends and family. When all eyes turn toward me, I raise my glass in a toast. "What an exciting time to be alive!"

Everyone cheers amidst the explosive blasts of the fireworks, and I knock back my drink as I Join with Ada, my joy intensifying as her hopes and dreams blend with my own.

We're together, we're alive, and the entire universe will soon be our home.

SNEAK PEEKS

Thank you for reading! If you would consider leaving a review, it would be greatly appreciated.

Neural Web concludes the *Human++* series, but more books of mine are coming soon. If you'd like to be notified when they're out, please sign up for my new release email list at www.dimazales.com.

Other series of mine include:
- *The Last Humans* — futuristic sci-fi/dystopian novels similar to *The Hunger Games*, *Divergent*, and *The Giver*
- *Mind Dimensions* — urban fantasy with a sci-fi flavor
- *The Sorcery Code* — epic fantasy

I also collaborate with my wife on sci-fi romance, so if you don't mind erotic material, you can check out *Close Liaisons*.

If you enjoy audiobooks, please visit my website to check out this series and our other books in audio format.

And now, please turn the page for a sneak peek at *Oasis (The Last Humans: Book 1)*, *The Thought Readers (Mind Dimensions: Book 1)*, and *The Sorcery Code*.

EXCERPT FROM *OASIS*

My name is Theo, and I'm a resident of Oasis, the last habitable area on Earth. It's meant to be a paradise, a place where we are all content. Vulgarity, violence, insanity, and other ills are but a distant memory, and even death no longer plagues us.

I was once content too, but now I'm different. Now I hear a voice in my head, and she tells me things no imaginary friend should know. Her name is Phoe, and she is my delusion.

Or is she?

Fuck. Vagina. Shit.

I pointedly think these forbidden words, but my neural scan shows nothing out of the ordinary compared to when I think phonetically similar words, such as *shuck, angina,* or *fit.* I don't see any evidence of my brain being corrupted, though maybe it's already so damaged that things can't get any worse. Maybe I need another test subject—another 'impressionable' twenty-three-year-old Youth such as my-self.

After all, I might be mentally ill.

"Oh, Theo. Not this again," says an overly friendly, high-pitched female voice. "Besides, the words do have an effect on your brain. For instance, the part of your brain responsible for disgust lights up at the mention of 'shit,' yet doesn't for 'fit.'"

This is Phoe speaking. This time, she's not a voice inside my head; instead, it's as though she's in the thick bushes be-hind me, except there's no one there.

I'm the only person on this strip of grass.

Nobody else comes here because the Edge is only a couple of feet away. Few residents of Oasis like looking at the dreary line dividing where our habitable world ends and the deserted wasteland of the Goo begins. I don't mind it, though.

Then again, I may be crazy—and Phoe would be the reason for that. You see, I don't think Phoe is real. She is, as far as my best guess goes, my imaginary friend. And her name, by the way, is pronounced 'Fee,' but is spelled 'P-h-o-e.'

Yes, that's how specific my delusion is.

"So you go from one overused topic straight into an-other." Phoe snorts. "My so-called realness."

"Right," I say. Though we're alone, I still answer with-out moving my lips. "Because I *am* imagining you."

She snorts again, and I shake my head. Yes, I just shook my head for the benefit of my delusion. I also feel compelled to respond to her.

"For the record," I say, "I'm sure the taboo word 'shit' affects the parts of my brain that deal with disgust just as much as its more acceptable cousins, such as 'fecal matter,' do. The point I was trying to make is that the word doesn't hurt or corrupt my brain. There's nothing special about these words."

"Yeah, yeah." This time, Phoe is inside my head, and she sounds mocking. "Next you'll tell me how back in the day, some of the forbidden words merely referred to things like female dogs, and how there are words in the dead languages that used to be just as taboo, yet they are not currently forbidden because they have lost their power. Then you're likely to complain that, though the brains of both genders are nearly identical, only males are not allowed to say 'vagina,' et cetera."

I realize I was about to counter with those exact thoughts, which means Phoe and I have talked about this quite a bit. This is what happens between close friends: they repeat conversations. Doubly so with imaginary friends, I figure. Though, of course, I'm probably the only person in Oasis who actually has one.

Come to think of it, wouldn't *every* conversation with your imaginary friend be redundant since you're basically talking to yourself?

"This is my cue to remind you that I'm real, Theo." Phoe purposefully states this out loud.

I can't help but notice that her voice came slightly from my right, as if she's just a friend sitting on the grass next to me—a friend who happens to be invisible.

"Just because I'm invisible doesn't mean I'm not real," Phoe responds to my thought. "At least *I'm* convinced that I'm real. I would be the crazy one if I *didn't* think I was real. Besides, a lot of evidence points to that conclusion, and you know it."

"But wouldn't an imaginary friend *have* to insist she's real?" I can't resist saying the words out loud. "Wouldn't this be part of the delusion?"

"Don't talk to me out loud," she reminds me, her tone worried. "Even when you subvocalize, sometimes you imperceptibly move your neck muscles or even your lips. All those things are too risky. You should just think your thoughts at me. Use your inner voice. It's safer that way, especially when we're around other Youths."

"Sure, but for the record, that makes me feel even nuttier," I reply, but I subvocalize my words, trying my best not to move my lips or neck muscles. Then, as an experiment, I think, "Talking to you inside my head just highlights the impossibility of you and thus makes me feel like I'm missing even more screws."

"Well, it shouldn't." Her voice is inside my head now, yet it still sounds high-pitched. "Back in the day, when it was not forbidden to be mentally ill, I imagine it made people around you uncomfortable if you spoke to your imaginary friends out loud." She chuckles, but there's more worry than humor in her voice. "I have no idea what would happen if someone thought you were crazy, but I have a bad feeling about it, so please don't do it, okay?"

"Fine," I think and pull at my left earlobe. "Though it's overkill to do it here. No one's around."

"Yes, but the nanobots I told you about, the ones that permeate everything from your head to the utility fog, *can* be used to monitor this place, at least in theory."

"Right. Unless all this conveniently invisible technology you keep telling me about is as much of a figment of my imagination as you are," I think at her. "In any case, since no one seems to know about this tech, how can they use it to spy on me?"

"Correction: no Youth knows, but the others might," Phoe counters patiently. "There's too much we still don't know about Adults, not to mention the Elderly."

"But if they can access the nanocytes in my mind, wouldn't they have access to my thoughts too?" I think, suppressing a shudder. If this is true, I'm utterly screwed.

"The fact that you haven't faced any consequences for your frequently wayward thoughts is evidence that no one monitors them in general, or at least, they're not bothering with yours specifically," she responds, her words easing my dread. "Therefore, I think monitoring thoughts is either computationally prohibitive or breaks one of the bazillion taboos on the proper use of technology—rules I have a very hard time keeping track of, by the way."

"Well, what if using tech to listen in on me is also taboo?" I retort, though she's beginning to convince me.

"It may be, but I've seen evidence that can best be explained as the Adults spying." Her voice in my head takes on a hushed tone. "Just think of the time you and Liam made plans to skip your Physics Lecture. How did they know about that?"

I think of the epic Quietude session we were sentenced to and how we both swore we hadn't betrayed each other. We reached the same conclusion: our speech is not secure. That's why Liam, Mason, and I now often speak in code.

"There could be other explanations," I think at Phoe. "That conversation happened during Lectures, and someone could've overheard us. But even if they hadn't, just because they monitor us during class doesn't mean they would bother monitoring this forsaken spot."

"Even if they don't monitor *this* place or anywhere outside of the Institute, I still want you to acquire the right habit."

"What if I speak in code?" I suggest. "You know, the one I use with my non-imaginary friends."

"You already speak too slowly for my liking," she thinks at me with clear exasperation. "When you speak in that code, you sound ridiculous and drastically increase the number of syllables you say. Now if you were willing to learn one of the dead languages…"

"Fine. I will 'think' when I have to speak to you," I think. Then I subvocalize, "But I will also subvocalize."

"If you must." She sighs out loud. "Just do it the way you did a second ago, without any voice musculature moving."

Instead of replying, I look at the Edge again, the place where the serene greenery under the Dome meets the repulsive ocean of the desolate Goo—the ever-replicating parasitic technology that converts matter into itself. The Goo is what's left of the world outside the Dome barrier, and if the barrier were to ever come down, the Goo would destroy us in short order. Naturally, this view evokes all sorts of unpleasant feelings, and the fact that I'm voluntarily gazing at it must be yet another sign of my shaky mental state.

"The thing *is* decidedly gross," Phoe reflects, trying to cheer me up, as usual. "It looks like someone tried to make Jell-O out of vomit and human excrement." Then, with a mental snicker, she adds, "Sorry, I should've said 'vomit and shit.'"

"I have no idea what Jell-O is," I subvocalize. "But whatever it is, you're probably spot on regarding the ingredients."

"Jell-O was something the ancients ate in the pre-Food days," Phoe explains. "I'll find something for you to watch or read about it, or if you're lucky, they might serve it at the upcoming Birth Day fair."

"I hope they do. It's hard to learn about food from books or movies," I complain. "I tried."

"In this case, you might," Phoe counters. "Jell-O was more about texture than taste. It had the consistency of jellyfish."

"People actually ate those slimy things back then?" I think in disgust. I can't recall seeing that in any of the movies. Waving toward the Goo, I say, "No wonder the world turned to this."

"They didn't eat it in most parts of the world," Phoe says, her voice taking on a pedantic tone. "And Jell-O was actually made out of partially decomposed proteins extracted from cow and pig hides, hooves, bones, and connective tissue."

"Now you're just trying to gross me out," I think.

"That's rich, coming from you, Mr. Shit." She chuckles. "Anyway, you have to leave this place."

"I do?"

"You have Lectures in half an hour, but more importantly, Mason is looking for you," she says, and her voice gives me the impression she's already gotten up from the grass.

I get up and start walking through the tall shrubbery that hides the Goo from the view of the rest of Oasis Youths.

"By the way"—Phoe's voice comes from the distance; she's simulating walking ahead of me—"once you verify that Mason *is* looking for you, *do* try to explain how an imaginary friend like me could possibly know something like that… something you yourself didn't know."

Oasis is currently available at most retailers. If you'd like to learn more, please visit www.dimazales.com.

EXCERPT FROM
THE THOUGHT READERS

Everyone thinks I'm a genius.

Everyone is wrong.

Sure, I finished Harvard at eighteen and now make crazy money at a hedge fund. But that's not because I'm unusually smart or hard-working.

It's because I cheat.

You see, I have a unique ability. I can go outside time into my own personal version of reality—the place I call "the Quiet"—where I can explore my surroundings while the rest of the world stands still.

I thought I was the only one who could do this—until I met *her*.

My name is Darren, and this is how I learned that I'm a Reader.

Sometimes I think I'm crazy. I'm sitting at a casino table in Atlantic City, and everyone around me is motionless. I call this the *Quiet*, as though giving it a name makes it seem more real—as though giving it a name changes the fact that all the players around me are frozen like statues, and I'm walking among them, looking at the cards they've been dealt.

The problem with the theory of my being crazy is that when I 'unfreeze' the world, as I just have, the cards the players turn over are the same ones I just saw in the Quiet. If I were crazy, wouldn't these cards be different? Unless I'm so far gone that I'm imagining the cards on the table, too.

But then I also win. If that's a delusion—if the pile of chips on my side of the table is a delusion—then I might as well question everything. Maybe my name isn't even Darren.

No. I can't think that way. If I'm really that confused, I don't want to snap out of it—because if I do, I'll probably wake up in a mental hospital.

Besides, I love my life, crazy and all.

My shrink thinks the Quiet is an inventive way I describe the 'inner workings of my genius.' Now that sounds crazy to me. She also might want me, but that's beside the point. Suffice it to say, she's as far as it gets from my datable age range, which is currently right around twenty-four. Still young, still hot, but done with school and pretty much beyond the clubbing phase. I hate clubbing, almost as much as I hated studying. In any case, my shrink's explanation doesn't work, as it doesn't account for the way I know things even a genius wouldn't know—like the exact value and suit of the other players' cards.

I watch as the dealer begins a new round. Besides me, there are three players at the table: Grandma, the Cowboy, and the Professional, as I call them. I feel that now almost imperceptible fear that accompanies the phasing. That's what I call the process: phasing into the Quiet. Worrying about my sanity has always facilitated phasing; fear seems helpful in this process.

I phase in, and everything gets quiet. Hence the name for this state.

It's eerie to me, even now. Outside the Quiet, this casino is very loud: drunk people talking, slot machines, ringing of wins, music—the only place louder is a club or a concert. And yet, right at this moment, I could probably hear a pin drop. It's like I've gone deaf to the chaos that surrounds me.

Having so many frozen people around adds to the strangeness of it all. Here is a waitress stopped mid-step, carrying a tray with drinks. There is a woman about to pull a slot machine lever. At my own table, the dealer's hand is raised, the last card he dealt hanging unnaturally in mid-air. I walk up to him from the side of the table and reach for it. It's a king, meant for the Professional. Once I let the card go, it falls on the table rather than continuing to float as before—but I know full well that it will be back in the air, in the exact position it was when I grabbed it, when I phase out.

The Professional looks like someone who makes money playing poker, or at least the way I always imagined someone like that might look. Scruffy, shades on, a little sketchy-looking. He's been doing an excellent job with the poker face—basically not twitching a single muscle throughout the game. His face is so expressionless that I wonder if he might've gotten Botox to help maintain such a stony countenance. His hand is on the table, protectively covering the cards dealt to him.

I move his limp hand away. It feels normal. Well, in a manner of speaking. The hand is sweaty and hairy, so moving it aside is unpleasant and is admittedly an abnormal thing to do. The normal part is that the hand is warm, rather than cold. When I was a kid, I expected people to feel cold in the Quiet, like stone statues.

With the Professional's hand moved away, I pick up his cards. Combined with the king that was hanging in the air, he has a nice high pair. Good to know.

I walk over to Grandma. She's already holding her cards, and she has fanned them nicely for me. I'm able to avoid touching her wrinkled, spotted hands. This is a relief, as I've recently become conflicted about touching people—or, more specifically, women—in the Quiet. If I had to, I would rationalize touching Grandma's hand as harmless, or at least not creepy, but it's better to avoid it if possible.

In any case, she has a low pair. I feel bad for her. She's been losing a lot tonight. Her chips are dwindling. Her losses are due, at least partially, to the fact that she has a terrible poker face. Even before looking at her cards, I knew they wouldn't be good because I could tell she was disappointed as soon as her hand was dealt. I also caught a gleeful gleam in her eyes a few rounds ago when she had a winning three of a kind.

This whole game of poker is, to a large degree, an exercise in reading people—something I really want to get better at. At my job, I've been told I'm great at reading people. I'm not, though; I'm just good at using the Quiet to make it seem like I am. I do want to learn how to read people for real, though. It would be nice to know what everyone is thinking.

What I don't care that much about in this poker game is money. I do well enough financially to not have to depend on hitting it big gambling. I don't care if I win or lose, though quintupling my money back at the blackjack table was fun. This whole trip has been more about going gambling because I finally can, being twenty-one and all. I was never into fake IDs, so this is an actual milestone for me.

Leaving Grandma alone, I move on to the next player—the Cowboy. I can't resist taking off his straw hat and trying it on. I wonder if it's possible for me to get lice this way. Since I've never been able to bring back any inanimate objects from the Quiet, nor otherwise affect the real world in any lasting way, I figure I won't be able to get any living critters to come back with me, either.

Dropping the hat, I look at his cards. He has a pair of aces—a better hand than the Professional. Maybe the Cowboy is a professional, too. He has a good poker face, as far as I can tell. It'll be interesting to watch those two in this round.

Next, I walk up to the deck and look at the top cards, memorizing them. I'm not leaving anything to chance.

When my task in the Quiet is complete, I walk back to myself. Oh, yes, did I mention that I see myself sitting there, frozen like the rest of them? That's the weirdest part. It's like having an out-of-body experience.

Approaching my frozen self, I look at him. I usually avoid doing this, as it's too unsettling. No amount of looking in the mirror—or seeing videos of yourself on YouTube—can prepare you for viewing your own three-dimensional body up close. It's not something anyone is meant to experience. Well, aside from identical twins, I guess.

It's hard to believe that this person is me. He looks more like some random guy. Well, maybe a bit better than that. I do find this guy interesting. He looks cool. He looks smart. I think women would probably consider him good-looking, though I know that's not a modest thing to think.

It's not like I'm an expert at gauging how attractive a guy is, but some things are common sense. I can tell when a dude is ugly, and this frozen me is not. I also know that generally, being good-looking requires a symmetrical face, and the statue of me has that. A strong jaw doesn't hurt, either. Check. Having broad shoulders is a positive, and being tall really helps. All covered. I have blue eyes—that seems to be a plus. Girls have told me they like my eyes, though right now, on the frozen me, the eyes look creepy— glassy. They look like the eyes of a lifeless wax figure.

Realizing that I'm dwelling on this subject way too long, I shake my head. I can just picture my shrink analyzing this moment. Who would imagine admiring themselves like this as part of their mental illness? I can just picture her scribbling down *Narcissist,* underlining it for emphasis.

Enough. I need to leave the Quiet. Raising my hand, I touch my frozen self on the forehead, and I hear noise again as I phase out.

Everything is back to normal.

The card that I looked at a moment before—the king that I left on the table—is in the air again, and from there it follows the trajectory it was always meant to, landing near the Professional's hands. Grandma is still eyeing her fanned cards in disappointment, and the Cowboy has his hat on again, though I took it off him in the Quiet. Everything is exactly as it was.

On some level, my brain never ceases to be surprised at the discontinuity of the experience in the Quiet and outside it. As humans, we're hardwired to question reality when such things happen. When I was trying to outwit my shrink early on in my therapy, I once read an entire psychology textbook during our session. She, of course, didn't notice it, as I did it in the Quiet. The book talked about how babies as young as two months old are surprised if they see something out of the ordinary, like gravity appearing to work backwards. It's no wonder my brain has trouble adapting. Until I was ten, the world behaved normally, but everything has been weird since then, to put it mildly.

Glancing down, I realize I'm holding three of a kind. Next time, I'll look at my cards before phasing. If I have something this strong, I might take my chances and play fair.

The game unfolds predictably because I know every-body's cards. At the end, Grandma gets up. She's clearly lost enough money.

And that's when I see the girl for the first time.

She's hot. My friend Bert at work claims that I have a 'type,' but I reject that idea. I don't like to think of myself as shallow or predictable. But I might actually be a bit of both, because this girl fits Bert's description of my type to a T. And my reaction is extreme interest, to say the least.

Large blue eyes. Well-defined cheekbones on a slender face, with a hint of something exotic. Long, shapely legs, like those of a dancer. Dark wavy hair in a ponytail—a hairstyle that I like. And without bangs—even better. I hate bangs—not sure why girls do that to themselves. Though lack of bangs is not, strictly speaking, in Bert's description of my type, it probably should be.

I continue staring at her. With her high heels and tight skirt, she's overdressed for this place. Or maybe I'm under-dressed in my jeans and t-shirt. Either way, I don't care. I have to try to talk to her.

I debate phasing into the Quiet and approaching her, so I can do something creepy like stare at her up close, or maybe even snoop in her pockets. Anything to help me when I talk to her.

I decide against it, which is probably the first time that's ever happened.

I know that my reasoning for breaking my usual habit—if you can even call it that—is strange. I picture the following chain of events: she agrees to date me, we go out for a while, we get serious, and because of the deep connection we have, I come clean about the Quiet. She learns I did something creepy and has a fit, then dumps me. It's ridiculous to think this, of course, considering that we haven't even spoken yet. Talk about jumping the gun. She might have an IQ below seventy, or the personality of a piece of wood. There can be twenty different reasons why I wouldn't want to date her. And besides, it's not all up to me. She might tell me to go fuck myself as soon as I try to talk to her.

Still, working at a hedge fund has taught me to hedge. As crazy as that reasoning is, I stick with my decision not to phase because I know it's the gentlemanly thing to do. In keeping with this unusually chivalrous me, I also decide not to cheat at this round of poker.

As the cards are dealt again, I reflect on how good it feels to have done the honorable thing—even without anyone knowing. Maybe I should try to respect people's privacy more often. As soon as I think this, I mentally snort. *Yeah, right.* I have to be realistic. I wouldn't be where I am today if I'd followed that advice. In fact, if I made a habit of respecting people's privacy, I would lose my job within days—and with it, a lot of the comforts I've become accustomed to.

Copying the Professional's move, I cover my cards with my hand as soon as I receive them. I'm about to sneak a peek at what I was dealt when something unusual happens.

The world goes quiet, just like it does when I phase in... but I did nothing this time.

And at that moment, I see *her*—the girl sitting across the table from me, the girl I was just thinking about. She's standing next to me, pulling her hand away from mine. Or, strictly speaking, from my frozen self's hand—as I'm standing a little to the side looking at her.

She's also still sitting in front of me at the table, a frozen statue like all the others.

My mind goes into overdrive as my heartbeat jumps. I don't even consider the possibility of that second girl being a twin sister or something like that. I know it's her. She's doing what I did just a few minutes ago. She's walking in the Quiet. The world around us is frozen, but we are not.

A horrified look crosses her face as she realizes the same thing. Before I can react, she lunges across the table and touches her own forehead.

The world becomes normal again.

She stares at me from across the table, shocked, her eyes huge and her face pale. Her hands tremble as she rises to her feet. Without so much as a word, she turns and begins walking away, then breaks into a run a couple of seconds later.

Getting over my own shock, I get up and run after her. It's not exactly smooth. If she notices a guy she doesn't know running after her, dating will be the last thing on her mind. But I'm beyond that now. She's the only person I've met who can do what I do. She's proof that I'm not insane. She might have what I want most in the world.

She might have answers.

The Thought Readers is now available at most retailers. If you'd like to learn more, please visit www.dimazales.com.

EXCERPT FROM
THE SORCERY CODE

Once a respected member of the Sorcerer Council and now an outcast, Blaise has spent the last year of his life working on a special magical object. The goal is to allow anyone to do magic, not just the sorcerer elite. The outcome of his quest is unlike anything he could've ever imagined—because, instead of an object, he creates Her.

She is Gala, and she is anything but inanimate. Born in the Spell Realm, she is beautiful and highly intelligent—and nobody knows what she's capable of. She will do anything to experience the world… even leave the man she is beginning to fall for.

Augusta, a powerful sorceress and Blaise's former fiancée, sees Blaise's deed as the ultimate hubris and Gala as an abomination that must be destroyed. In her quest to save the human race, Augusta will forge new alliances, becoming tangled in a web of intrigue that stretches further than any of them suspect. She may even have to turn to her new lover Barson, a ruthless warrior who might have an agenda of his own…

———————

There was a naked woman on the floor of Blaise's study.

A beautiful naked woman.

Stunned, Blaise stared at the gorgeous creature who just appeared out of thin air. She was looking around with a bewildered expression on her face, apparently as shocked to be there as he was to be seeing her. Her wavy blond hair streamed down her back, partially covering a body that appeared to be perfection itself. Blaise tried not to think about that body and to focus on the situation instead.

A woman. A *She*, not an *It*. Blaise could hardly believe it. Could it be? Could this girl be the object?

She was sitting with her legs folded underneath her, propping herself up with one slim arm. There was something awkward about that pose, as though she didn't know what to do with her own limbs. In general, despite the curves that marked her a fully grown woman, there was a child-like innocence in the way she sat there, completely unselfconscious and totally unaware of her own appeal.

Clearing his throat, Blaise tried to think of what to say. In his wildest dreams, he couldn't have imagined this kind of outcome to the project that had consumed his entire life for the past several months.

Hearing the sound, she turned her head to look at him, and Blaise found himself staring into a pair of unusually clear blue eyes.

She blinked, then cocked her head to the side, studying him with visible curiosity. Blaise wondered what she
was seeing. He hadn't seen the light of day in weeks, and
he wouldn't be surprised if he looked like a mad sorcerer
at this point. There was probably a week's worth of stub-
ble covering his face, and he knew his dark hair was un-
brushed and sticking out in every direction. If he'd known
he would be facing a beautiful woman today, he would've
done a grooming spell in the morning.

"Who am I?" she asked, startling Blaise. Her voice was
soft and feminine, as alluring as the rest of her. "What is
this place?"

"You don't know?" Blaise was glad he finally managed
to string together a semi-coherent sentence. "You don't
know who you are or where you are?"

She shook her head. "No."

Blaise swallowed. "I see."

"What am I?" she asked again, staring at him with
those incredible eyes.

"Well," Blaise said slowly, "if you're not some cruel
prankster or a figment of my imagination, then it's some-
what difficult to explain…"

She was watching his mouth as he spoke, and when
he stopped, she looked up again, meeting his gaze. "It's
strange," she said, "hearing words this way. These are the
first real words I've heard."

Blaise felt a chill go down his spine. Getting up from
his chair, he began to pace, trying to keep his eyes off her
nude body. He had been expecting something to appear. A
magical object, a thing. He just hadn't known what form

that thing would take. A mirror, perhaps, or a lamp. Maybe even something as unusual as the Life Capture Sphere that sat on his desk like a large round diamond.

But a person? A female person at that?

To be fair, he had been trying to make the object intelligent, to ensure it would have the ability to comprehend human language and convert it into the code. Maybe he shouldn't be so surprised that the intelligence he invoked took on a human shape.

A beautiful, feminine, sensual shape.

Focus, Blaise, focus.

"Why are you walking like that?" She slowly got to her feet, her movements uncertain and strangely clumsy. "Should I be walking too? Is that how people talk to each other?"

Blaise stopped in front of her, doing his best to keep his eyes above her neck. "I'm sorry. I'm not accustomed to naked women in my study."

She ran her hands down her body, as though trying to feel it for the first time. Whatever her intent, Blaise found the gesture extremely erotic.

"Is something wrong with the way I look?" she asked. It was such a typical feminine concern that Blaise had to stifle a smile.

"Quite the opposite," he assured her. "You look unimaginably good." So good, in fact, that he was having trouble concentrating on anything but her delicate curves. She was of medium height, and so perfectly proportioned that she could've been used as a sculptor's template.

"Why do I look this way?" A small frown creased her smooth forehead. "What am I?" That last part seemed to be puzzling her the most.

Blaise took a deep breath, trying to calm his racing pulse. "I think I can try to venture a guess, but before I do, I want to give you some clothing. Please wait here—I'll be right back."

And without waiting for her answer, he hurried out of the room.

———————————

The Sorcery Code is currently available at most retailers. If you'd like to learn more, please visit www.dimazales.com.

ABOUT THE AUTHOR

Dima Zales is a *New York Times* and *USA Today* bestselling author of science fiction and fantasy. Prior to becoming a writer, he worked in the software development industry in New York as both a programmer and an executive. From high-frequency trading software for big banks to mobile apps for popular magazines, Dima has done it all. In 2013, he left the software industry in order to concentrate on his writing career and moved to Palm Coast, Florida, where he currently resides.

Please visit www.dimazales.com to learn more.

www.ingramcontent.com/pod-product-compliance
Lightning Source LLC
Chambersburg PA
CBHW072203130726
47910CB00011B/1795